THROUGH THESE EYES

BLIND FAITH SERIES, BOOK TWO

N.R. WALKER

COPYRIGHT

Cover Artist: N.R. Walker and Samuel York
Blind Faith © 2013 N.R. Walker
Published by BlueHeart Press
Fourth edition: 2021

ALL RIGHTS RESERVED:

This literary work may not be reproduced or transmitted in any form or by any means, including electronic or photographic reproduction, in whole or in part, without express written permission, except in the case of brief quotations embodied in critical articles and reviews.
This is a work of fiction and any resemblance to persons, living or dead, or business establishments, events or locales is coincidental.
The Licensed Art Material is being used for illustrative purposes only.

WARNING

This book contains material that is intended for a mature, adult audience. It contains graphic language, explicit sexual content, and adult situations.

Trademarks:

All trademarks are the property of their respective owners.

DEDICATION

For Lisa Fisher...

N.R.
WALKER

THROUGH
These Eyes

CHAPTER ONE

"CARTER, for God's sake, would you hurry up?"

I smiled into the bathroom mirror as I pulled on one of his shirts. "Keep your pants on."

"If you don't hurry the fuck up, I'll be keeping them on," Isaac called back to me from down the hall. "Permanently."

I snorted. "Well, if I had my own clothes here…" I trailed off, waiting for him to bite back, knowing this conversation – one we'd had many times – annoyed him.

"I'll go start the car," I heard him mumble, and I laughed. Then the front door closed.

Shit.

"Isaac!" I stumbled out of the bathroom door, hopping on one foot, trying to put on my shoe, trying to stop him from getting in behind the steering wheel and starting my car. I almost fell down the hall, with my shoe half on and my jeans undone, to find Isaac still standing inside at the front door.

Looking gorgeous in his pricey jeans, expensive shirt and tight-fitted, designer sunglasses, the self-righteous bastard smiled. "Thought that might get your attention."

Standing up straight, wedging my foot into my shoe and doing up the fly on my jeans, I looked at my boyfriend. My blind boyfriend. Then I looked at the golden Labrador at his feet, his guide dog. "Well, Brady," I said to the dog. "It seems Isaac thinks he's funny."

Isaac grinned, smugly. "Are you finally ready?" he asked, again. He held out my wallet and keys. "You know my sister doesn't have a baby every day, Carter. I'd like to get to the hospital some time before my niece starts middle school."

Instead of taking my wallet and keys, I took his face in my hands and kissed him. "Shut up and get in the car."

By the time we had Brady harnessed into the backseat and were on our way to Carney Hospital, he was still complaining. "Seriously, Carter. How long should it take?"

"I was at work," I said, *again*. "I had to get changed! I could hardly turn up in my work clothes." Spending my days as a vet, tending to an array of animals, didn't make for clean work clothes. I changed gears and weaved through some traffic, looking from the cars in front of me to Isaac. "You know, if I had my own clothes at your place, it wouldn't take so long. I wouldn't have to go through your wardrobe to find clothes that fit me."

Isaac sighed dramatically. "Haven't we had this conversation?"

Yes. Yes, we had. But he didn't want me to move in with him. At all. It had stung when he'd first told me he didn't want me to live with him. I'd brought it up, considering we'd been together for a year, thinking it was the next step for us, thinking it was what he'd want. But he didn't. He liked his independence, he'd said. He liked things just the way they were. He didn't want us to be in each other's pockets, he'd said. It hurt to know he didn't want me to move in, but since then, the subject had now become a bit of a joke between us.

Usually, I'd make a joke of it and he'd sigh or change the subject. Or tickle me. Or throw something at me.

"Yes, we have had this conversation before."

"And how long are we going to continue to have it?"

"Until you agree for me to move in."

"So a long while, then?"

I chuckled and shook my head. "Apparently." I reached over the console and took his hand. "What time did you get the call about Hannah?"

"Carlos phoned me at work this morning to say she'd gone into labor, but not to hurry, because they thought it'd be hours," he said. "But then he called me again after lunch to tell me it was all over."

I looked at the clock on the dash, and like he could see what I'd just done, he added, "That was over an hour ago."

I knew he was anxious. His sister meant the world to him, and the new addition to the Brannigan clan was the best news they'd had in a long time. I lifted our joined hands and kissed his knuckles.

"I did leave work four hours early. I got to your place as fast as I could."

He sighed again, and squeezed my hand. "It's okay. The bus took forever anyway."

"Why won't you let me drive you to work?"

"Because you don't need to be driving out of your way for me, when you live five minutes from your work," he said. "And I'm a big boy. I can catch the bus to work if I want to."

I looked at the man in the passenger seat beside me, at his dark brown hair, his chiseled jaw and trademark Armani sunglasses. The beautiful, stubborn, completely infuriating man. "It's hardly out of my way. It'd take me twenty minutes tops," I started, but he cut me off.

"Carter," he said sternly, in that I-can't-believe-I-have-to-say-this-out-loud tone he gets when he thinks he's stating the obvious. "Brady and I are just fine on the bus, thank you."

I held in a sigh and bit back the exasperated comment that threatened to snap at him. You'd think after being together for over twelve months I'd be used to it by now. But no, I wasn't really. I wasn't often offended by his snide comments anymore, but the frustration still weighed in.

Dropping any conversation pertaining to how independent he was, I asked, "So did Carlos tell you what they called the baby?"

"No," he shook his head and smiled softly. "Just that mother and daughter were doing well."

When I pulled the car over and to a stop, Isaac turned his face toward to me. "Why did we stop? We haven't been driving for long enough to be at the hospital. Carter, what the hell are you doing? We're late enough!"

I waited for his little tirade to be over. "I'm aware of that, Isaac," I said slowly. "I stopped at a florist so we could bring Hannah some flowers. Is that okay?"

Isaac sighed. "Why didn't you tell me?"

"Because I just saw it and decided it was a good idea."

He sighed. "Just don't take long."

"Wouldn't dream of it." I rolled my eyes dramatically, though that silent trait was lost on him. Two minutes later, I opened the passenger door of the Jeep and handed Isaac the ridiculously overpriced teddy bear and bouquet of pink flowers with matching balloon. He pulled his face back in surprise, so I kissed his cheek. "Now you can't say I've never given you flowers."

I got back in behind the wheel and Isaac was smelling the flowers. After I'd pulled the Jeep out into traffic and we were nearly at the hospital, he said, "You haven't, you know."

"I haven't what?"

"Given me flowers."

I looked from him to the traffic in front of us, back to him, trying to decide if he was serious... I mean, no, I'd never brought him flowers, but I was trying to decide if he cared. "Would you like me to? Bring you flowers?"

"Not if I have to ask you for them."

"Then I shall bring you flowers." I chuckled, and shook my head. "When you don't expect it."

"Well now you've mentioned it, I'll be expecting it."

I sighed out a laugh. "Will I *ever* win an argument?"

Isaac smiled. "Not if I'm the one you're arguing with."

I laughed as I drove my Jeep into the parking lot of the hospital. Pulling into a spot, I turned the ignition off. "Well, come on. Let's go meet the newest Brannigan."

Isaac grinned and got out, holding the teddy bear and flowers, while I unhooked Brady's harness. I gave the dog a good ruffle on the forehead and he grinned, with his tongue lolling out the side of his mouth. As soon as he was free, he went to Isaac's side of the Jeep and waited patiently for Isaac to click him into his harness.

It was a routine we'd done hundreds of times. Me driving, Isaac in the passenger seat, dogs in the back. My dog, a Border Collie called Missy, normally shared the back-seat with Brady, but not today. Brady was on his own.

A beautiful dog for a beautiful man.

I walked around the car and took the flowers and bear, so Isaac could hook up Brady. When he was done, I said, "Come on, the maternity ward is this way," taking his hand and leading the way.

As we walked across the courtyard, I remembered the last time I was at this hospital. I'd come to pick Isaac up and take him home. He'd decided to do some trail hiking by himself on a remote path, with Brady of course, and slid down an embankment, spending a cold winter night outside. What started out as a foolish exercise to test his relationship with his guide dog—and to prove a point to me—ended up being a humbling reality check. The upside to him nearly freezing to death that night, was that he learned to appreciate what a marvelous dog Brady is.

The barriers Isaac put up to protect himself were coming down, little by little. There was still the occasional defensive remark aimed at the heart, or pride of those around him, but for the most part, he was finally starting to allow himself love; to love those around him, and more importantly, allow himself to be loved.

And coming back here, to the same hospital he was admitted to after his overnight ordeal, was a little ironic. That ordeal was like the ending of one part of his life, and now coming back here to see his brand new niece was like a new beginning.

As we walked into the building, Isaac wrinkled his nose. "Never thought I'd be happy to be back here."

"I was just thinking the same thing."

"Ugh, the smell is disgusting."

I know his sense of smell was more heightened than mine, but I had to agree. "Yep, it is."

We approached the nurse's station, and just as the nurse opened her mouth to speak to us, Isaac said, "Dear God. It smells like old food, dirty laundry and cheap disinfectant."

. . .

HER MOUTH FELL open and I smiled at the rather alarmed, probably offended nurse. "Good afternoon," I greeted her cheerfully. "We're here to see Hannah Brannigan-Peroni and Carlos Peroni. They had a little baby girl today."

"Room twelve," she replied. She looked at me, the flowers in my hand, then to Isaac, then to Brady and back to me and smiled. "Down the hall, turn right."

I was used to Isaac saying things in front of others that could be construed as rude – whether on purpose or not – but upon seeing he was blind, they quickly forgave any indiscretions. Part of me thought that was the very reason he did it, either that or he simply didn't give a shit.

With Isaac, either scenario was likely.

After a squeeze of his hand and a quiet 'this way', we headed down the hall. I walked into the room first, knocking gently on the door. "Up for visitors?"

"Oh, hey," came Hannah's soft reply. "Please, come in."

Hannah was lying on the bed, Carlos sitting in the chair beside her, and a tiny little bundle of pink blankets in a crib next to them. Isaac's sister looked tired, but she smiled brightly when we walked in. I walked over to the bed, leading Isaac. I held up the flowers, teddy bear and balloon proudly, like I'd made it myself, and put it on the side dresser. I kissed Hannah and whispered, "Congratulations," then stood aside, giving Isaac room to be with his sister.

He felt along the bed for her. She reached out, taking his arm, and they embraced for a long time. I moved to the other side of the bed, shook Carlos's hand, offering my congratulations, then peeked in at the tiny bundle of pink.

I looked over to Isaac, but he was still hugging Hannah and almost whispering in her ear with his hands on her face. "I'm so proud of you," he told her.

Poor Hannah started to cry. Happy tears, of course, but tears all the same. She swatted his arm, but then kissed his cheek. "Did you want to have a hold of her, Uncle Isaac?"

He gasped quietly. "Oh, I um... I'm not sure that's a good idea."

"Nonsense," Hannah said flatly. "Carter, bring over one of those chairs," she pointed to the chairs along the wall, under the TV. I did as instructed, and once Isaac was seated, Hannah asked, "Carlos, honey, could you please..." she waved her hand from the crib to Isaac, "...do the honors."

Carlos gently picked up the bundle of blankets, and like he was carrying the most precious gift in the world, he handed his newborn baby to Isaac. Isaac took the baby in his left arm, holding her close to his chest, and with his right hand, ever so gently traced his fingertips along the edge of the blanket and across the sleeping baby's cheek. He skimmed lightly across her forehead, down to her tiny button nose.

Without looking up, he asked, "What's her name?"

Hannah took a moment. "Ada."

Isaac gasped quietly, but he nodded. "It's perfect," he murmured. It took me a second to realize he was crying, before he took his sunglasses off and wiped at his tears. "I'm sorry," he said softly. "I don't know why I'm crying."

I knelt beside him and kissed the side of his face. "Don't apologize."

He turned his face to mine. His sky-blue, unseeing eyes and wet lashes were beautiful. He spoke quietly. "Ada was our mother's name." He leaned down and kissed the sleeping newborn baby. "Is she beautiful?"

I looked at little Ada. "Isaac, she's perfect."

He nodded again, and fresh tears filled his eyes. He

opened his mouth to say something, but closed it again and whatever was on his mind remained unsaid.

I looked at Hannah, to find her wiping her eyes. She shrugged and smiled. "I don't need a reason to cry, I'm a hormonal train wreck."

Carlos kissed her forehead then he smiled at me. "Hannah's a trooper. My God, she went through hell today. Swore like a sailor, threatened the medical staff with physical bodily harm, and she's never been more amazing."

I smiled at him and how adoringly he looked at his wife. And when I looked back at Isaac, he was utterly engrossed in Ada.

"She smells unlike anything I've ever smelled," he said quietly, in awe at the little human in his arms.

Then Ada started to wake and fuss, making a tiny squeaking sound. "Oh!" Isaac's face shot up. "What happened? What did I do? Is she okay?"

I grinned. "She's waking up, that's all," I reassured him. "I think she wants her mommy."

"Oh," he mumbled. "Carter, can you take her?"

Shit. "Sure!" I replied quickly. "Here, I'll hand her to Hannah." I took Ada carefully, all seven tiny pounds of her, not really sure how to hold her. "I've held lots of newborns," I told them. "Granted, they were all four-legged."

Hannah chuckled as she took her new daughter. "We should go," I told her. "You look tired, Hannah. We can come back tomorrow." I kissed the top of her head. "You did real good. She's beautiful."

When I turned to Isaac, he was fiddling nervously with Brady's collar. Following my line of sight, Hannah looked over to him. She frowned and asked, "Isaac honey, you okay?"

"Yes, I'm fine," he answered a little too brightly.

She looked at me and rolled her eyes. "Have you been getting to and from work okay?"

"Yeah, that's all fine," he told her. "And the groceries have been delivered just fine, there's still a freezer full of your cooking. You've got your hands full now. Don't you worry about me."

Hannah looked at me and shook her head, but she answered him. "Okay, just let me know if you need anything."

Not only was Hannah his sister, she was also his official caregiver. So while she has some time off adjusting to being a new mom, Isaac was doing it all on his own. He'd flat out refused a stand-in caregiver, so Hannah had prepared, cooked and frozen a lot of dinners, she'd organized fresh bread and milk, fruit and vegetables to be delivered every few days, and he had to get himself to and from work on the bus.

Of course I offered to help in each and every one of these aspects, but was promptly shot down. Isaac was blind, yes. But he was also independent, and very, very stubborn.

If anyone did anything for him without him asking, such as suggest driving him to and from work, or do the laundry, or cook dinner, they'd have their head ripped off and handed to them. Or so I found out.

I did help him a little, but in the last two weeks since Hannah was bedridden in later pregnancy and was unable to work, he'd been doing just fine. Hannah had planned to take four weeks or so off after the arrival of the baby, but had planned to at least start driving him to and from work as soon as possible. She hated that he had to catch a bus. He could have taken a cab every day, but declared the waiting in Boston morning traffic with a meter running was just wasting money.

Not that that should have bothered him. He had plenty.

But Isaac was Isaac. Proud, stubborn, gorgeous, and utterly amazing. It wasn't about wasting money. It was about proving his independence.

He stood up and pulled gently on Brady's harness. I walked over to him and took his free hand. "You okay?" I asked him quietly.

He nodded. "Yeah."

"We'll come back tomorrow, okay?"

"Sure."

After we'd said goodbye and were walking back to the car, I told him, "I know you wanted to stay, but Hannah needed to feed little Ada, then try and get some sleep. I figured being so new to breastfeeding, she wouldn't want an audience. She looked really tired."

"Yeah, I guess," he said. His disappointment was palpable.

I squeezed his hand. "We'll come back tomorrow."

He nodded, and was quiet on the way back to his house. It was obvious he was upset, and knowing him as well as I did, I knew not to push him.

He'd say what was on his mind if I gave him time.

It didn't take long. We were having dinner, and after he'd pushed his food around his plate for long enough, he put down his fork. "Can you describe her for me?"

Describe her? "Ada?"

He nodded sadly.

Oh, Isaac.

"I couldn't see much," I told him honestly. "She was more blankets than baby. But she had dark hair, pale skin and a cute little button nose."

He nodded and sighed. "She smelled gorgeous."

"She is gorgeous. But her looks will change almost every day," I told him. "I'll fill you in on how she looks tomorrow."

I thought he'd at least smile, but he didn't. I picked up our plates and took them to the sink, and when he didn't follow, I walked back and took his hand, pulling him to his feet. I wrapped my arms around him. "Isaac, baby, you okay?"

He shrugged.

"Isaac?"

He sighed into my chest. "I've been blind for almost nineteen years..." He trailed off.

"And?"

"I mean, I've always wanted my sight back, but there's only been a handful of times when I'd have honestly killed to be able to see."

Oh, Isaac.

I tightened my arms around him and kissed the side of his head. "And today was one of those days." It wasn't a question.

He nodded against me, and his voice was quiet, "Just once, ya know? If I could see her, just once."

I wasn't sure what I could say to make him feel better about himself, so instead I just held him. For the longest time, we just stood in his kitchen with our arms around each other. Eventually, I took him to bed, where instead of making love, I wrapped my arms around him again, kissed his lips then his closed eyelids, and told him he was perfect.

I could tell he didn't believe me. When I told him he was perfect, or called him gorgeous, he never believed me.

"What will it take for you to me believe me when I say that?"

Laying in my arms, he nuzzled into my neck. He never answered.

THE NEXT AFTERNOON, after I'd done my usual Thursday afternoon house-calls, I picked up some flowers for Isaac. He made the fact well-known that I'd never given him flowers, so I stopped in at the florist on my way to his house, with hopes they'd cheer him up.

"I'm after some flowers for someone special," I told the lady behind the service counter.

"Ah," she smiled knowingly. "Red roses are special."

"Do they smell nice?" I asked.

"Well, most flowers these days are de-pollinated beforehand," she told me, "so they don't make a mess, it also means they don't smell quite as good."

"Well, it doesn't really matter what they look like," I told her. "But they need to smell beautiful."

She walked around to my side of the counter and over to a particular stand. "These smell divine," she said, lifting a bouquet to her nose and inhaling deeply. "But they're expensive."

Of course they are.

"I'll take them."

"Do you want to know what kind they are?"

I shrugged. "Doesn't really matter."

She gave me an odd look, took them to the counter and proceeded to ring up the sale. I handed over my credit card, and she smiled at me. "She must be special."

I smiled. "Yes, he is."

It took a second for my words to register, but I didn't wait for a response. I took my card, the flowers and called out, "Thanks!" as I walked out the door.

I grinned all the way to Isaac's place, looking forward to giving him his first bouquet of flowers.

But my smile died when I pulled into his drive, because parked in front of his house were two police cars. One car had its blue lights flashing, the other sat dormant, the front door of the house was open with someone in white coveralls dusting for prints.

With my heart in my throat, I grabbed the stupid flowers off the front seat, jumped out of the Jeep, and ran for the house.

CHAPTER TWO

"ISAAC!"

I ran into his house, ignoring the man dusting for prints on the front door. "Isaac?"

"Carter?" his voice came from the living room. "I'm in here."

He was on the sofa, and he turned to face me. Brady sat on the floor between his legs, and Isaac's hands grasped his collar. An official looking guy, not in uniform, was sitting beside him, but stood to meet me.

He looked down at the flowers in my hand, then at my face. "Detective Zinberg," he introduced himself.

"Carter Reece," I answered absently. I was looking at Isaac. "What happened?" Isaac didn't answer, so I looked at the detective. "What happened?"

He smiled tightly at me, and again, looked at my hand.

I followed his gaze to my hand, and at the stupid fucking flowers. I held them up. "I bought these." Then I sat down next to Isaac and took his hand. I realized then, he wasn't wearing his trademark sunglasses. His eyes were closed. I know how he hated not wearing his sunglasses in front of others. "Isaac, please tell me what happened? Are you okay? Is Brady okay? What happened?"

Detective Zinberg cleared his throat. "Mr Reece?"

"It's Doctor," I automatically corrected him. "Doctor Reece. I'm a vet."

"Okay, *Doctor* Reece," he amended. "Can I ask what you're doing here?"

I shook my head. "What?"

"What are you doing here?"

"I was taking Isaac to see his sister," I answered in a daze. "She just had a baby."

"He's my boyfriend," Isaac added flatly.

The detective nodded thoughtfully, his expression didn't give much away, but he wrote something down in his notepad. I hadn't even notice he had a notepad. My mind was having trouble focusing.

"Can someone please tell me what happened?"

Detective Zinberg looked directly at me. "There was a home invasion-"

"A what?" I cut him off, and turned to Isaac. My blood ran cold. "Jesus, Isaac! Are you okay?"

"I'm fine," he replied curtly. "This will take twice as long if you're going to make the detective repeat everything."

I blinked, and blinked again, still trying to get my head around what happened. I couldn't believe it. Home invasion. Jesus, fuck. "Isaac..."

"Carter, I'm fine," Isaac cut me off. "Detective, please continue. I'd like to get this over with."

The detective looked at me, then back to Isaac. "Let me recap. So you got off the bus, and you believe you were followed."

"Yes," Isaac said. I knew that tone. His patience was wearing thin. "I heard someone follow me."

My stomach twisted.

"But you got inside the house, yes?"

"Yes."

"But you were pushed from behind?"

Oh fuck, no.

Isaac nodded. His voice was quiet. "Yes."

"Tell me what happened from there."

I tried to listen, tried counting to ten in my head before I lost my shit, while trying not to be physically sick.

"I unlocked the front door and stepped inside with Brady, but before I could close it, I was pushed in the back." Isaac spoke quietly, holding my hand in one of his, and Brady's collar in his other. "I fell into the foyer, and just sat up against the hall wall with Brady."

Oh, God.

The detective prompted him. "Did he speak to you?"

Isaac cleared his throat. "He said if I knew what was good for me, I'd stay where I was." Then he corrected, "His words were, 'If you know what's good for you, blind man, you'll stay down, and keep your fucking dog on a leash'."

I put the flowers on the sofa next to me and squeezed the bridge of my nose to the point of pain with my free hand.

"Your dog," Detective Zinberg started.

"Brady," Isaac corrected him. "His name is Brady."

Zinberg nodded. "Brady stayed with you?"

"Of course," Isaac said. "I held him. I didn't want him getting hurt or kicked."

I groaned. Imagining him huddled on the floor, holding onto Brady. "Fuck."

Detective Zinberg gave me a sympathetic smile, before turning back to Isaac. "Mr Brannigan, how long do you think he was in the house for?"

"It felt like an hour," he said. "But it was probably five minutes."

"Do you know if he took anything?"

"Not like I can have a look around now, is it?" Isaac bit back at him.

I squeezed his hand. "I might be able to help," I offered. "To see if something's missing at a glance."

The detective nodded. "Yeah, that'd help."

"He took my sunglasses," Isaac said softly. "When he left."

"While you were sitting in the foyer?" Detective Zinberg asked. "As he walked out?"

"Yes."

My stomach knotted, and I swallowed down the urge to vomit and scream. "He touched your face?" I asked, trying to sound calm, but my voice croaked.

"He snatched them off me," he clarified. He seemed so vulnerable, like his one weakness was so exposed. So *not* like my Isaac. I hated seeing him like this.

The detective made notes in his notepad, then he added, "We can take the footage off the bus, but there's no saying the culprit got off the bus with Mr Brannigan, or was waiting. Without a physical description..."

Isaac's face spun to the sound of the detective's voice. His mood went from vulnerable to pissed off in half a second. "So then ask me more pertinent questions, *Detective*. No, I can't see, but Jesus Christ, I'm not fucking useless!"

That got a facial expression from the detective. "I never assumed you to be useless, Mr Brannigan."

I squeezed his hand, but his anger was justified, considering what he'd just been through, and then the officer telling him his statement was worthless without a visual description.

"Yeah, right," Isaac scoffed disbelievingly. "I might be blind, but I can give descriptions."

"Such as?"

"He wore hiking boots, the hard-soled kind. Carter has a pair like them; they sound the same. He spoke with an inflection, to suggest he's from the Upper East Side. He didn't sound like a street thug. I'd even say from the way he spoke that he was educated. And he smelled like rolled tobacco, the port wine-scented kind."

Despite everything, I smiled proudly at Isaac. Detective Zinberg blinked in surprise, but dutifully made notes. "Doctor Reece, your hiking boots. Where are they?"

"Um," I tried to think. "Um, at my place, I think. When did we go hiking last?" I asked Isaac. Jesus, my mind couldn't keep up. "No, wait, they're here, in the garage," I said, remembering. "They were too muddy to wear inside, so I left them in the garage."

"Here?" the detective asked.

"Yes."

He looked up and called out to another officer who was somewhere in the house, asking them to look for my boots in the garage and to bag them.

"Bag them?" I asked. "What for?"

"It's just protocol."

I couldn't believe it. "Do you think I had something to do with this?"

"Detective Zinberg," Isaac hissed. "If you're implying Carter was somehow the man who came here today, you're very mistaken."

Huh? "No, Isaac," I said, shaking my head. "I'm sure he didn't mean it like that."

Isaac squeezed my hand, and before the detective could answer, Isaac told him, "I said they were the same type of shoes, not the same gait. I can't see, but I can tell you the man who was here earlier walked different. His footfalls were heavier, somewhat off-kilter, like he had a limp. And Brady growled the entire time. Brady would never growl at Carter." He absently stroked the dog's neck. "And he smelled different. He reeked of stale tobacco and sweat. Carter doesn't smell like that at all."

The detective stared at him disbelievingly. "You know people by how they *smell*?"

Isaac's brow pinched. "Yes, of course! You'd be surprised how other senses take precedence." Isaac shrugged, then told the detective, "Like how you smell of coffee and cheap aftershave."

I pulled on his hand. "Isaac."

Isaac's only response was to raise his chin, just a fraction.

"My daughter gave me this aftershave," Detective Zinberg admitted, trying to lighten the mood, I think.

Isaac answered flatly. "I suggest you tell her you dropped it."

"Okay, Isaac," I said softly. "That's enough." I grimaced apologetically at the somewhat stunned officer.

Zinberg smiled at me. "Doctor Reece, we might do a look around to see if we can notice anything that might be missing?" he nodded pointedly to the doorway.

"Sure." I squeezed Isaac's hand, kissed his cheek and told him I wouldn't be far. Before I stood up, I leaned in and whispered in Isaac's ear. "Do you want my sunglasses? They're in the car. I'll get them for you."

He shook his head. "I'm fine. Thank you."

I squeezed his hand. "I know how you prefer to wear them."

"I'm fine."

I dropped it, knowing it would only further irritate him. Though it was obvious he wasn't fine, at all.

I followed Zinberg into the foyer. I spoke quietly, not sure if Isaac could hear, or if he was too distracted. "Isaac tends to lash out when he's upset," I said by way of an apology.

"He's been through quite an ordeal."

I nodded, and looked over at him where he sat on the sofa. He was still clutching Brady's collar, and he was pale.

I looked back at Zinberg. "Detective, how did this happen?"

"Mr Brannigan said he'd caught the bus every day for two weeks?"

"Yeah, he wouldn't let me drive him," I told him. "He's very stubborn."

"I can tell," the detective said with a smile. "It wouldn't be a far stretch to think the person of interest noticed a blind guy on his own, watched him for a few days and figured out his routine, taking him for an easy target."

Fuck. "What do we do now?"

"Well, we'll run fingerprints, pull the CCTV from the bus, speak to possible witnesses," he said, rather formally. "But first we need to confirm any items that might have been stolen."

"Okay," I agreed. "Where do you want me to start?"

"We can start in the formal living room first," Detective Zinberg said, with a glance to the room on the right of the foyer, the room Isaac hardly ever used. It was a large room with a formal lounge suite and a large wooden, antique-looking writing desk. The drawers were askew, and a police officer was dusting for prints.

Then the bedrooms, both bathrooms, sunroom and finally back to the lounge room where Isaac was still sitting. From what I could tell, it was all smaller, pocketable items, or items that could be stashed in a backpack like his expensive sunglasses, iPod and laptop.

"Items that can be pawned or sold," Detective Zinberg had explained. "The bathroom cabinets were ransacked for any type of prescription medicines. It looks like he was after anything with a street resale value."

"It shouldn't be too hard to find a guy trying to pawn off laptop with a screen reader, or with a Braille cover on the keyboard, surely?" I asked.

"Detective?" Isaac's quiet voice interrupted us.

"Yes, Mr Brannigan?"

"I've been going over what happened in my head. I've been trying to place a sound he made," he said, still holding on to Brady. "It was a metal clicking noise. I heard it twice. I think he unlocked some windows."

I turned to the detective, who had one of his uniformed officers confirm a bedroom window and the sunroom window were indeed unlocked. "Why would he do that?" I asked, though I was fairly sure I already knew.

Zinberg looked at me, and told me seriously. "It would suggest he intends to come back."

Oh, fuck.

Isaac took a deep breath, and I was quick to sit back down beside him and take his hand. "You're coming to my place tonight."

He shook his head defiantly. "I won't be run out of my own house."

"Then I'll stay here with you," I told him.

"Carter, I'll be fine," he said. "The alarm will be activated."

"I don't care, Isaac," I told him flatly. "You're not staying here tonight by yourself."

He clenched his jaw. "I don't need a babysitter."

"I'm not babysitting you," I told him, trying to sound calm. "But I'll be fucking damned if you're here by yourself and that asshole comes back."

Isaac took a deep breath, and spoke through gritted teeth. "I don't *want* you to stay here."

His usual defense of saying hurtful things had no effect on me right then. I wasn't giving in. Not this time. "Then I'll stay to keep an eye on Brady. As his vet, it's my professional opinion that he needs overnight observations. He's been through quite an ordeal today."

Isaac opened and closed his mouth a few times before he said, "You won't let this go, will you?"

"Not this time."

"Whatever, Carter. I'm not up for the argument. You can take the spare room." Then he added, "And you can stop fucking smiling. You didn't win that one."

"I'm not smiling."

Isaac growled. "You can't lie for shit."

Grinning, I said, "I'll go home, grab Missy, and some clothes and come straight back. I'll be fifteen minutes, the police won't leave until I get here." I looked at Detective Zinberg, and he gave me a nod.

And true to my word, fifteen minutes later, I walked back into Isaac's house, just as the detective was leaving. The first patrol car was gone already, but Detective Zinberg had waited for me to get back.

It was only when my dog, Missy, bounded over to where they were still sitting on the sofa, that Isaac let go of Brady.

He stood slowly and I slid my arm around his waist. "Hey, told you I wouldn't be long."

Zinberg bid us farewell with promises to be in touch if there was any news or developments, or if they had any more questions. He gave me his card, told us to call him any time, and he left. I closed the door behind him, set the security alarm and walked back to Isaac.

I kissed his cheek. "You okay?"

He nodded.

"We'll need to call Hannah."

"Ugh. Really? I don't want to have this conversation with her," he said. "She'll worry herself sick and she's just had little Ada. She's still in hospital..."

I took his face in my hands and kissed him chastely. "Did you want to have a shower, and I'll call her and tell her what happened," I offered, knowing a hot shower would do him a world of good. "By the time you call her back, she'll have had some time to calm down."

After a short pause, he gave me a small nod. "Okay."

I tidied up his bathroom a little—the police weren't exactly trying to be clean when they dusted for prints on everything—and once the water was running, I phoned his sister.

It wasn't an easy phone call.

There was shocked silence, then she yelled, and then she cried, telling me she could leave the hospital at any time; she'd be there in half an hour. I told her Isaac was upset, but he was safe.

In the end, I asked to speak to Carlos, telling him to calm Hannah down, and to come over tomorrow. I told him to tell her that Isaac would call her later tonight, how he was, above all else, really pissed off, and given that Hannah had just been through childbirth two days earlier, they were both too emotional and it really, really wouldn't end well.

I suggested that maybe tomorrow, when Hannah lectured him about being a stubborn ass for not allowing me to drive him to work, he'll have had a night's sleep to deal with it. Carlos agreed. "They're being discharged from hospital in the morning," Carlos said. "We'll come around after Ada's lunchtime feeding."

I thanked him, and disconnected the call. By the time Isaac walked back into the living room, I had a damp cloth and a cleaning spray, trying to clean up the print dust residue from the windowsill.

"Are you cleaning?" Isaac asked. His sense of smell was almost as good as his hearing.

"Yeah, that black dust the police use is everywhere," I told him.

"Oh."

"It won't take me long," I reassured him. "I ordered some dinner. Chinese food."

He nodded, sitting down on the sofa. He was dressed in sleep pants and an old t-shirt. He was quiet and sullen. There was a frustrated anger just under the surface. I knew him and every mood he could throw at me. Admittedly, his mood swings, in particular his temper, have been fairly tame these last six months. But I was used to them.

I knew he lashed out at those closest to him. Actually, whoever was there in that particular moment, who just might happen to say the wrong thing. And the looming silence is usually directly proportionate to the size of the temper storm about to hit.

For two whole hours, he never said a word. I'd ask him something, and he'd either shrug or ignore me altogether. He had a very brief, one sided phone conversation with

Hannah, which only served to darken his mood, and then I put my foot in it after dinner. He didn't eat a bite, just pushed his food around his plate with his fork before pushing it away and standing up.

"Isaac, please. Talk to me."

And he snapped.

"Don't tell me what to do, Carter!" he said loudly. "I said I'm fine, and I mean it."

But he wasn't fine. That much was obvious. "Isaac, you're not fine."

"This is why I didn't want you here!" he yelled at me. "You're trying to tell me what I'm feeling now? Christ, Carter, this is why I don't want you to move in! Do you get it now? Is that what you wanted to know?" he sneered at me. "Why I don't want you here all the time? Because I can't stand to have people tell me what I can and can't do, and what to feel!"

I blinked, shocked at his outburst. It had been a while since he'd unleashed on me like that, and regardless of how angry he should be, it stung to have it directed at me.

He stomped to his room, slamming the door behind him, while I sat at the kitchen counter, blinking, staring at where he'd just stood.

Though it'd been a while since I'd seen them in full force, I was used to his moods. He didn't come out of his room. I didn't hear a peep from him for the next few hours. After I'd rechecked that all the windows and doors were locked properly and the alarm was set, I finally fell asleep in the spare room. Only to be woken two hours later to the sound of Isaac screaming.

CHAPTER THREE

"CARTER!" His shrill voice cut the silence. "Carter!"

I flew out of bed and raced into his room in a sleepy daze. My heart was hammering, or had stopped beating all together, I wasn't sure which. I didn't know what to expect, whether there was someone in his room, whether he was hurt, or whether someone was about to jump out and attack me.

"Isaac!" I said, flinging his door open and flipping on the light switch. My eyes were still adjusting to the light. He was sitting in the middle of his bed, clutching at the sheet tangled around his waist. "Isaac, I'm here. Did you hear something, are you hurt?"

He shook his head and a soft sob escaped him. "No."

I walked over, knelt on the bed and touched his hand. "Hey," I said softly.

His hand gripped mine tightly and his voice was whisper soft. "...scared."

Oh, Isaac.

I quickly sat beside him, and wrapped my arm around him. I pulled us back so we were lying down. I tugged the sheet up over us, then the blanket, and wrapped my arms tightly around him, while he snuggled his face into my neck.

He started to cry.

"Don't be scared," I murmured against his ear. "I've got you, baby."

"I'm so stupid," he said between sniffles.

"Ssh," I tried to soothe him. "You're not stupid."

"Why do I push you away when I need you the most?" he asked. "Why do you put up with me?"

"Because I love you."

He cried harder. "I treat you like shit."

I couldn't help but chuckle. "Not all the time."

He sniffled. "I was awful to you tonight. I'm sorry."

I kissed the side of his head. "You had an awful day."

He nodded against my neck with a wave of fresh tears.

"Isaac?" I hedged quietly. "Did you have a bad dream?"

He nodded again. "My dream... He came back and you weren't here," his voice was a bit muffled against my neck. "You left, because I told you to go. And he hurt Brady."

I pulled the blanket over his shoulder and snuggled him further against me. "It was just a dream. You're okay, Brady's okay."

"Can you check on him for me?"

I smiled and kissed his forehead. "Of course."

Throwing back the covers, I padded out through the kitchen to the sunroom. Brady and Missy were on their beds, awake, no doubt because of Isaac yelling. Both dogs looked up at me when I walked into the room. Confirming Brady was safe and well, I snuck back into bed with Isaac.

"He's fine," I reassured him. "Tucked in with Missy."

He seemed to breathe out in relief, quickly snuggling back into my side. Using my arm as a pillow, he snaked his arm around my waist, and buried his face back into my neck. I traced circles on his back and his breathing became deeper.

Despite the circumstances, I smiled. It wasn't too long ago he was so distanced from his guide dog, Brady. He loved him, he always had. But he was hesitant to acknowledge it, in a feeble attempt to save himself from a broken heart when the time should come that Brady died. He'd lost two other guide dogs since being blinded at the age of eight, and the last time, with his beloved Rosie, nearly broke him.

In the last six months, he'd come so far with Brady. And today was testament to that. The way he held onto him, protected him from the intruder, and then the way he'd held onto his collar, wanting him close by for most of the afternoon. But now, even in his dream, his concern was for Brady.

Thinking he'd fallen back asleep, I kissed the side of his head again.

He sighed. "I'm sorry for making you sleep in the spare room."

I chuckled. "You're forgiven. Just don't make me do it again. I belong in here with you."

He nodded against my neck, but never said anything. His breathing soon evened out and he slept.

I fell asleep wondering what today's events would mean for Isaac; for his independence, for his confidence. Selfishly, then I wondered what that meant for me. I wondered how much he'd push me away, how much he'd hurt me with his words, with that temper of his.

I woke up alone.

I WALKED into the living room, heading toward the kitchen. Well, the coffee machine, to be exact. Isaac was sitting on the sofa, writing something with his Braille punch-pad. It's technical term was a slate template, or something like that, but because he slid the paper into it, then used the pear-shaped stylus to punch Braille holes in it, I'd long ago dubbed it his punch-pad.

He heard me coming. "Coffee machine is on."

I kissed the top of his head as I walked past. "Thanks. Want one?"

"Um, sure."

So with two cups of coffee in hand, I sat down beside him. "What list are you making?"

He put down his punch-pad, and I gently handed him his coffee. "Oh, just some things I need to do today."

I turned side on, folded my leg up and under my ass and put my spare hand on his thigh. "Like what?"

"Call my insurance company, my bank, change PIN's and passwords, buy a new laptop, new glasses."

I rubbed his thigh. "Make your fantastic boyfriend breakfast."

He smiled as he sipped his coffee. "I'm pretty sure that's not on my list."

"It should be."

"You're not working today?"

It wasn't unusual for me to work some Saturdays. "No, not this weekend. I'm all yours."

"Hannah said she'll be here after lunch," he reminded me. "So, if it's okay with you, I'd like to organize what I can this morning."

"Of course it is," I told him. "On one condition."

He shook his head, and tried not to smile. "What?"

"We save time and water, and shower together."

SOMETIMES I JUST WANTED TO PUNCH SOME people. And this was one of those times. The computer salesperson at the electronics store was an ass. He spoke to Isaac loud and slow, like he presumed him to be mentally inept, or deaf.

Isaac was used to it. It happened all the time apparently. But even after us being together for a year, it was something I knew I'd never get used to.

It infuriated me to no end.

The salesman looked at Isaac, then at Brady, then to me. "Can I help you?"

I put my hands up. "Nah, not me. Isaac, what are you after?"

The salesman smiled, as though it were some kind of joke.

"I'm after a new laptop, preferably eight gig memory and a one terabyte hard drive. It needs to have multi-core processors, and have a sound card for synthetic speech. My last laptop had an Intel i5 and it was fine, but going on two years old. What's the latest version?"

The salesman stared at Isaac then blinked slowly. "Um."

I waved my hand in front of his face, garnering his attention. "Oh, sure," he said, turning on his heel. "We have the latest model. It has the i7, I think, but the Mac has a bigger screen..." he trailed off, glancing at Isaac, obviously wondering whether he should have said that or not.

"Screens and monitors are of no use to me," Isaac said simply. "I'll also need an external hard drive and a carry case in leather, if you have it. Thank you."

The salesman blinked in shock again and looked at me like I should give permission. Instead, I gave him a what-the-hell-are-you-waiting-for glare and he scurried off to the back room.

I shook my head. "What an asshole."

Isaac smiled. "It's not his fault he's an idiot."

I laughed. "Anyway, why are you nice to *him*, but you give *me* hell all day long?"

"Because you're *not* an idiot," he answered. "Or an asshole."

"So let me get this right," I joked. "You'd be nicer to me if I were an asshole to you."

Isaac chuckled. "I'd consider it."

"You're unbelievable."

"So you've told me."

I rolled my eyes just as my favorite salesman came out carrying a large rectangular box and put it on the sales counter. "Come on," I said, putting my hand on his arm. "Your new laptop awaits."

Despite having to go to Boston's city centre, shopping for his new glasses was much more fun.

I never imagined I'd ever go into a store like it. Well, not on my income. I mean, I earned good money, but Armani?

I felt underdressed and under classed walking inside, but Isaac just waltzed on in, with Brady, of course. A salesman—a young, good-looking, rich-looking guy—walked right up to him, never taking his eyes off him. "Good morning, how may I be of assistance?"

Isaac smiled. "Sunglasses?"

"This way," he said, leading us toward a brightly lit wall cabinet of sunglasses. "The summer range this year is amazing."

"My last pair were the GA 675," Isaac told him.

"Ah," the salesman, whose nametag declared him to be Michael, said. "Very stylish."

"I can't take credit for picking them." Isaac turned his face toward me and smirked. "But I've been told they suit me."

I looked at Michael and shrugged. "They do. Well, they did."

The salesman grinned at me, then pulled a pair of glasses off the wall. "Well, good style never goes out of fashion. Here's the newer 675, just like your old pair."

Isaac had worn my sunglasses out today, so I stepped up closer, and told him, "Take your glasses off so we can try these new ones on."

Isaac took my not-so-expensive glasses off and handed them to me, and when Michael handed the new glasses to Isaac, he saw how blue his eyes were. He looked at me, a little surprised at just how beautiful his unseeing eyes were. I smiled at him.

"How are they?" Isaac asked, facing us wearing the sunglasses.

I smiled. "Perfect."

He lightly traced his fingers on the frames. "They feel the same."

I couldn't deny it. He looked hot. "Well, actually, they look better than your last pair."

Michael softly cleared his throat, interrupting this little moment between us. He waggled his finely plucked eyebrows. "Can I take those for you, or would you like to wear them now?"

"I'll wear them now, but if you could take off any tags," Isaac told him, handing him back the glasses. "Carter, did you want a shirt or something?"

Pfft. Not likely. "Ah, no. I'm all good."

"Some sunglasses?"

I looked at my old pair of cheap sunglasses in my hand. I actually could use some new shades. "Um, well..."

"Here," Michael said, pulling a pair of glasses off the wall. "Let's try these on." I turned toward him and he slid the expensive glasses onto my face. "Oooh, they look good on you."

I looked in the mirror. "Eh, they're a bit big. Something smaller?"

He picked another pair. "These will accentuate your jaw line."

I tried them on, and he was right. I had to admit, they looked good. "Mm, I like these."

"They suit you," Michael said. "They make you look... hot."

Isaac cleared his throat. "Are you two finished? Would you like some alone time?"

Michael looked positively horrified, like he'd just committed some professional misdemeanor. Isaac was pouting. I laughed, "Yes, I'm finished."

Michael hurried off to the service counter ahead of us, and I took Isaac's arm and followed Michael. Isaac sighed. "Do you always flirt with the sales assistants?"

"Oh, all the time," I said sarcastically, rolling my eyes. I put my sunglasses down on the counter. "I'll take these."

"I'll pay for his," Isaac said.

"No, you won't," I said flatly.

Isaac sighed again and pulled his wallet out of his back pocket, then deftly skimmed his fingertip over his cards and pulled out his credit card. He held it out in Michael's general direction. "Both pairs, please."

"Isaac," I started.

He smiled. "Are you really going to argue with a blind man in public?"

At this point, Michael's mouth fell open. I chuckled. "Since when do I ever *not* argue with you?" I looked at the poor sales assistant. "It's okay, Michael. He loves it when I argue with him."

Isaac lifted his chin defiantly. "Remind me again why I put up with you?"

"Because you love me," I told him. "And I'm great in bed."

This time Isaac's mouth fell open, and he hissed, "Carter!"

Michael smiled as he completed the transaction. I tried to ignore what it cost in total, and our shopping expedition was over.

After we'd got Brady harnessed into the back seat and were out in traffic, Isaac started. "So, Michael was cute, was he?"

I couldn't help but smile. "Oh, sure," I admitted. "For an eighteen year old, make-up wearing college kid."

"You were very cozy with him."

"Cozy?" I scoffed. "Oh, my God. Are you jealous?"

He shook his head. "Jealous? Do you not know me at all?"

I smiled, but that was just it. I did know him. I knew him well enough to know something wasn't right. He was trying too hard to be funny. His jokes, his smile, it was all too forced. Yesterday, the home invasion... as much as he said he was fine, he really wasn't.

That's the thing about Isaac. Not one to talk openly, he'd prefer to bottle it up, let it fester, then lash out at whoever was closest. He'd been working on it over the last six months, he'd been trying to talk more openly, but he thought it showed vulnerability and that was something a blind man had enough of.

"Yes, I do know you, Isaac," I said, reaching over the console and taking his hand. "So, care to tell me what really bothered you with Michael?"

He was quiet for a while, and I thought he was just going to ignore me, so I changed the subject. "Thank you for the glasses, by the way. You didn't have to buy them for me."

He was still quiet, and when I looked from the traffic in front of me to him, I saw he was gnawing on his bottom lip. "Isaac?"

"He said the glasses will accentuate your jaw line."

"So?" I asked, trying to figure out his angle. "He also said I was hot, so he clearly would say *anything* for a sale."

Again, silence.

I squeezed his hand. "Isaac, please talk to me."

He swallowed hard, obviously trying to get the words right in his head first. "It's little comments like that... to anyone else it wouldn't mean anything. But he just said it, 'these will accentuate your jaw line' so flippantly."

"I'm sure he meant nothing of it, Isaac."

"No, Carter," he shook his head. "*Oh, these will do, they'll look good on you, you're hot.* Don't you get it, Carter? He's *seen* your jaw line. He *sees* what looks good on you."

"Isaac," I said, lifting his hand to my cheek. "Oh, baby."

He shook his head. "It's silly, I know. But I just... wish..."

"It's not silly. Nothing you feel is silly."

He shrugged and was silent again. It wasn't until we were almost back to his house when I asked, "You know Hannah and Carlos will be at your place soon. Should we grab some lunch?"

Finally, he spoke. "Sure."

When Hannah arrived, with Carlos and two-day-old baby Ada in tow, she almost tackled her brother as she raced into the living room to see him. Isaac spent the better part of an hour going over every detail of yesterday's ordeal. He got mad, Hannah got upset, and he reassured her a hundred times he'd be fine.

Hannah apologized again for being overly emotional, but given she'd just had a baby two days ago, I thought she was doing quite well. She felt guilty for not being able to drive him to and from work. "But I'll be here first thing Monday morning to take you."

"No you won't," Isaac and Carlos said in unison.

"I'll drive you," I told him.

"No one is driving me!" Isaac cried. "I'll be fine."

"You're not catching the damn bus again," Hannah snapped at him. She'd started pacing, and Carlos urged her to take it easy.

"I'll take a cab," he offered weakly. "I don't need a babysitter."

I shook my head at this impossible man. "Why won't you let me help you?"

Isaac turned to the sound of my voice. "What?"

"No matter what I say, no matter what I offer, you say no. Why is that?"

He turned away from me, which was his way of silently telling me he had no intention of answering.

"I'm serious, Isaac," I pushed my point. "I offer to drive you, you say no. I offer to move in, you say no."

"You what?" Hannah asked, clearly surprised.

Isaac sighed. "Carter..."

I stared at Hannah. "He didn't tell you I asked him if I could move in? But that was weeks ago..."

Isaac's voice was low, his warning clear. "Carter..."

An awkward silence fell over us, until Hannah looked at me and Carlos. "Can I have a word with Isaac, please?"

I withheld a sigh. I doubted this would end well.

Carlos looked over at the baby carrier, where Ada was still sleeping soundly. "Carter and I will take the dogs out the back," he said. He told Hannah, "Just give me a holler if you need me, or if Ada wakes up."

We walked out into the backyard, with both dogs running off for a sniff of God-knows-what. "How's Hannah?" I asked.

"She's okay," Carlos answered. "Exhausted, worried about Isaac. She feels so guilty."

I nodded. "Yeah, I can see that."

Carlos was always so patient, always so understanding about his wife's bond with her brother. I wondered if her built-in need to protect Isaac, to run to his aid, was a toll on their marriage.

"Does it bother you?" I asked him. "That Hannah seems to put Isaac before everyone else."

Carlos smiled. "No, not at all. She adores him, and she's looked after him ever since I've known her. It was like a package deal."

"You're a saint."

"Hardly." He laughed. "I don't have to tell you how stubborn he can be, and sometimes I wish he could see just how much he hurts her."

I nodded. "Yeah, I know."

Carlos looked at me for a long moment. "Did he really say he doesn't want you to move in with him?" he asked. "I thought you two were going strong."

I sighed. "Yeah, me too."

"He's just scared."

"I thought that too," I admitted. "But I'm starting to wonder if it's not something else."

"Carlos?" Hannah called out from inside. "Can you come here a sec?"

Carlos walked in, and I followed him, presuming their little chat was over. But it wasn't. While Carlos took little Ada for a diaper change, I found myself standing in the sunroom while Isaac and Hannah briefly paused mid-way through their rather heated discussion. They didn't know I was there. I didn't mean to eavesdrop, I just kind of froze...

"You love him," Hannah said. "I know you do."

"Of course I do," Isaac answered.

"Then why?" she asked. "Why not let him live with you? No bullshit this time, Isaac. I want the truth."

I think my heart just about stopped. I wasn't sure if I wanted to hear his answer, but my feet couldn't seem to move.

Isaac's voice was quiet. "I don't want him to see how blind I really am, how much of a burden I am. If he lives here, he'll see how much I struggle."

"Oh, Isaac," Hannah said. "You've been together for a year! He knows you."

He answered so softly, I almost didn't hear him. "I want to be normal for him."

I moved then, my feet suddenly kicked into gear. I had to go to him. I walked in through the kitchen and straight over to him in the living room. He heard me coming and turned toward the sound of my footsteps. "Carter?"

I cupped his face in my hands and pulled him against me. "I just want to be with you," I told him. "Isaac, baby, I know you're blind. I won't ever think any less of you. I couldn't." I pulled his face back and kissed his cheek. "It's the opposite for me. The more I get to know you, the more amazing you are."

He frowned. "I knock things over sometimes."

"So do I. Just last week, I dropped a whole packet of ground coffee."

"I don't want you to realize how much hard work I am. When you're at your place, then visit me or stay overnight, you see me in snippets. You put me on some pedestal, tell me how perfect I am, but I'm not."

"I spend three or four nights a week here and every weekend. What will I see that I don't already?"

He frowned. "How much of a burden I can be."

I kissed his forehead and pulled him against me again. "Never. Isaac, you're the most independent and insanely stubborn man I've ever met." And the most amazing.

"I want you to move in, I do. I need you..."

"But?"

He sighed. "I'm impossible to live with."

"I'll take my chances."

"You need your head read."

"Is that a yes?"

He was quiet for a long time, then he nodded. "Promise you won't hate me?"

"Never."

"Promise you won't leave me?"

"I promise." I kissed the side of his head. "Promise you won't push me away."

"Promise." Then he amended, "Well, I'll try..."

"That's all I ask."

"Are you sure?"

"Absolutely."

"Carter?"

"Yeah?"

"Move in with me."

CHAPTER FOUR

HANNAH SAT down with Carlos to feed baby Ada, while we sat on the other sofa. Isaac sat side on to me, with one leg tucked under himself, as he held my hand and kept smiling into my shoulder. It was kind of adorable.

Even Hannah would look over at him occasionally and smile. "So," she asked, looking at me. "When will you move in?"

"Oh, well, I'll have to give notice on my rent, find somewhere to store most of my stuff, so maybe in two weeks?"

Isaac sat up straight. "Two weeks?"

"Officially," I said, trying not to grin at his disappointment. For someone who'd resisted this move for weeks, he was now very excited by the idea. "I can go home and grab some things this afternoon. Tonight will be my first night, officially."

"Oh," Isaac said, but then his smile faded. "You're going to bring all your stuff here, aren't you?"

I laughed at his oh-shit realization. "No, I'll put most of it in storage or something. Don't worry, I won't rearrange your furniture or anything."

Isaac bit my shoulder playfully. "Not funny."

When Ada was fed and content, she was promptly handed to her besotted uncle. He was so amazed by this tiny baby. He'd hold her close to his face, taking in that new-baby smell that astounded him. And every little snuffle or squeak from Ada, Isaac would smile.

So, while Hannah and Carlos were still there, I headed home to collect a few things. I'd wanted to move in with Isaac for months, and now it was finally happening. It wasn't lost on me that he'd had an attacker in his house the day before and this could be his knee-jerk reaction to that. But he said he wanted me to move in, he had wanted me to move in with him for a while, he was just scared.

He didn't want me to realize how blind he was.

Of all the silly things.

Two bags of clothes, toiletries and some of Missy's things and I was done. The rest could wait.

And when I got back to Isaac's, Hannah was going through some papers, talking to who I quickly deduced was a bank. She was requesting password changes and instructing that all withdrawals until further notice had to have telephone verification from Isaac.

"What's going on?" I asked, leaving my bags in the foyer.

Isaac was still on the sofa holding Ada. "Hannah was looking through the paperwork in the desk that that guy went through. Apparently, there are some financial documents missing."

I walked in and sat down next to Isaac, putting my hand on his leg. "We'll need to call that detective."

Isaac nodded before leaning down and sniffing little Ada. "Ah, Hannah?"

"Yeah."

He crinkled his nose. "Um, the most amazing smelling little creature in the world doesn't smell so wonderful."

Carlos laughed. "Here," he said, leaning down and taking his daughter. "I'll take her."

Isaac settled back on the sofa and reached for my hand, and turned toward me. He was smiling. "Did you grab everything you need?"

I found myself smiling back at him. "Yeah, we can pick up anything else tomorrow or after work during the week."

He played with my fingers on the hand he was holding. "So, now we officially... *cohabitate*, what are you cooking for dinner?"

I chuckled and kissed the knuckles on his hand. It was usually a lot of fun when Isaac was feeling cheeky, but given the events of the last twenty-four hours, I was a little unsure of *how* he should be acting.

How is a blind person supposed to act after being attacked in their own home? It wasn't a violent attack, but terrifying nonetheless. His one safe haven had been breached. The one place where he felt secure, where he could let his guard down, had been violated.

I just went with it, with his mood. He seemed unfazed, even happy to have me move in. Yes, the incident with the intruder had thrown him, and he had a nightmare last night, but today he seemed almost jovial.

I also knew, if he kept ignoring the elephant in the room, he was likely to fall apart. When, how, or what the catalyst would be, was anyone's guess.

He might very well talk openly about his ordeal, he was getting better with his reluctance to talk. Or he could bottle it up until I said the wrong thing, and then proceed to rip my head off. That's the thing about Isaac Brannigan. It really could go either way.

"I thought I might grill some fish," I suggested, answering his question about dinner. "We can eat out on the back patio, then we can have a swim," I leaned in and whispered, "naked."

He gave me a shy smile. "I like those kinds of swims."

"I know you do."

Hannah cleared her throat. "Before you two get too carried away, don't forget to call that detective guy and tell him about the missing documents." She was starting to pack up the diaper bag, getting ready to leave. "You can tell him the bank's been notified and no fraudulent transactions had been processed so far."

She looked tired, and Isaac seemed to know. "Go home and get some rest, Hannah. I appreciate your help, but we'll be just fine. Thank you," Isaac said kindly.

"Isaac," she said seriously. "Please promise me you won't be taking the bus anymore."

"I'll be driving him to and from work every day," I answered, reinforcing the issue with Isaac. "Except for Thursday nights. I have house-calls and can't get there by the time he's finished."

"I can take care of Thursdays," Hannah said.

"You just had a baby," I reminded her, though I doubted she needed reminding. "He can cab it until you're ready."

"Are you both finished?" Isaac cried. "I'm quite capable of organizing myself!"

I took his hand in both of mine. "Isaac," I said firmly. "When it comes to your safety, we need to make sure we're covered, okay?"

"I'm not useless," he said again.

"You're far from useless," I replied.

"Then don't treat me like I am," he snapped. "I won't be scared off because of one guy."

"*One guy* who could have very well hurt you," I stated calmly. "What's to say next time he's not armed, or high on drugs? Isaac, we take this one time as a warning and learn from it. And we're not being scared off. You don't change being you, being independent, we just change tactics, that's all."

"I'm hardly independent when you two keep organizing everything on my behalf."

"You're more independent than you realize," I told him. "And stubborn. Have I ever mentioned how stubborn you are?"

Isaac sighed. "You're not going to let this go, are you?"

"No," I said adamantly. "I will negotiate on everything else, but not this. Not when it comes to your safety." We'd had similar conversations to this before, so he knew this was my one sticking point.

"What else is there to negotiate on?" he asked incredulously.

"There's plenty!" I told him. "Like who does what household chores, how much I pay you for rent and utilities..."

"You'll pay me no such thing."

"Yes, I will."

The sound of Hannah laughing made us both turn to where she and Carlos stood watching us argue. She shook her head. "Are you sure you two haven't been married for fifty years?"

She walked over to the sofa, leaned down and kissed the top of her brother's head. "I love you, Isaac. I'll call you tomorrow." Then she looked at me. "I'll call you Carter, and we'll work out Thursdays for picking him up."

"Sure thing," I told her. "Take that gorgeous little girl home and get some rest."

Pulling Isaac to his feet, we walked them out, said good-byes, shut and locked the door behind them.

I slid my arms around his waist, pulling him against me, and pressed my lips to his. "We have all night to talk about the mundane stuff. Let's get dinner ready, then take that swim."

WE SWAM SOME LAPS, which became a bit of a race. Isaac could out-swim me. He was fitter, he was faster. So it was only right that my highly strategic distract-Isaac-with-sex-tactic would be my only chance at any kind of ego salvage.

It probably wouldn't be so bad if Isaac didn't gloat like a frat boy.

If he was wearing swimming trunks—or any kind of clothing—I'd have pantsed him. But he wasn't wearing anything, except for that damn gloating grin. So I splashed him. Then I tried to wrestle him, but he threw me off, laughed at me, gripped me around the top of my arm and pulled me around and under the water instead.

So, coming up for air, and winning the only way I could, I pushed him up against the edge of the pool and kissed him. Hard.

At least he stopped laughing.

And when I pulled his legs up and wrapped them around my waist, he wasn't laughing at all.

I could tell by the way he kissed me, the way his fingers clawed at my shoulders, my back and through my hair, he wanted it. He needed it.

I broke away from his mouth, only to have him kiss feverishly down my neck. "Isaac, we need to go inside."

He nodded, taking in ragged breaths.

Out of the pool, I wrapped a towel around him, took his hand and led him through the house to his room.

To our room.

He stood before me, and I took my time drying him off, ensuring every inch of his skin was dry, and kissed. Kneeling in front of him, I wiped down his feet, up his calves, his thighs, leaving soft kisses in my wake. And when I replaced the towel with my tongue, licking his sac, rubbing my cheek and lips along his cock, his fingers threaded through my hair.

He guided me, showing me what he wanted, how he wanted it.

Without sight, his responses to touch, to sounds, were enhanced. If I licked him, twirled my tongue over his shaft, or moaned, his responses were my reward.

He'd groan, buck, writhe. And it would spur me on. The more he did it, the more I wanted it. Each reaction was honest, tactile, immediate.

I stood up and kissed his neck, then whispered in his ear. "Lie down on the bed for me."

I led him to the bed and grabbed supplies from the bedside table. I crawled over to where he was now lying down, settling between his legs. I kissed up his stomach, sucked his nipple into my mouth, then trailed wet kisses up his chest, neck and jaw. My voice was rough, "I think you need to come twice tonight."

He shivered from head to foot.

"Once in my mouth," I said, nipping below his ear. "Once when I'm inside you."

His hands found my face, and he pulled my mouth to his, caressing his tongue against mine. I settled my weight on him and his legs fell open, his hips thrusting into mine.

I could almost taste the desperation on his tongue.

I knew he wouldn't last long.

It only took a few passes of my mouth on his cock, a few twirls of my tongue and two fingers inside him to make him come the first time.

I'd never tire of the way he came. How his body would succumb to the pleasure, how his body would tense and the sounds he made.

How he tasted.

As he lay there completely boneless, I made my way back up his body and delved my tongue back into his mouth. "Taste you."

He groaned, his body still spent. "Carter."

My body tingled. I loved how he murmured my name like that. Deep, husky, sated.

"I haven't finished with you yet," I told him.

Goosebumps covered his skin. He shivered.

"Cold?" I asked with a smile.

He shook his head and whispered, "No."

"Roll over for me," I urged him, helping him onto his stomach.

I trailed my tongue down his spine, to the crack of his ass, spreading him with my hands so I could tongue his hole.

Isaac groaned, fisting the sheets and lifting his ass for me. He loved it. When I had two slicked fingers inside him, he was mumbling incoherently, and when I swiped his gland over and over, he was begging me. "Please, Carter. Please."

I flipped him over onto his back and folded his legs up to his chest. I leaned over him so I could kiss him and he quickly tried to wrap his legs around me, groaning in frustration when I denied him.

"I'm not ready," I told him. I took his hand and wrapped

it around my engorged cock so he could feel it was bare. He squeezed me while I tore at the condom wrapper with my teeth, and quickly took hold of the backs of his thighs, holding his legs open for me. "Carter, please."

He was getting desperate. I pressed my sheathed cock against his ready hole. "Is that what you want?"

He nodded, lifting his hips, widening his legs. So I pushed inside him slowly, letting him breathe through the intrusion.

It took every ounce of self-control not to thrust in completely. "Baby, you okay?"

He nodded, letting go of his legs only to wrap his arms around me instead, and we started to move together.

Leaning over him, I had one elbow at the side of his head, and the other wrapped under his shoulder, my hands holding his head and face while I kissed him. His hard cock was pressed between us, sliding in his precum. I was so far inside him, and he was holding me so tightly, all I could do was rock my hips into him.

He held me tighter.

His legs gripped me harder.

"Fuck."

"Carter... coming," he grunted.

He flexed violently. All I could do was hold on while he clamped down around me, shaking as his orgasm rocked us both. His neck corded as his mouth fell open in a silent scream, and he spilled hot and thick between us.

Pleasure surged through me, with cold fire in my bones and lights behind my eyes, as I filled the condom deep inside him.

I don't know how long we rocked together. Long after I'd pulled out of him. We just lay together, all wrapped around each other. The sex between us was always intense.

Sometimes it was frenzied fucking, sometimes lazy love-making. But it always intense.

Tonight's intensity was not anything out of the ordinary. At least I didn't think it was, until I saw the blunt scratches down my back. I knew Isaac was holding on to me tightly, I knew he was a little frantic, desperate even, but I'd never had war-wounds before. I smiled at the reflection in the bathroom mirror, before taking a warm, damp cloth back to bed.

Laying back down beside him, I took his hand and placed it over the scrape marks up my back. Even half asleep, he perked up, running his delicate fingers over the raised tracks.

"What's that?"

I laughed. "Your fingernails."

He gasped and ran his hand all over my back, searching for further scratches. "Does it hurt?"

I kissed him softly. "Not at all."

"Why are you smiling?"

"Because it's funny," I told him. "And hot."

His hand stopped moving. "Hot? But I marked you." He sat up in bed. "I'll get some cream for the scratches."

I pulled him back down and snuggled into him. "No you won't. You'll stay here with me."

He sighed and ran his hand gently over my back. "Are you sure you're okay?"

"Yes," I reassured him. "And Isaac?"

"Yeah."

"I like it when you mark me."

"DETECTIVE ZINBERG? IT'S ISAAC BRANNIGAN."

I brought the two coffees with me into the living room and sat down beside him on the sofa.

"You told me to call if I thought of anything else," Isaac went on to say. "About the man who came into my house."

Isaac explained how Hannah had realized there was some banking documents missing, but the bank had been notified and no funds were missing. Then Isaac explained the accounts held quite a sum of money. I heard the detective ask something, and Isaac shifted in his seat. He was never comfortable discussing his money. "There was a compensation payout for the accident, the same accident that claimed my sight and my mother's life. My father had the foresight to let a financial adviser manage the funds. There are term deposits, high-interest accounts and stocks and shares." Isaac almost sneered. "Though I'm sure this information you've already found out."

I could hear the murmur of the detective's deep voice through the phone as he continue to speak, and though I couldn't make out many words, it sounded like the police had spoken to someone about the home invasion.

Isaac frowned. "Was that necessary? I told you the physical description was of a man who walked with a limp."

The detective spoke again, but Isaac shook his head, obviously not too pleased with what Zinberg was saying. With an exasperated sigh, Isaac thanked him and disconnected the call.

I lifted his coffee mug and placed it in his hand. "What did he say?"

"He said they spoke to Joshua Lindstrom."

"As in the Joshua you work with?"

"Yes," Isaac said, shaking his head. "What am I supposed to say to him tomorrow at work?"

Isaac loved his job as a teacher at Hawkins School for

the Blind. I'm not surprised he was worried about his reputation. "You tell him its procedure, and if he has nothing to hide, then he has nothing to worry about."

Isaac shrugged and sighed before sipping his coffee. "It's embarrassing."

"You've nothing to be embarrassed about, baby."

He shrugged one shoulder, silently telling me he didn't agree, so I changed the subject. "Well, it's Sunday morning. What did you want to do today?"

"Did you need to get anything from your place?"

"Yeah, I guess," I answered. "I thought we could do something a little more... romantic."

Isaac smiled as he sipped his coffee. "What did you have in mind?"

"Grocery shopping."

The coffee cup stopped half way to his mouth and his face turned toward me. "What?"

I chuckled. "Come on, we live together. It's a couple thing to do."

"Grocery shopping?"

He said it like I'd asked him to donate a kidney. "Yes, grocery shopping."

"But I have groceries delivered."

"It'll be fun."

"Fun?" he scoffed. "Do I need to get the dictionary for you again?"

I laughed. "We'll swing past my place and grab a few things, then we can go to the market."

He put his cup down on the coffee table. "Do you promise me you'll make it up to me later?"

I took his chin in between my thumb and forefinger and stole a coffee flavored kiss. "I promise."

THE MARKET WAS BUSY, there were people every-where and Isaac wasn't familiar with it at all. Even with Brady, he was out of his comfort zone, but I never ventured too far from him.

"Smell this," I said, lifting the mango to his nose. "Smell good?"

"Mmm," he hummed.

I leaned in. "Mangos should be eaten whilst naked," I whispered. "That way when the juice runs down your chin, your neck and your chest, I can lick it off."

Isaac's mouth opened and closed, and he cleared his throat. "Then we better get a few."

I grinned. "And you thought this wouldn't be fun."

He shook his head. "You do realize everything in our cart is phallic, yes?"

I looked in the cart. Bananas, carrots, zucchinis, cucum-bers, sweet potato. "Strawberries and mangos aren't," I told him.

"No, but what you want to use them for is rather... non-dietary."

Laughing, I picked up a whole pineapple and handed it to him. "I hope not, because I'm coming up blank with what I can do with a pineapple."

Isaac grinned and whispered, "If you get the canned, sliced pineapple rings, you could eat them off my-"

I burst out laughing, surprised at his blatant sexual remark. "How many rings do you think will fit?"

A blush crept over his cheeks and he bit his bottom lip. "We'll need two tins at least."

I bit back a groan. "I have a sudden craving for pineap-ple," I told him, just as someone interrupted us.

"Isaac?"

Isaac turned to the sound of another voice calling him by name.

"It's Joshua. Joshua Lindstrom."

The man was about our age—maybe a bit older than our twenty-seven years—tall, lean, with short sandy-colored hair and blue-grey eyes.

"Josh?" Isaac cleared his throat, his cheeks were still tinted with his earlier embarrassment. "What are you doing here?"

The man looked down at his hand-held basket. "Just grabbing a few things." Then he looked down at the pineapple Isaac was still holding. "Fresh pineapple, huh?"

"Oh, I um..."

I stepped in. "Here, I'll put that back. He prefers the canned stuff," I said, taking the fruit. Isaac cleared his throat, and smiling, I held out my hand to our guest. "I'm Carter Reece."

"Joshua Lindstrom." He shook my hand and gave me a tight smile, but he was obviously wondering what I was doing here with Isaac. Instead, he turned back to Isaac. "Please tell me what happened on Friday afternoon, Isaac. I had the police asking me questions—"

"I'm really sorry about that," Isaac interrupted. "I had no idea they'd question you. The police wanted to know if I'd recently met any new people at work..."

"It's fine, Isaac," Joshua said, patting his arm. "Is everything okay?"

"Oh, yeah," Isaac said dismissively.

"Isaac," I said. "I'll just go to the deli. I'll meet you back here."

I figured giving him some time with his work colleague, letting him explain what happened, was a good idea. I didn't know if this Joshua guy knew Isaac was gay, and I didn't want to put Isaac in an awkward position with someone he worked with.

As I stood in the line at the deli, I couldn't help but watch them. And that Joshua guy kept looking at me. Not in a good way, he wasn't checking me out or anything. It was like he was sizing me up as competition. He made no attempt to hide it, just a smug, what-are-ya-gonna-do-about-it look he kept giving me while he talked to Isaac.

I'd always been one to give people the benefit of the doubt, not one to judge without knowing. But I had a gut feeling about him.

I didn't like him.

I didn't like him at all.

CHAPTER FIVE

WAKING up next to Isaac was the perfect way to start a day, and in particular a Monday. He was still sleeping, so with a kiss to the back of his head, I got up, let the dogs out, set the coffee machine going, showered and got ready for work.

I sipped my coffee, thinking about last night. How we ate nothing but fruit, licking mango juice from places mango juice strictly should not go, sliding rings of pineapple on Isaac's engorged dick then eating them off and finally ending up in the shower, both of us sticky messes. And then what we did in the shower...

"You're up early," Isaac's croaky morning voice came from behind me as he walked into the kitchen.

"Hey you." I smiled at him, carefully placed his coffee in his hand and kissed his cheek. "Good morning."

"I woke up and you weren't there."

"Gee, I've only officially lived here for two days and you missed me already?"

"Don't get used to it," he mumbled, sipping his coffee.

"I'll be obnoxious soon enough and you'll wonder why on earth you wanted to live with me."

I shook my head at him. "Oh, please. I already know how obnoxious you are."

"You know, you're probably not supposed to agree with me," he said. "On the obnoxious thing, you know, being my boyfriend and all."

I laughed. "I believe the correct term is *live-in* boyfriend, and I adore your obnoxicity."

"That's not a word."

"Is too."

"Since when?"

"Since I just made it up."

Isaac shook his head at me, took another sip of coffee and put his cup down on the counter. "I'm going to have a shower." He turned and walked back through the living room to the hall. "Maybe, by the time I get back, you'll have had enough caffeine to actually fuel that sense of humor."

"Isaac?"

He stopped, and waited. "Yeah?"

"I love your obnoxicity, with or without caffeine."

"You're absurd."

"Go and have a shower, or we'll be late," I told him. "I'm organizing what we'll be having for dinner tonight."

He turned to face me. "Do I want to know what we're having?"

"That second can of sliced pineapple."

I PULLED the Jeep into the parking lot of Isaac's work. Hawkins School for the Blind was an amazing facility. A school to vision-impaired kids from ages six to adults. Isaac taught Braille English, reading and writing, and he loved it.

I'd been to his work a few times. Most of his colleagues knew we were together, and none of them seemed too bothered by it. They accepted Isaac for who he is, not that he paraded his sexuality by any means, but they seemed more tolerant to things considered outside the norm. Certainly when it came to being judgmental.

I got out of the Jeep and unharnessed Brady as Isaac got out on his side. I walked around to his side as he clicked Brady into his guiding harness, and I noticed a man standing near the entrance doors watching us. I spoke low, so only Isaac could hear me. "That Joshua guy's waiting for you."

Isaac stood up straighter. "Is he?"

"Yeah, he's near the front door," I told him. "I'll walk you to the path, and you can find your way from there."

As we crossed the lot and made our way to the path leading to the front door, Joshua walked up to meet us. I wondered if my first impression of him was off, whether he was a concerned colleague, wondering if he thought *I* could be implicated in Isaac's home robbery.

Joshua said good morning to Isaac, then to me, and he smiled. It was amicable. Pleasant, even. And I wondered if my first impression of this guy was wrong. I didn't know him. Isaac seemed to like him, and Isaac could tell the sincerity of people by their tone and the cadence of their voice. He was the most perceptive person I knew. So, I decided to try and play nice.

"Good to see you again," I said to Joshua. Then I turned to Isaac, and said, "Isaac, I'll meet you here just after five."

But then as I got to the Jeep, I turned around to look at them, and they were just walking through the door. Joshua held the door open, put his hand on Isaac's arm and looked back at me with that smug smile before walking inside.

So the guy was a douche.

I shook my head incredulously, and put it out of my mind and made my way to work. I was met by my assistant, Rani and our receptionist, Kate, as they had their pre-customer coffee. "Good morning, ladies."

"You're awfully smiley for a Monday," Rani said. "Good weekend?"

"Yes, it was. It was very busy," I answered automatically, thinking of me moving in to Isaac's. And then I remembered the reason, the catalyst for the move. "Well, it didn't start out too great, but it ended well."

They both stared at me, waiting for me to elaborate.

"Hannah had a little baby girl, seven-pound Ada Brannigan-Peroni. Isaac had an uninvited guest in his house. He was a bit shaken up, had a few things stolen, and then I moved in with him."

Both women blinked. "Whoa, hold up," Rani said. "Isaac had an intruder? In his house?"

I nodded. "Yes."

"Is he okay?" Kate asked, rather alarmed. "Was he there when it happened? Oh, my God. Was he hurt?"

"Yes, he was there," I told them. "But he's okay. A bit shaken up at first, but you know what he's like. He's tough. The guy who broke in didn't hurt him, just took some stuff for resale."

"God, that must have been terrifying for him," Kate said with her hand over heart. "Is that why you moved in?"

I smiled. "No, not really. It was just what got us talking about the reasons he originally didn't want me to move in." I knew that didn't make much sense, so I explained. "I've wanted to move in with him for a while, but he was always hesitant. He didn't want me to see how much his blindness affected his everyday living. But he knew stuff like that's never bothered me."

"Oh, of course it wouldn't bother you," Rani said. "Isaac's such a sweetheart."

I smiled at her. "Yes, he is rather." Both women grinned at me, with a collective 'awww.' I glanced at my watch. "Come on, first appointment will be here any minute. We'd better get organized." Then I thought of something. "Rani, don't let me forget. I need to call my realtor at lunch time."

"Sure."

"I'll need to cancel the lease on my house."

She smiled at me, probably because I was still smiling. I turned to the receptionist behind the front counter, trying to at least act like the boss. "Kate, which lucky customer is seeing me first today?"

I'D NEVER REALLY SPENT many Monday nights at Isaac's. It was typically a night we spent at our own places after the weekend together. I was cutting up some salads to go with the grilled chicken, and decided to ask, "So, what do you normally do on Monday nights?"

Isaac sat at the kitchen counter. "Usually some prep work for class, then hit the treadmill or cross trainer." One of the spare rooms was set up with gym equipment. Isaac liked to stay fit and in shape, but didn't want to go to a gym, so he set up his own.

"Did you speak to Hannah today?" I asked him.

"Yeah, she was good. Little Ada was fussing when I called at lunch time, so we didn't speak for long."

"Are you sure she's doing okay?" I asked. "She was really worried about you."

Isaac nodded. "She's an organizer and a worrier by nature."

I tipped all the chopped salad ingredients from the board into a bowl. "What does that Joshua do at your work?"

Isaac tilted his head. "He does technology integration, like an occupational therapist type of job. He helps students become more tech savvy, using normal technology and vision impaired technology together."

I hummed. "That's pretty cool."

Isaac smiled and shook his head. "You're a terrible liar. Why did you really ask?"

I didn't want to come out and say the guy was an ass. I needed to word it more carefully. I sighed. "I just don't know how to take him, that's all."

"He's a nice guy," Isaac said.

"But he's only been there for a few weeks?"

Isaac paused for a moment. "He's not employed by us. He contracts out for the company that makes the screen readers and the software that makes it work. We buy the product, they send out someone to help us integrate it into everyday use. He has a three month contract with us, then he's off to the west coast, I think he said."

Well, I felt better knowing he wasn't a permanent fixture at the school. But it reminded me of something. Isaac was going to arrange a new screen reader to replace his stolen one. "Did you get a new screen reader today?"

"Yeah," he said with a nod. "Josh told me to bring my new laptop in tomorrow and he'll set it all up for me."

Josh.

He'd now gone from Joshua to Josh.

"That's nice of him."

Isaac laughed. "Carter, you need to work on your ability to lie with conviction."

I smiled, knowing he'd see through me. "Isn't it a good thing that I can't lie?"

"Tell me why you don't like him."

I shrugged, figuring I had nothing to hide from him. "He looks at me like I'm..." I searched for the right analogy "...like I'm gum on his expensive shoes."

Isaac nodded thoughtfully. "It is really awful to step in gum."

I gasped, and walked around to his side of the counter. I took his face in my hands and kissed his smiling lips. "Not funny, Isaac."

He opened his legs and pulled me into him. "How can he not like you?"

I brushed my nose along his. "Maybe he doesn't like gum."

Isaac chuckled. "It doesn't matter if you're not his flavor. You're my flavor."

I kissed him, tracing my tongue along his before pulling his bottom lip between mine. "I like it when you call me yours."

"And you have the scratches down your back to prove it."

I pecked his lips. "Those scratches are faded. We might need to work on some more."

He rubbed my calf with his foot and ran his hands over my face. He traced along my eyebrows, my cheekbones, my jaw. "Are you beautiful? You feel beautiful to me."

I looked into his blue, unseeing eyes. "Me? Beautiful? No, not compared to you."

He ran his thumb over my lip. "I bet you're beautiful."

"You'd be disappointed if you ever saw me."

Isaac's breath hitched, and he whispered. "Never." His eyes closed and his face fell. He shook his head. "Never."

This conversation took a downward spiral, his mood along with it. I lifted his face and kissed him sweetly. "You see me just fine."

He tried to smile, but settled on a shrug instead. "Dinner almost ready?"

"Yeah. Come out the back with me while I grill the chicken?" I asked. "It's still pretty warm outside, maybe we could take a swim after dinner?"

"I normally hit the gym on Mondays," he said again. "And I'll need you to help me with some labels."

Labels? "Sure. What labels are those?"

"On the groceries we bought yesterday," he said quietly. "Hannah usually labels everything for me."

Shit. I should have remembered that. "Of course."

He shrugged one shoulder. "It's little things like that'll remind you you're living with a blind man."

I kissed him, then whispered low in his ear. "I love this blind man."

"I know you do," he said with a sad smile. "I love you, too." He stood up from the stool, and pecked my lips. "I'm going to get changed."

"Okay," I said as cheerfully as I could. "I'll go fire up the grill."

I stood on the back patio, grilling chicken, wondering how our conversation had gone from light and funny, to Isaac being withdrawn and sullen. I knew he struggled some days, with his blindness, with his misconceived notion that he was a burden to those around him.

So with dinner had, work-outs done, we made labels.

Isaac's Braille label maker was easy to use. The keypad had the standard alphabet with Braille on each button so an able-sighted person or a blind person could type in words using the standard alphabet and it would print out Braille, or he could type in Braille to print out labels.

It made identifying tins and jars of food in the pantry much easier for him, and in particular, differentiating between strawberry and raspberry jelly, apple juice from orange juice, or a tin of sliced peaches from baked beans. It was also ideal for labeling bathroom stuff, like shaving cream, shampoo and boxes of toothpaste. He was familiar with most shapes and sizes, and of course the smell, but to differentiate between a small tube of cold-sore cream from superglue was the difference between living comfortably or a trip to Emergency.

The everyday stuff able-sighted people took for granted.

This was what Isaac didn't want to subject me to. Me having to watch him make his house safe for the everyday stuff. He thought it would somehow make me see how disabled he was.

Which was ridiculous. There wasn't anything he did that would make me think that. Just the opposite, in fact. In seeing the everyday adversity he took on, just made me love him even more.

"Can I have a go?" I asked, and took the label maker from him, just to get a feel for it. I wanted to practice.

Because after we'd gone to bed and Isaac had fallen asleep, I got back up and added some labels of my own. Adding an 'I love you' to a tin of beans, or 'Good morning, sexy' to his morning jelly jar would be a nice surprise and make him smile.

I woke up the next morning to gentle kisses down my back as Isaac crawled over me to go start his morning routine. Knowing he shaved first, I gave him a few minutes before joining him, and when I heard the shower start, I followed him into the shower. I took over soaping him up, which of course led to soapy hand jobs.

Isaac was still light-headed and he swayed, before resting his forehead on my chest. "I think we should start every day like this," he said with a blissed-out chuckle.

"Yes, please. I'm all for that." I kissed the side of his head. "You better get out and let me get showered and shaved, or we'll both be late for work."

"Coffee?"

I smiled and kissed his lips. "So, all I have to do every morning, is make you come, and you'll make me coffee?"

"Seems a fair trade to me." He took my spent cock in his hand. "Though you weren't left out at all."

I groaned at his touch. "Go. Make me coffee or we'll both be calling in sick for work."

He pouted, but left me to finish my shower and when I walked out into the kitchen, he was there, dressed in his well-fitted gray suit, making breakfast.

My coffee cup was full and waiting, and he handed me a piece of toast. The jar of strawberry jelly was on the counter, and I wondered if he'd read my messages I'd stuck on pretty much everything.

Then he picked up the jar and ran his fingers over the Braille label, again and again. "I don't know if it's the most romantic notion, or the cheesiest."

"Oh," I said with a smile. "No, the cheese has a different message."

He smiled shyly. "Did you put love notes on everything?"

"Yep."

"It was very sweet of you."

"So, am I romantic, cheesy or sweet?"

Isaac smiled. "I think you could be all three."

I stepped in close, but instead of kissing him, I reached around and stole his piece of toast. "If that's a compliment from you, I'll take it."

His mouth fell open. "You stole my toast."

"I did," I said while I bit into his breakfast.

"Romantic, cheesy, sweet and stealer of toast."

This time I kissed him. "And you love me."

He sighed dramatically, and a smile played at his lips. "Should I go through the entire pantry to find what else you wrote?"

"Nope, we don't have time," I told him. "Plus, it'll make for a nice surprise when you find them." I took a mouthful of my coffee. "We'd better get going. Oh," I added as an afterthought, "don't forget your laptop so what's-his-name can take a look at it."

Isaac put his empty cup and plate in the sink. "If I didn't know any better Carter, I'd think you might be jealous."

"Pfft. What's to be jealous of?" I asked. "He's a douche, and I'm awesome."

Isaac laughed. "I'm so glad you're not conceited or anything."

I drained my coffee cup. "Come on, grab Brady. Your awesome, romantic, cheesy, conceited live-in boyfriend needs to drop you off at work."

He grabbed Brady's harness off the hook and called Brady to come. I grabbed his laptop and as we walked outside, locking the door behind us, he said, "You forgot sweet."

I grinned at him. "You *do* think I'm sweet!"

"And amazing and wonderful, though I'd never tell you that," he deadpanned. "God forbid you get an ego."

I grinned all the way to work, until I pulled into the

parking lot at his school. Because Joshua was there, waiting for him.

Just like he was every day that week. And every afternoon when I picked him up, except for Thursday when I had house-calls and Isaac took a cab, but he was there. Always there, always waiting with a smile.

A snide smile. A fake smile, and insincere conversation. He was polite enough, and to Isaac it would seem he was being pleasant. But the looks he gave me were of pure disdain. I'd just smile at him and pretend I didn't see the glances.

But on Friday afternoon when I arrived to pick Isaac up after work, Joshua wasn't there. As always, Isaac and Brady stood outside on the path near the lot, and my mood brightened when I realized Joshua wasn't with them.

"Hey," I greeted Isaac and Brady warmly. "Ready to go home?"

"Hi," Isaac answered with a smile. "Sounds good."

And then I saw him. Joshua. "Isaac!" he called out from the door.

I groaned, and Isaac grinned. "Be nice."

He ran over to where we were standing and ignoring me completely, he touched Isaac's forearm. "Isaac, I was hoping I'd catch you."

"What is it, Josh?"

"Well," he started. He looked at me, then back to Isaac. "I was wondering if you'd like to go out, for dinner or drinks."

My mouth fell open. I couldn't believe the audacity of this guy! He seriously just pissed me off. He just asked my boyfriend out. *While I was standing there!*

"Um," Isaac stalled. "Thanks for the offer, but we have plans."

"Oh," Joshua mumbled. He looked between me and Isaac again, and he obviously just figured out we were together. His mouth formed a small 'o' shape. "Oh."

I still hadn't closed my mouth. "Yeah. Oh."

Isaac took a small step closer beside me, either to show Joshua he was with me, or to pacify me. Possibly both.

"Oh, my God," Joshua said. "I'm really embarrassed." He even had the decency to look it. He ran his hand through his hair. "I'm really sorry, I didn't mean to... oh, shit."

Isaac laughed. "It's fine, Josh. You weren't to know."

Well, I didn't exactly think it was fine. And of course he knew. He wasn't... well, he wasn't blind. I put my hand on Isaac's arm, looked at Joshua and said, "I thought you knew."

"No, actually," Joshua answered, looking at me. "I wasn't sure. I thought you might have been a friend, or someone who drove for him." He tilted his head and almost smiled. "Isaac never mentions you."

I stared at Joshua. There were a dozen things I could have said, and wanted to say, to shut this asshole up, but I figured that was what he wanted. He was goading me, trying to get a reaction. So instead I just smiled and spoke as sweetly as I could, though it could have been through clenched teeth. "Of course he doesn't." I turned to Isaac, with my hand still on his arm and said, "You ready, babe?"

Isaac was smiling. "Sure."

We said goodbye, well, Isaac said goodbye, I might have sneered, and when we got Brady harnessed in the back seat of the Jeep and pulled out of the parking lot, Isaac laughed.

"Something funny?"

"He asked me out!"

"I know!"

"No one's ever asked me out before!"

I looked from the car in front of me to Isaac. "What? What the hell am I?"

Isaac laughed. "You know what I mean."

"No," I scoffed. "No, I don't. Don't you remember, *I* asked you out?"

He chuckled. "Of course I remember, I just meant no one else has asked me out."

I almost growled. "Do you want someone else to ask you out? *Like Joshua.*"

Isaac laughed again. "You're jealous."

"He asked you out!" I cried. "*In front of me!*"

"I know!"

"It's not funny, Isaac."

"Oh, please. Yes, it is."

"No, it really fucking isn't."

He grinned hugely, looking rather pleased with himself. He continued to smile like that while we walked the dogs, swam in the pool, and ate dinner. After we'd cleaned up the kitchen, I stood against the kitchen counter and kissed him lightly. "You know," I told him, "if you weren't so cute when you're smug, I'd be really pissed off. That guy is an ass."

Isaac ran his hand up my chest and fisted my shirt at the collar, pulling our faces closer. "You're cute when you're jealous."

"I'm not jealous," I offered weakly.

"Yes, you are," he stated. He pressed his nose against mine so I could feel his breath on my lips. "I'll admit, it's nice to have an admirer, but I don't like him like that. Just remember, I'm with *you*, not anyone else. I *live* with you. Sleep next to, wake up next to. Share my bed," he whispered with a soft kiss to my lips, "with you."

I pulled him against me. "I might be a little bit jealous."

"Just a little?"

"Maybe a lot."

"I don't want him."

"No?"

"No," he murmured, trailing his nose along my jaw. "You, no one smells like you."

I knew he loved my smell. I told him it was my deodorant and aftershave, but he said it was just me. "I think I need reminding," I said breathily, as his lips found the skin under my ear.

I lifted my chin to give him access, and he gently bit my neck. "Reminding of what?"

"That you want me." I said with a groan as he kissed my neck with his lips, his tongue, his teeth. Fuck.

Then his hands were on my sides and he turned me around, so I faced the kitchen counter, and he pushed himself against me. I could feel his hardening dick against my ass. His nose pressed into the back of my head and his lips were on the nape of my neck. "Can you feel how much I want you?"

I groaned shamefully and leaned back into him. "Yes."

"Do you want me to show you how much I want you?"

Oh, fuck. Isaac would only get all dominating every once in a while, usually preferring me to take the lead in the bedroom. Sometimes he'd take charge, and it drove me fucking wild. "Yes," I gasped. I could barely speak. "Please."

Isaac pushed me into the counter, grinding his cock against my ass and with a handful of my hair, pulled my head back. He whispered low in my ear. "Then lead us to the bedroom. Unless you want me to fuck you here."

Jesus.

I have no recollection of moving, of taking his hand and leading us to our room, but before I knew what the hell I'd done, I was stripping off and Isaac's hands were on my back.

He pushed me toward the bed, where I knelt, naked. Waiting.

I loved the way he kept a hand on me, feeling where I was, which way I was facing. When he needed his hands to undress, he kissed my shoulder, the back of my neck, always a part of his body touching mine.

For a man who couldn't see, he knew my body like he knew his own.

He stood behind me with his feet on the floor, while I knelt on the bed. When the last of his clothes were off, his hands held my hips while he kissed between my shoulder blades. His voice made me shiver. "Lie down for me."

I crawled forward, laid down on my stomach and spread my legs wide. When I heard the bedside drawer open and the familiar rustle of foil, my stomach clenched and shivers ran down my spine.

The bed dipped when he knelt between my legs and I gripped the bed covers in anticipation. I might have groaned.

"So keen for it." Isaac chuckled. Then slickened fingers ran down the crack of my ass and pressed against my hole. "Is this what you want?"

I lifted my hips for him. "God, yes."

I wanted him, I wanted him inside me. I wanted him to have me, mark me, claim me. Fuck me.

When he sank his cock into my ass, he sank his teeth into my shoulder. He made me his, with every thrust, every scrape of his nails, and nip of his teeth and his lips. And when he pulled out of me and flipped me over, he pulled my legs up to our chests and pushed back inside me, only this time he kissed me, softly, deeply.

He sucked on my neck, my collar bones, and kissed every inch of skin he could reach, and when he rasped out dirty words of love and lust in my ear, I came. Untouched, my cock spilled between us, and he followed soon after.

As he wrapped me up in his arms to sleep, there was no doubt in my mind.

I was his.

CHAPTER SIX

THE NEXT MORNING, when I looked in the mirror, I laughed out loud.

I was his, all right. I had the scratches, bite marks and love bites to prove it.

"Here," I said, taking his hand and touching his fingers to the love bites over my neck and collar bones. "And here." Then I turned around and he ran his fingertips over the scratches and the teeth marks on my shoulder.

"I'm so sorry."

"Don't ever be," I told him. "I wanted it. You gave it to me."

He shook his head. "Still, I'm sorry."

I smiled at the reflection. "I'm not."

"Are you sore?" he asked softly. "Was I too rough?"

I kissed him softly. "Absolutely not. You were perfect." I smacked his ass playfully. "Go put the coffee machine on. I need to shave, and we have a lot to do today."

And by a lot to do, I meant packing up the rest of my stuff before the movers came in. They were only taking it to storage, but I had some clothes, photos and personal papers to grab. The rest of the furniture, television, appliances and other household crap was going into storage not too far from Isaac's. There really wasn't any need to bring anything else other than personal belongings, Isaac's house had everything. But if I needed anything, it wasn't too far away.

By mid-afternoon, I'd just opened the back door of the Jeep when my cell rang. I checked the screen. Shit. Mark. My best friend, besides Isaac, of course. I haven't spoken to him in two weeks.

"Hey."

"Where the fuck have you been?"

I smiled into the phone. "I've missed you too."

"You always call me. What's more important than calling me?"

It was typical Mark. The universe rotated around him, apparently. "Well, actually, I'm moving in with Isaac."

"No way!" he cried. "He finally caved in, did he? You must be really good at sucking dick."

I laughed. "One of my many talents."

"So what brought on the change of heart?" Mark asked. He knew Isaac had originally said no to me moving in with him.

Just then, after having unclipped Brady from his harness in the back seat, Isaac walked toward the back of the Jeep. "Here," I said to him. "Can you carry these inside?" Resting the phone between my ear and shoulder, I handed a box to Isaac, making sure his hands held it securely. "The door leading inside is open."

Isaac stood there with the box. "You know I'm blind, right?"

I kissed his cheek with a chuckle. "Yes, but you're not useless."

I watched him walk gingerly to the door that led from

the garage to the laundry. "Mark?" I said into the phone. "Sorry about that. Yeah, something happened to make him change his mind."

I told him a very brief version of the intruder in Isaac's house and our conversations that followed. How it turned out he was just worried that me living with him would make me see just how blind he is.

"That doesn't make any sense," Mark huffed. "Of course you know how freakin' blind he is."

"I never said it made sense."

I carried another box inside and slid it onto the kitchen counter. "Did you want to talk to him while I grab the last of my things?" I asked. "He's right here."

I handed my cell phone to Isaac. "Mark wants to say hi."

As I walked back through the sunroom to the laundry and into the garage, I grabbed my duffel bag of clothes and I could hear Isaac's side of the conversation. He was laughing at something Mark had said. More than likely it was the dick-sucking comment.

I took my bag through to the bedroom and when I walked back into the living room, Isaac was sitting on the sofa. Brady was at his feet, resting his chin on Isaac's knee, enjoying a gentle scratch behind the ear.

I smiled to myself as I sat on the sofa beside him. Putting my hand on the backrest, I ran my fingers through his hair, gently massaging the back of his head. He turned his face toward me as he talked to Mark. He was smiling. "Yeah, it's been good. I think I'll keep him around."

I pretended to be offended, gasping so he'd hear my reaction. I gave him a none-too gentle scratch on the back of his neck, making him smile at me as he spoke into the phone. "Of course you can stay here when you visit... oh, sure. Carter won't mind taking the spare room..."

"Yes, I will!" I interrupted.

Isaac held the phone down from his mouth to speak to me, but making sure Mark could hear him. "Mark said he'll stay in my bed with me."

"No, he won't!" I cried. Leaning over, I spoke into the phone. "No, you won't!"

We could hear Mark laugh, long and loud through the cell phone. "Oh, Carter. You're so easy."

Isaac spoke into the phone. "Yes, he is easy."

I gasped for real this time, and covering his hand in mine, I peeled the phone from his fingers. "Are you two finished?" I asked them both, knowing Mark would hear through the phone. "I'm not easy."

Isaac leaned toward me and called out so Mark would hear. "Yes, he is. And he's got the love bites to prove it."

Mark was laughing so loud, I doubt he heard me tell him to "shut the fuck up" before I hung up on him. I took Isaac's smiling face in my hands and pulled him close to gently peck his lips with mine. "I'm regretting ever introducing you two."

"You love that we get on so well."

I kissed him again. "I can't believe you told him I have love bites."

"Oh, who are you kidding?" Isaac scoffed. "Mark loves that kind of talk, and you know it."

My best friend is bi-sexual. A self-proclaimed sex enthusiast, who "wasn't fussy" if he bedded a guy *or* a girl. My best friend with a mind that took permanent residence in the gutter. My best friend, Mark, who was never fazed that I fell in love with a blind guy. My best friend, who weaseled his way into Isaac's heart and adored him completely. Just as Isaac adored Mark.

"Anyway," Isaac added. "He's pissed off you never called

him to tell him you'd moved in here, and that you didn't tell him about the guy who broke into my house. But he'll be visiting next month, so you'll hear *all* about it then." He sighed. "Oh, and he wants you to send photos of your hickies to his phone."

"He did not," I countered. "You're making that up."

Isaac grinned. "Maybe. But I'm sure he'd appreciate the sentiment."

I leaned in and kissed him quickly. "The marks on my body are for you and you only." I stood up and walked into the kitchen. "Lunch first, then I'll unpack the rest of my stuff. I might take Missy for a run when it cools down a little later." I pulled the cold cut ham from the fridge and some tomatoes. "Did you want to go to the movies tonight?"

"Um, sure."

There was a cinema not too far away that was Audio Description friendly. Where blind people, and able-sighted people, could enjoy movies. Blind people simply wore head-phones that gave audio descriptions of what was on screen. We'd been several times over the last twelve months. "I get to pick which one we watch, because the last one you picked was crap."

Ignoring my jibe at him, Isaac put his hands on either side of Brady's face and touched his face to the dog's. "Don't you listen to him. He's the one with crappy taste in movies, not me."

"Did you want ham and tomato on rye, with or without cheese?"

"Without cheese, thanks."

"And my taste in movies is just fine."

Isaac laughed as he got up and walked into the kitchen. "You're allowed your opinion on that," he said, going to the fridge and pulling out the jug of iced-tea. "Even if you're wrong."

I sliced the tomato and slapped his sandwich together. "Here's your lunch. Extra cheesy."

He poured two glasses of tea, delicately using his fingers to gauge the rim of the glass. "And here's your tea. Extra tasteless." He pushed one glass over toward me. "It matches your movie selecting skills."

"Yeah, thanks," I deadpanned. "I thought you were about to say my boyfriend selecting skills."

Isaac bit into his sandwich and spoke with his mouth full. "Nah, your boyfriend selecting skills are awesome." He swallowed his food. "Your sandwich making skills could use some work though."

I laughed and shook my head at him. "You're very sassy today."

"All part of my charm."

I bit into my sandwich and instead of prolonging this sassy banter, which he would undoubtedly win, I kissed him. Just a quick peck.

"Did you just kiss me with sandwich in your mouth?"

"I did," I answered as I swallowed my food.

"That's gross."

I grinned. "All part of my charm."

WHILE I'D SORTED through my clothes and made some space in Isaac's wardrobe and then filed my folders of personal papers with his folders on the desk in the formal lounge, Isaac talked to Hannah on the phone. They were organizing a brunch for tomorrow.

Who was I to argue? I certainly wouldn't argue with one Brannigan, let alone two.

I walked back into the living room dressed in my running gear, as Isaac and his sister were discussing the politics of parking downtown for people with prams. Although he would have heard me walk in, I put my hand on his shoulder to interrupt his conversation. "Just taking Missy for a run," I told him. I collected the dog lead from the back sunroom and called Missy inside.

She was excited, bouncing at the sight of me with her lead. I clipped her lead on, kissed Isaac's forehead on the way out and told him I'd be an hour or so and we hit the sidewalk at a steady jog.

It felt good. No, scratch that. *Life* was good. And as my feet thumped out an even rhythm as I ran, I got lost in my thoughts. Things with Isaac were going great, he and Mark got on well, Hannah and Carlos finally have little baby Ada, and I loved my job.

But it was Isaac that made me smile. I was living with him, the man I loved. He was doing so well; his moodiness was tame compared to when we first met, he was learning to talk about things that bothered him instead of bottling them up, he was learning that good things, like love, are worth the risk. Even his relationship with his guide dog Brady was great.

Even the frightening incident with the intruder in his home didn't seem to faze him too much. He was understandably shaken at first, and yes, he'd had resulting nightmares the first night, but seemed to simply pick himself up, dust himself off and take it in stride.

I knew he was strong and resilient. He'd faced so much adversity in his twenty-seven years and yet he never truly waivered. Sure, he balked sometimes. We all did. He has fears just like everyone else, but he never let his lack of sight stop him from living. He loves his job, he's fit and active, and has some good friends.

It was no surprise that I admired him. I made no attempt to hide it. He was a remarkable man. Even with his temper, his moods, his defensive walls and his mind-boggling ability to be condescending, arrogant and charming at the same time, he was still perfect.

Perfect for me, anyway.

I'd been so lost in my thoughts, I didn't realize how long I'd been running. I checked my watch and realized it had been almost an hour. I could feel the sweat running down my back as I ended the five mile loop at the park, just a short walk from Isaac's. Though it was late afternoon, the summer sun still had some sting to it, and Missy was panting hard. I found a tap and cupped my hands under the running water to give her a drink.

She loved running, walking and trail hiking, loved being outside and I ran or walked her most evenings. But it was hot, so after she and I had had a drink, we walked back to Isaac's giving us time to cool down.

When we walked into the driveway, there was a car parked out front, which I didn't recognize. The thought of Isaac being alone with some stranger made my heart rate spike.

"Come on," I said to Missy, as I started to jog down the drive. I opened the front door and walked inside, not caring if I appeared rude. "Isaac!"

"We're out the back," came his response.

We're. As in *we are*. We.

He sounded happy enough, and I felt a bit foolish for thinking he was in some kind of danger. I walked through the kitchen to the back sunroom and then to the back patio, and I saw who exactly the unknown "we" party was.

I couldn't believe it.

Half of me was completely stunned, and the other half of me wasn't surprised one fucking bit.

Because sitting at the patio table with Isaac, was Joshua Lindstrom.

I unclipped Missy and let her out the back door before me, and I watched as she trotted over to the shade of the trees and sprawled out in the longish grass.

I walked over to the table and gently ran my hand on Isaac's shoulder, letting him know I was there, when he said, "Josh called not long after you'd left. He hasn't been here long. He just wanted to come by and apologize."

Only then did I look at Joshua. "What for?" I asked, still shocked this guy had the audacity to just turn up. At Isaac's house.

"I wanted to apologize to both of you," Joshua started. "I didn't mean to offend either of you yesterday when I asked Isaac out for dinner. I didn't realize you were together."

I smiled at him. He knew damn well we were together. I could feel my blood start to boil and was just about to ask him what fucking angle he was playing, when Isaac spoke. "Carter, will you join us?"

"No, I'm all sweaty," I answered. "I might cool off in the pool. I'll just go get changed."

"Okay," Isaac replied hesitantly. I knew my lack of apology-accepting didn't go unnoticed, and by the way Josh looked at me, I knew he didn't miss it either.

I went into the walk-in-closet, stripped off and snatched my swimming trunks off the shelf, grumbling to myself. Apologize, my ass. This guy was really rubbing me the wrong way. And as I walked out, I caught sight of my naked torso—my love-bite covered, fingernail-scratched torso—and for the briefest of moments, I considered putting on a t-shirt to cover them, then I thought fuck it. I smiled.

I wanted him to see it.

I grabbed a towel, threw my dirty running gear in the laundry on my way out and walked back outside. The look on Joshua's face was fucking priceless.

He tried to hide his surprise, and he recovered pretty quickly, but he stared. I was fairly tanned, but still the purple blotches across my chest, shoulder and lower neck were in stark contrast to my skin. There was no mistaking them for what they were.

I had 'Property of Isaac Brannigan' stamped all over me.

I couldn't *not* smile as I dived into the cool water. I only swam one lap, feeling the water cooling my heated skin, and I was still smiling at Joshua's reaction when I got out of the pool.

I towel-dried off roughly, wrapped the towel around my waist, leaving my torso on display, and all but fell into the chair beside Isaac with a groan. "Sorry about that," I said casually. "Who's less-than-bright idea was it to run five miles in this heat?"

Isaac smiled. "That would be yours."

"Oh, right," I said, putting my hand on his thigh. "It was too."

I looked at Joshua and gave him a smug smile. He was looking at me with a look I couldn't really place. It was a mix of disbelief, distaste, annoyance and admiration. He smiled at me, somewhat pleasantly. "Carter, I meant what I said before. I wanted to clear the air, that's all."

I nodded, and because I was obligated to respond, I told him, "No hard feelings."

Isaac cleared his throat softly. "Excuse me, nature calls,"

he said. "Won't be long." He tapped my thigh twice, which felt like a syllable equivalent "be nice" warning to me.

I watched as he walked inside and when the back door was closed behind him, I looked at Joshua. "What are you really here for?"

He smiled and looked down at his hands. "Believe it or not, I actually did come here to apologize."

"And if I don't believe you?"

Joshua shrugged. "You don't have to. I guess I'd probably be the same if I was in your shoes, but I don't mean to cause any problems," he said, looking at me directly. Then he even looked a little sheepish. "It's just that I... well, I move around a lot, travel a lot with my job, and it's not very often I meet some guys who I can relate to. I mean, I meet guys for a casual hook up," he said, blushing at the admission. "But not for conversation, or discussions on work issues, politics, or just current affairs, ya know?"

I looked at him a little disbelievingly. "You want to talk?"

"Well, yeah," he replied with a shrug. "It gets lonely on the road. I met Isaac through work, as you know, and we got talking about books and... and it was good to have an intelligent conversation with someone about something that interested me, and the fact he was gay too made it easier, ya know?" He looked at me and gave me a half smile. "I don't want to cause problems, truly. I feel like a bit of an ass, to be honest."

I smiled at that. Here he was, admitting to just wanting a friend. Someone he could talk to, about books and issues that affected the blind community—both things Isaac was passionate about—and a fellow gay man at that. Who was I to stop Isaac being friends with people he got on well with and had things in common with?

I still didn't really know what to make of him. He

appeared to be speaking the truth, but there was always that underlying feeling of something not being right in there somewhere that I couldn't put my finger on.

He seemed to say all the right things, he looked honest enough, and he worked traveling the country, visiting schools for the blind to help them. Theoretically, he should be a real nice guy. And if Isaac worked with him and became friends with him, then it was no business of mine to begrudge that. So I made the decision to make an effort with Isaac's new friend.

He was only here for another two months or something. How bad could it be?

Isaac walked back out and as he sat down, I stood up. "Who wants a drink?"

And just like that, I was offering a metaphorical olive branch to Joshua. But when I stood up—because I couldn't help myself—I turned and walked toward the door just to make sure he could see the scratches down my shoulder and love bite on the back of my neck.

I said I was making an effort. I never said I'd be a saint about it.

I came back out with three bottles of water and some pretzels to share, and they were having a discussion on what sounded a lot like work to me. Something about the evolution of eBooks and screen readers, and how it revolutionized reading new releases and classics alike for blind people. Isaac was smiling as he spoke, and as I listened to them debate, and I joined in occasionally.

Joshua asked Isaac about his time at Hawkins and conversation soon turned to Isaac's job. I loved watching him talk about his classes and the kids he taught. His whole face lit up and he used his hands animatedly. Sitting there listening to him talk with my hand on his thigh, I found myself smiling, staring at him.

Joshua looked at me from across the table and smiled, before looking away seemingly embarrassed at witnessing my blatant adoration for Isaac.

I certainly wasn't about to apologize for it.

"Is something the matter?" Isaac asked, unsure of the awkward silence.

I took his hand and gave it a squeeze. "I just love watching you talk about your job," I told him. "I think I made Joshua uncomfortable by the way I was staring at you."

"Oh, no," Joshua said quickly. "It's just... I don't get to see a gay couple together very often. It's... well, it's nice."

"Oh," Isaac said, sitting up straighter. "Sorry."

"Don't apologize," I told him.

Isaac turned toward me. "Were you drooling over me again?"

I laughed at him, and looked to Joshua. "Thankfully, he's only a *little* bit conceited."

Joshua smiled, and after a thoughtful pause, he asked, "So, you two have been together for a while?"

"Just over a year," I told him.

He seemed surprised by this. "And you live together?"

"Yep," I said. "But that's only very recent."

"Yeah," Isaac said with a sigh. "He wore me down eventually."

I chuckled. "I seem to recall the words 'move in with me' coming from your mouth."

"Only because you pestered me into it," Isaac said with a sniff.

I looked at Joshua and rolled my eyes. "Conceited *and* obnoxious!"

Isaac grinned and squeezed my hand. "Oh yes, but you knew that long before you moved in with me."

Joshua was smiling at us, and I shook my head, telling him, "I never win these types of conversations."

He chuckled. "No, I don't presume you would."

"Don't let him fool you, Joshua," Isaac said with a smile. "Carter gives as good as he gets."

Joshua's eyes flickered to the love bites on my naked chest, then back to my face. "I can see that."

I grinned, probably far too smugly, and looked around the yard at the passing afternoon. "Well, I better go get showered and get these dogs fed if we're gonna make that movie."

Isaac's hand instinctually went to his watch. He flipped open the glass cover and read the time with his fingertips. "Oh, it's only four."

"Yeah, but we'll have dinner somewhere first."

"Okay," he said with a shrug. "But if you're picking the movie, then I get to pick the restaurant."

"Deal."

I stood up and looked at Joshua, hoping he'd take it as his cue to leave. Thankfully, he did. "I better leave you guys to it," he said, standing up. "Thanks for having me around this afternoon."

Thanks for inviting yourself was more like it.

Isaac stood up. "You're welcome, Josh. It's been a nice afternoon."

"It has," he replied politely.

We all walked back inside and I organized dinner for Brady and Missy, while Isaac walked Joshua to the front door. I'd filled the dogs' bowls and Isaac met me back in the kitchen. "Did he just call you out of the blue and say he wanted to see you?"

Isaac leaned against the kitchen counter. "Yeah. He said he felt bad about asking me out in front of you," Isaac explained. "He wanted to apologize to both of us."

I washed my hands in the sink. "I was surprised to see him, that's for sure. I thought he might have watched me leave," I added, half joking, half not.

He was quiet for a moment then he added, "He's a nice guy. I think he's lonely, that's all."

I walked over to him and put my hands on the tops of his arms. "Maybe. But at least he knows we're together now."

"He does," Isaac agreed, and he put his hands on my waist. When his fingers felt bare skin, his hands crawled up my sides and over my chest. "Have you been shirtless all this time?"

I laughed. "Yep. Since I went for a swim."

"In front of Josh?"

"Yep," I said, still grinning. "Love bites and all."

Isaac gasped and his mouth fell open. "Carter!"

"And now he knows, without a lick of doubt, that we're together."

"Oh, Carter..." he whined. "Now he's going to think I'm some kind of deviant."

"As long as he knows you're *my* kind of deviant, I don't care."

His shoulders fell. "I work with him!" Then his eyebrows furrowed. "What do you mean, *your* kind of deviant?"

"Yours, as in belongs to you."

"You don't *belong* to me."

"Ah, but I beg to differ. It says Isaac was here. And here," I said, taking his hand. I touched his fingertips over the love bites on my chest. "And here," I moved my hand as I spoke. "And here."

He groaned and rested his forehead on my chest. "What am I supposed to say to him on Monday?"

I lifted his chin with my fingers. "You hold your head up high and you tell him you're very loved."

He smiled at that. "I still can't believe you did that."

"Would you prefer it if I left some 'Carter was here' marks on your neck and chest instead?"

He gasped again. "You wouldn't dare!"

"If your friend Joshua wouldn't get the hint, then yes, I totally would."

He grinned and pushed me gently. "Go and shower. Get dressed. Dinner at Lucia's and movies tonight is on you."

"Oh, yay!" I cried sarcastically as I walked through the living room to the hall. "The one time you *let* me pay and you pick one of the most expensive restaurants in Boston."

"Consider yourself lucky," he called out after me.

I got to the bedroom door and yelled out, "You could consider yourself lucky if you join me in this shower."

I stripped out of my board shorts when I got to the en-suite bathroom and by the time I turned the taps on, he was behind me.

"HOW WAS THE MOVIE?" Hannah asked. We'd had a brunch of cut sandwiches and pastries, sitting outside in the shade of the veranda at their house, while the dogs sprawled out on the lawn.

"Pretty good," I said. "I liked it."

"It was crap," Isaac added. He was sitting across the outdoor patio table from me with little Ada snuggled against him. He looked particularly good today, dressed in a white polo shirt, khakis and his trademark sunglasses. He grinned in my general direction. "Carter likes movies with action and violence."

I rolled my eyes and took a mouthful from my bottled water. "Not that I don't find artsy, foreign films riveting."

Carlos laughed and said, "Hannah and I have similar conversations."

Hannah raised an unimpressed eyebrow at her husband. "That's because your favorite actors are Stallone and Arnie."

"So?" he defended himself. "What's wrong with that?"

Isaac scoffed. "Oh, dear Lord. I thought Carter's taste in movies was bad."

Carlos fell back in his seat and shook his head at me. "It's not our fault they have no taste in cinematic mastery."

And our morning of banter went on until lunch time, when I suggested we should be on our way. "I have to drop into my old place and make sure the movers have taken everything," I told them. "The cleaners come in tomorrow. The realtor already has someone interested in renting it."

"Oh, so there's no turning back now," Hannah said with a smile. "No regrets?"

My response was immediate. "None."

"Yet," Isaac added. "It's only been a week. Give him time."

"Stop being an ass, Isaac," she retorted. Then she looked at me, "If he's an ass to you, you let me know."

I laughed and told her, "I think I've got him figured out." She looked tired, but I knew better than to tell her that outright, so I said, "You should to get some rest while Ada does."

She smiled at me and Carlos rolled his eyes. Hannah

and Isaac were so much alike. Stubborn and independent. Brannigan traits to a tee.

She smiled and kissed us both and we shook hands with Carlos, and Isaac said he wouldn't bother harnessing Brady into his guiding harness to go to the Jeep. Instead he used my arm as a guide and I led him to the passenger door. I clicked both dogs into their harnesses and we were on our way.

When we arrived at my old address, we unclipped the dogs and this time Isaac clicked Brady into his harness. We went inside to find the house, as expected, completely empty. I walked through the rooms, looked in cupboards and wardrobes. There was no trace of me ever being here.

Isaac stood, leaning against the kitchen counter with Brady at his feet. "It's echoey and cold," Isaac said. "It doesn't feel like your place at all."

I walked over to him and pecked his lips. "That's because it's not my place. Not anymore. My place is with you, at your house."

He smiled, almost sadly. "Are you sure you want to do this?"

"Do what?"

"Give up your place?"

"What?" I asked, looking around the empty room. "Are you having second thoughts?"

"No," he shook his head and reached his hand out to lay it flat against my chest. "I'm not having second thoughts."

"Then what's the matter?"

He shrugged. "I don't want *you* to regret moving in with *me*."

"Why would I?" I asked.

"Because I'm blind."

I picked up his hand and kissed it. "We've been through this before, Isaac. I don't care that you can't see."

He sighed dramatically. "You're insufferable."

I chuckled, glad this downturn in conversation was over. "No, I'm amazing and awesome."

"And you told Josh that *I* was the conceited and arrogant one."

"Because you are."

"And you're not?"

"Nope," I said. "I'm amazing and awesome."

"If I agreed to that, it doesn't mean you win this conversation."

I laughed and took his face in my hands to kiss him. "Yes, it does. I so won that one."

He tried not to smile. "One out of about two hundred isn't bad."

I did a little happy dance. "Yeah, but you think I'm amazing and awesome."

"Are you finished?"

"Not even close."

Isaac sighed again and pulled gently on Brady's harness. "Come on, Brady. We don't need to be here for this," he said flatly. "No doubt we'll hear all about it for quite a while."

I smiled as I followed him out, locking the place up behind me for the last time. When we got back to his place, I went through the inventory the movers had emailed me, checking and double-checking what I'd itemized against what they'd packed, while Isaac curled up on the sofa with a book.

When I was done, I crawled up his body, sneaking in underneath the book and snuggling in against him. When I'd sufficiently annoyed him enough, instead of reading, he tried to teach me some more Braille.

With his fingertips slowly guiding mine, he showed me letters and words and while I was getting the basics, Isaac declared me to be his slowest student ever. So I tickled him instead, until he was laughing and wriggling and writhing underneath me, which of course ended in a make-out session on the sofa, which of course ended in the bedroom.

And that's how the second week of us living together went. Fun, kisses, laughs, talks about everything and nothing in particular and it was pretty fucking perfect.

But then when I got home on Thursday night after my house-calls, when Isaac was supposed to cab it home, I pulled into the drive to find a car parked out in front of the house. Isaac obviously got a lift home from work.

From Joshua.

CHAPTER SEVEN

I PARKED IN THE GARAGE, knowing both Isaac and Joshua would hear the automatic garage door open. Hell, Isaac could hear my Jeep come down the street. But I didn't know what I'd be walking in on.

I didn't know whether to be angry or scared; two years ago, I'd innocently walked in on my then live-in-boyfriend and found him in our bed with another guy.

Isaac knew all about my relationship with Paul and how it ended, and I never once thought Isaac would be the kind to cheat. I *knew* him. I *knew* this man, and I knew in his soul he wasn't capable of such an act, but it didn't stop the cold ache of dread in my belly as I walked inside.

It was almost like deja vu.

I came in through the internal garage door, through the laundry to the sunroom. I could hear them before I could see them; voices from the living room discussing medical research into something, but the conversation stopped when I walked into the room.

I put my bag on the kitchen counter and was greeted rather enthusiastically by Missy and then Brady. I gave both dogs a pat and walked into the lounge room. Going for casual, I greeted both men with, "Hey."

Isaac smiled back at me. "Carter," he said, sitting with one leg bent under the other. He patted the seat next to him, motioning for me to sit there. "You're a little late. Everything okay?"

I almost fell into the seat beside him. "Yeah, it's okay. I'll tell you about it later," I told him, looking over at Joshua. I gave him a half-hearted smile. "Joshua."

"Hello again," he said rather cheerfully. "Hope you don't mind, I offered Isaac a lift home. Save on cab fare."

"Mind? No, I don't mind at all," I lied with a smile. I looked back at Isaac and put my hand on his knee. "How was your day?"

"Good," he answered brightly. "We were just discussing medical advancements with different eye surgeries. It's all rather interesting." Then he put his hand on my thigh. "You sure everything's okay? You don't sound like you're okay."

"Yeah, I'm fine," I said with a sigh. Then changing the subject completely, I asked, "What do you want to do for dinner?"

Isaac tilted his head, obviously wondering what was going on with me, yet very aware of Joshua sitting in the room. "Let's order in, yes? You pick. I don't mind."

This was Isaac being sweet. He knew I wasn't up for any argument. I smiled at him and rubbed his thigh, then looked over at Joshua to find him smiling at us. "I can go," he said quickly. "Carter, if you've had a bad day..."

"No, it's okay. I'm sure Carter won't mind," Isaac interrupted, speaking to Joshua. "I was rather interested in those information sites you were talking about."

Too bad if I did mind, I thought to myself. And as much as it pissed me off that he was here, it pissed me off even more that I'd thought of Isaac in the same vein as my no-good, cheating ex-boyfriend Paul. "I don't mind," I said again. "Truthfully, I don't mind. I'm thankful for you driving Isaac home."

Isaac gave my thigh a reassuring, gentle squeeze, but Joshua stood up. "No, I really should be going anyway. Isaac, I can give you that information at work in the morning. There's no rush. Anyway, it looks like you two could use some alone time right now."

"Joshua," I said, standing up as well. "You don't have to leave, really, I'm fine."

"It's no problem," he said quickly. "I need to get going anyway."

Isaac stood up beside me. "If you're sure..."

He was sure, apparently, because he left. I still didn't know what to make of him. If he was such an asshole, why would he leave on my behalf? I still didn't necessarily like the guy, but he may have just redeemed himself a little.

I closed and locked the door behind him. "I didn't mean to chase him off," I said to Isaac as I walked back into the living room. Isaac was sitting on the sofa and I sat beside him.

"No, that's okay," he replied. "I know you didn't. He said he had to leave."

I leaned in and gave him a quick kiss. "You enjoy his company."

"Only as a friend, Carter-"

"Oh, I know that," I said, cutting him off. "That's not what I meant. I meant you like his company, as in you get along well, that's all."

"Yeah, we do get along," he admitted. "He knows so much about what we do at Hawkins and what other schools do across the country. He knows all the new technology and programs and the latest developments and research. I find it interesting."

I leaned my head on the back of the sofa and looked at him. "I know you do, baby. That's really great."

He put his hand out, reaching for mine. "Tell me, what happened today."

I took a deep breath and sighed. "It's Mrs Yeo. She really wasn't well today."

"Oh."

"Yeah, I asked if there was someone I could call, but she said she'd be fine."

"What was wrong with her?"

"Sounded like a chest infection. She was coughing and wheezy. She really wasn't well, and she's so small and frail."

"She doesn't have any family, does she?"

"I think she mentioned a nephew?" I said, trying to remember. "But jeez, he'd have to be in his sixties, at least." I sighed. "I just worry about her, that's all."

"Did you want us to visit her this weekend?" he asked. "We can drop in and check on her tomorrow."

"I don't know," I said hesitantly. "Would that be over-stepping some professional boundary?"

"Carter," he chastised me. "You've been calling in to see her every two weeks for a year. We gave her a new cat when her old cat died! You even helped her bury her old cat. I think we *should* go and see her."

I smiled warmly at him and held his hand in both of mine. "You can't fool me, Mr Brannigan. You might want the world to think you're snobbish and arrogant, but I know how sweet you really are."

"Oh no," he said casually. "I'm arrogant. I'm even arrogant enough to admit it."

I leaned in and kissed him. "Well, would your arrogant self settle for Italian for dinner? I feel like pasta and salad."

"Sounds good."

WE CALLED in to see old Mrs Yeo on Saturday. She wasn't well, but appreciated the time we took to call in, and the chicken soup we brought with us. When we left, Isaac agreed that no, she didn't sound very well at all. She was going back to bed as we were leaving.

On Sunday, we went trail walking on the Wompatuck State Park trails. We both enjoyed the outdoors, hiking, and it was the Wompatuck trails where Isaac had spent a night out in the cold last winter. But we go back often, maybe every second weekend, taking the paved paths or the trails for hikers. For a blind guy hiking, the Isaac and Brady duo actually made a great hiking team.

And they both loved it. Isaac loved it. We'd take a backpack with lunch, Missy too, and the four of us would spend hours in the great outdoors.

Except without my hiking boots, we were limited to the paved paths, much to Isaac's chagrin. The police had taken them, and I still hadn't got them back.

We'd walked the popular path to take a seat by the small lake. "Why won't you let me just buy you another pair?"

"Because I'll get my perfectly good pair back from the police."

"I still can't believe he took them, or thought you were implicated."

"Yeah well, the more people they can discount the better."

"Mmm," he hummed thoughtfully and took a mouthful

of his water. "Still, I told that detective all he should have needed to know."

I chuckled. "Not everyone's as smart as you. You might need to be a little tolerant of those who trust only their sight."

Isaac growled out a huff. "Anyway, I'd like to know if they found anything. Not that I expect them to have."

"We should call the detective tomorrow," I agreed. "Even if just to remind him we're still here."

Isaac sighed. "I don't know what the point of it was, you know."

I frowned at him. "The point of what? Notifying the police? Because that sonofabitch deserves to be caught."

"No," Isaac said with a shake of his head. "The guy, who... who pushed me. I don't know why he took what he took. It doesn't make sense."

"Why's that?"

"He didn't take anything of real value," Isaac mused. "Sure the laptop and that are worth a bit of cash at a dodgy pawn shop, but nothing else. He took random stuff. Specific stuff."

"What are you thinking, Isaac?" I asked. "Do you think there's something else to it?"

He shrugged. "I really don't know."

He was quiet for a while, while my mind raced with possible reasons and scenarios as to what the intruder was after exactly. Before I could say anything, Isaac started talking about how the summer sounds varied to the other seasons. He asked me what I knew about migration and breeding habits of the birds he could hear.

"Um, I'm not entirely sure," I admitted. "I could give you an educated guess."

He clicked his tongue. "What kind of veterinarian are you?"

"Key word being veterinarian, not an ornithologist," I defended myself proudly. "I'm not an expert on birds."

"Oh, please," he scoffed impatiently. "Give me your educated guess on the Red-throated Loon."

"Well, given the size of the bird, I'd say it lays between two and three eggs, early spring. The fact it occupies deciduous trees when nesting is indicative that the bird migrates for winter."

Isaac grinned and nudged me with his elbow. "Sounds like more than an educated guess. Why didn't you just say that in the beginning?"

"Because I'm not exactly sure."

"Maybe not, but you could have told me anything, I wouldn't know the difference."

I shook my head. "Why on earth would I do that? You'd know if I were lying anyway."

He tilted his head as if considering it. "Probably. But your answer was pretty impressive."

I chuckled at him. "If you think that was impressive, you should hear my theory on the mating ritual of the male homosapian species."

"Homosapian or homosexual?"

"Either or," I told him. "I'm fluent in both."

He grinned at me. "Is there anything you don't know?"

I laughed out loud. "Nothing I'm not willing to learn tonight. Do you know of any willing participants I could do my practical examination on?"

He leaned into me, nudging me again with his elbow. "Well, possibly. Do you have anything in particular in mind?"

"Thought I'd start with a complete and thorough physical, bearing in mind some areas may only be examined by tongue alone."

Isaac picked up Brady's harness and stood up. "You ready to leave? I have a sudden urge to go home."

I chuckled at him. "Your wish. My command."

ISAAC PHONED Detective Zinberg on Monday after work and was told, basically, that although the detective wasn't there at that time, there were developments in the case and he'd be in touch in the next few days.

He spent the evening attached to his laptop, with both earphones in, listening to whatever he was 'reading' online. Joshua had given him some interesting reading apparently, and it kept him rather absorbed.

He sat lengthwise on the sofa with his laptop on his lap and his feet in my lap while I tried not to fall asleep watching some television. It wasn't unusual for Isaac to read a lot, he quite often sat for hours lost in a book, be it Braille or audio. He'd usually only have one earphone in, so he wasn't completely cut off from the world around him. But if he was with me, and I was watching television and he wanted to read—like tonight—he'd put both ear plugs in.

I tapped his leg, and he immediately pulled out one earphone. "Yeah, what is it?"

"It's late, babe. I'm just going to bed."

"Oh, I'm almost done here. I'll be in in a few minutes."

I yawned. "What are you reading?"

"Oh," he seemed to hesitate. "It's something Josh gave me. It's about different research and medical advancements in ophthalmology. It's really very interesting."

"Well, it sounds interesting, but I'm beat," I told him. "We can talk about it tomorrow if you like?"

"Um, okay. Sure."

I rubbed his shin through his sleep pants. "Okay, I'll turn everything off. Don't be too long."

"I won't," he answered, lifting his feet off me so I could stand up. He said, "Don't have too sweet a dream without me," before slipping the earphone back in, going back to his audio before I could reply.

I pointed the remote at the large flat screen, turning it off, and as I walked to the hall, I hesitated at the light switch. I always hated doing this, even though rationally I knew it made no difference to him, it still felt wrong to me. I hated the thought of turning off the lights while he was still up reading or listening to his screen reader, even though he'd reassured me it made no difference to him; his world was permanently dark.

I smiled sadly at him sitting on the sofa with his earphones in, because as much as I hated doing it, as much as it saddened me to do it, I turned off the lights and left Isaac sitting in the dark.

FOR THE NEXT FEW DAYS, we spent lazy nights at home. I drove him to and from work, we went for walks in the evenings and we talked, of course. Isaac was animated, as always, when he spoke of his work. And I had to admit, the introduction of Joshua and his industry knowledge, has sparked an enthusiasm in Isaac which I envied.

At night, he read a lot, more than usual, while I watched TV or read work journals or newspapers. We made dinner, made out, made love. It was kind of perfect.

I called in to see Mrs Yeo, as I did every other Thursday, and I thought she was doing better. She opened the door, looking a little pale, still wheezy, but she smiled when I arrived.

"Where's Isaac and Brady?" she asked.

"They'd be on their way home from work," I told her. "Hopefully not trying to cook dinner, because he's really not that good at it."

Mrs Yeo smiled. "My husband couldn't cook. Hopeless, he was. Not even make tea," she said in her broken English.

I gave Tiddles the cat a look over, though there was no need. It wasn't the cat's health that concerned me. I sat with the older woman for a little while, sipping green tea, and talking about something she'd read in the paper. I was pretty sure it was from last week, not that it mattered. She just enjoyed the company. Though the longer I stayed, the quicker she seemed to fade and as soon as was polite, I told her I should go.

"Say hello to your boy," she said to me as I was leaving. "You tell him he visit next time."

"I will," I told her with a reassuring smile. "I'll tell him you said so."

After expecting her to be worse, or at best, no better than the last time we saw her, I left happier that she seemed to have improved. But my mood soon soured as I pulled into the drive to find Joshua's car parked out front.

He'd obviously driven Isaac home, and I should have been grateful.

But it just irked me.

I was trying to like him, but I just couldn't warm to him. There was something about him I just couldn't put my finger on.

I walked in through the internal door from the garage to

find them sitting at the kitchen bench reading something in Braille.

They looked very happy, and that irked me too.

I wasn't typically a jealous guy. Well, I never thought myself to be jealous. I had no problem with Isaac spending time with friends. What I had a problem with, was when that *friend* didn't seem to be a friend at all.

Nevertheless, I smiled when I saw Isaac. I nearly always did.

Isaac turned his head to the sound of my feet, and he smiled. "Hey."

I walked over to him, and ignoring Joshua altogether, I kissed my boyfriend on the cheek. "Hey. Whatcha doin?"

Isaac smiled and tapped his fingers on the book in front of him. "Just doing some reading. You sound happier. How was Mrs Yeo?"

"She seemed better," I told him. "Still not great. She tired quickly."

"That's good, yes?"

"Yeah, I think so. Oh," I said as I remembered. "She told me to tell you to take some cooking lessons to 'keep your man happy'," I impersonated her poorly.

"Why would she say that?"

I kind of smiled at Joshua. "I might have told her your cooking was... experimental."

"Experimental?" Isaac repeated. Then he pouted. "And I was going to cook dinner tonight."

"Oh."

"Well, I'm not now," he said indignantly. "God forbid it be too *experimental*."

I smiled at him. "I happen to like experimental."

Isaac pursed his lips, knowing I was no longer talking about his cooking. "Well," he said, and cleared his throat and turned to face Joshua. "Please excuse Carter. He has no manners."

I chuckled. "Hi," I said by way of greeting.

He smiled tightly. "Hi."

Missy sat patiently at my feet, trying to contain her excitement at my being home. I gave her a good pat. It was a great excuse to show Joshua he wasn't worth my attention. "Hey girl," I cooed as I gently roughed Missy's face. "Want dinner or a walk first?"

"Does he always talk to his dog?" Joshua asked, presumably in good humor.

"Always," Isaac answered. "It took me a long time to realize that while we might be the only two humans in the room, sometimes the conversation is not with me."

Standing up straight, I smiled and shrugged. "Sorry, Isaac, do you want dinner or a walk first?"

Isaac sighed dramatically. "See what I have to put up with, Josh?"

I chuckled and shook my head. "You're not so hard done by, Isaac. I'll even let you cook dinner to prove it."

"Yeah, thanks."

"I'm considerate like that," I added, as I washed my hands in the sink. When I was done, I walked to the fridge. "Iced tea, water, a beer?"

Along with some drinks, I pulled out from the fridge some different cheeses and those little stuffed, marinated peppers Isaac loves from the deli, and then some wafer crackers from the cupboard. "I'm a little hungry. Here, help yourself," I offered to Josh. On a small plate, I cut a few pieces of cheese, added some stuffed peppers and some crackers, and put it in front of Isaac. "Your favorites; twelve, four and eight o'clock," I said, letting him know where abouts the food was on his plate. It was habit for me to do it, and figuring Joshua worked with blind people, I presumed hearing things described as per the clock face would be nothing new to him.

The corner of his lip twitched, almost in a smile. It was almost a sad smile. Reactions like that threw me with Joshua. Sometimes he'd be all smug and give me a daring glare, then other times he'd smile and seemed almost sorry.

I couldn't figure him out.

"Mmm" Isaac groaned. Then he spoke with his mouth half full, "Josh, you have to try these peppers. They're so good."

"They're his absolute favorite," I explained. "They're stuffed with ricotta and marinated in some kind of oil. Isaac would eat the whole tub."

Joshua did try one, then some cheese and then he picked up the cracker box. "What's that?"

"What's what?" Isaac asked.

Joshua grinned. "These labels on the cracker box."

"Oh," I said with a grin. "I had some fun with the Braille label maker."

"I can see that," Joshua said with a chuckle.

"Oh, dear God," Isaac said quietly. "What does that one say?"

Joshua ran his finger over the label. "It says 'hello handsome'."

I grinned. "I put little notes on the food."

Isaac groaned. "You should have seen what he put on the chocolate spread."

"He peeled the label off!" I told Joshua.

"Because it was rude," Isaac replied. "What if Hannah had have seen it?"

"I'm fairly certain Hannah knows all about... body painting in chocolate spread," I said, censoring what I was going to say because of Joshua. He seemed a little uncomfortable, or awkward, so it was also safe to assume he could imagine what I'd put on the note for chocolate spread. "Anyway," I added, changing the subject, "I'll take Missy for a run. I'll only be about an hour, so by the time I get back, dinner will almost be done."

Isaac scoffed. "Well, I will have called for takeout by then, yes."

"Deal." I walked around to his side of the kitchen bench, toward the hall. "I'll just get changed. Won't be long."

I quickly switched into some running gear and joined them back in the kitchen. They hadn't moved and were now talking about deli foods. I walked up to Isaac where he sat on a stool at the counter and kissed him softly on the lips. "I'll be back soon." Then I looked at Joshua. "Nice to see you again. Thanks again for driving Isaac home."

"No problem."

I called for Missy and clicked her lead onto her collar. "I've got my keys Isaac, so you can lock up if you want."

Pulling the front door closed behind me, we started an immediate jog. I wanted Isaac to know I trusted him by getting home and then leaving him there with Joshua. I wanted him to know, although Joshua wasn't my favorite person, I didn't mind if he was there.

But the slightly jealous side of me wanted Joshua to know Isaac was with me, hence the reason for the kissing him hello and goodbye. I always kissed him hello and goodbye, so that really was no different to any other day. Isaac certainly wouldn't think anything of it, but I wasn't going to stop doing it just because Joshua was there.

I wanted him to see it.

I wanted him to see that was how Isaac and I were together everyday.

Because just on the off chance the underlying thing I couldn't quite identify in Joshua was him trying to win over Isaac, then he'd see Isaac and I were very much together.

Did that make me possessive?

Probably.

Did I care?

Nope. Not one bit.

I loved Isaac. Loved him like I'd never loved another human being. And I'd be damned if some guy like Joshua would just blow into town and sweep him away.

As tolerant and pleasant as I was being to Joshua, I smiled when Missy and I jogged through the front gates and Joshua's car was gone.

I unlocked the door, walked inside and leant on my knees to catch my breath, to find a smiling Isaac on the sofa. He sniffed. "Dinner will be here in about ten minutes. Go shower. You stink."

I grinned, walked over and kissed him soundly. "Love you, too."

CHAPTER EIGHT

I PICKED Isaac up from work on Friday afternoon, looking forward to the weekend. He talked of his day, asked me about mine and we agreed on a quiet night, a nice dinner and some wine. We were almost home when he remembered something. "Oh, I almost forgot. I spoke to Hannah today. She called during my lunch hour. We're having lunch at home on Saturday."

"Okay. Sounds good."

"And I invited Josh."

Fuck.

"Is that okay?" he asked.

No, it's fucking not. "Yeah, of course."

"Sure? Because you hesitated..."

I didn't want to ruin our Friday night, so I came up with, "Of course I'm sure. Just thinking of ways I can dazzle him with my cookout skills."

Isaac shook his head at me. "You mean dazzle him with your ability to turn any kind of meat product into a carcinogenic bio-hazard."

I gaped and laughed at the same time. "I'm deeply offended!"

Isaac smiled. "Is that so?"

"Yes! I think that comment is going to cost you."

He was grinning now. "Cost me what?"

"A definite taste test."

"Hmm," he hummed with a nod. "If you insist."

"Oh, I insist." I pulled into the drive and waited impatiently for the automatic roller door to open. My groin was starting to ache at the thought of this impending taste test. I rolled the Jeep into the garage, turned off the ignition and jumped out.

Isaac laughed. "Impatient for something are we?"

Opening the back door, I leaned over the back seat to undo Brady's harness. "You started it."

Isaac licked his lips deliberately. "Don't know what you mean."

As soon as the harness was undone, Brady jumped out. "Good boy," I said to the dog. "Go find Missy. Daddy's gonna be busy for a little while."

Isaac's laugh died when I took his hand, followed Brady in through the access door and headed straight for the bedroom. I wasted no time in undoing my workpants. "You really shouldn't talk about tasting me when I'm driving."

Isaac's hand slipped under the elastic of my briefs and his fingers wrapped around me. I pushed my pants down over my hips and they slid down my thighs, and he kissed me as he used both hands to push my briefs down too.

"On the bed," I panted. "I want to taste you too."

Not a moment later, we were both on the bed, lying on our sides in a sixty-nine position with our pants around our thighs, our shoes still on. I slipped my arms around his hips, bringing him closer, so I could take him deeper.

Isaac's hands were everywhere. He knew my body better than I did. His fingertips had every inch of me mapped out, committed to memory. He knew exactly where a light trace of a finger would make me shiver. He knew where his blunt fingers pressed harder in my skin would make me groan. His lack of sight meant his knowledge of my body was purely tactile.

Like always, he kissed the star tattooed on my hip, as though he'd seen it with his very eyes and not just had me show him where it was. His fingers touched, caressed and probed and when he took the length of me in his mouth, his throat, my eyes rolled and I groaned around his shaft.

It felt so good. So, so fucking good.

Ignoring the beautiful tightening in my balls, I concentrated on him.

I loved the taste of him. I loved having him in my mouth, having him thrust gently into my throat. I loved how he moaned at my touch, my tongue.

But then he sucked deeper, pumped me harder, moaned louder. I pulled off his cock, crying out as I came, trying not to thrust too deep. He tightened his hold on me, took what I gave him, as I spilled down his throat.

Before the room had stopped spinning, before the haze in my mind was gone, he was back in my mouth, thrusting, swelling, coming. He groaned and writhed as I drank him down, and shuddered when I licked him clean.

"Mmm," he mumbled, rolling onto his back.

"Mmm, indeed," I agreed. I took his spent dick in my hand and gave him a pump and a squeeze. He convulsed, and I chuckled. "More taste testing later tonight, I think."

"Maybe we can get fully undressed next time."

I cupped his balls and probed my index finger down his perineum, making him squirm. "I think so too."

And after a swim, some dinner and some lounging on the sofa, we made our way to bed. Only this time when we made love, when I was buried inside him, his legs were wrapped around me, and I was slowly rocking my hips, thrusting gently into him, making love to him. He sucked in a shaky breath.

"Baby, you okay?"

He nodded, and then he whispered, "I wish I could see your face when you come."

Resting my weight on one elbow, I took his hand and put it to my face. It was his way of 'seeing' me. He traced his fingers across my eyebrows, my cheeks, my jaw. He slid his thumb along my bottom lip, edging it into my mouth.

Isaac brought his other hand to my face and kept them there, feeling my face, *seeing me*, until I came. He pulled me against him and kept me there, wrapping his arms around me. When I suggested I get up to clean us, he tightened his hold on me and shook his head.

"Stay."

LUNCH WITH HANNAH and Carlos was always funny. Isaac was sitting at the kitchen counter, holding little Ada, while Hannah and I finished getting lunch ready in the kitchen. Carlos was channel-flipping on the TV, searching for something sports related.

Hannah was telling us all about the most disgusting dirty diaper Ada had done to date, how it seeped up her back, into her hair and even down to her socks.

"Ew," Carlos groaned from the sofa. "It was so gross."

I laughed. "Yeah, this one time, we had a Dalmatian at the clinic with distemper. Poor thing had crapped so bad."

Hannah looked concerned. "Was it okay?"

"Oh, sure," I assured her. "He was fine with the right treatment. But the smell... dear God, we used about a month's worth of disinfectant to try and get rid of that smell. The owner had tried some homemade remedy they'd found online. It was some garlic and molasses concoction." I shook my head. "I can still smell it."

Hannah looked up from washing the lettuce in the sink and laughed. "Sounds gross."

Isaac lifted little sleeping Ada up to his face and inhaled like he always did. "Don't you listen to them, sweet little one. They're being immature and uncouth, talking about disgusting things. You stick with me, sweet heart."

Just then, the doorbell rang.

Hannah spun to look at me. "Expecting someone?"

"That will be Josh," Isaac said.

I smiled tightly at her. "That would be Isaac's work friend, Joshua," I explained further. "I'll go let him in."

Wiping my hands on a dish towel, I opened the front door. Joshua smiled and held up a white box, offering it with a smile. "I bought dessert."

I took the box and stood aside. "Come on in."

Walking back inside, I made introductions and was secretly pleased Joshua seemed a little uncomfortable. I don't know if it was that he wasn't expecting other people to be here, or if he wasn't used to walking in on such a family-type scene, but I think Hannah and Carlos being here threw him off guard. He lived most of his life on the road apparently, so it must have been a little unsettling.

His eyes certainly widened when he saw Isaac holding a baby. I grinned, rather pleased at his reaction. "And that little bundle of pink Isaac is holding, is Ada."

"Oh, this is the little niece you mentioned."

"The one and only," Isaac said. "She's the most amazing smelling creature in the world."

"Yeah," Hannah scoffed. "We were just talking about the amazing smells that ran into her socks."

"Will you two stop it?" Isaac scolded us. I laughed and Hannah grinned at me. Isaac sighed and turned in Joshua's general direction. "Excuse them. They're being crass."

"They're always crass," Carlos piped up from the sofa.

Joshua looked between us all, smiling but seemingly a little overwhelmed. He looked to the white cake box in my hand. "I um, I didn't know if I should have brought anything. I didn't want to turn up empty-handed."

I slid the box onto the countertop and opened the lid. It was a small cake of some sort.

"It's a butterscotch triple torte," Joshua said with a shrug. "Whatever that means."

Hannah peeked over my arm. "That means it's delicious and while I'd like to say you didn't need to bring anything, I'm kinda glad you did."

"I'll pop it into the fridge, yeah?" I asked. "Just need to make some room." I took the tray of homemade kebabs out of the fridge and put the cake in. "I made some kebabs for the grill. Here are some I prepared earlier," I said, using my best TV chef impersonation voice as I peeled back the foil.

"Excuse me," Isaac reprimanded me. "I did most of the skewering."

I shook my head and mouthed '*I did them*' to Hannah and of course Isaac picked up on it. "Did he just tell you all he did them?"

Hannah chuckled. "That's so we'll eat them."

Isaac's mouth fell open. "My cooking isn't that bad."

I walked around to his side of the kitchen counter and

kissed his cheek. I pretended Joshua wasn't watching us. "Of course not, baby. You cook just fine."

Isaac growled at me. "You can't lie for shit, Carter."

"That's why you love me," I said. Leaning in this time, I whispered in his ear quiet enough no one else could hear. "You love my nine inches of... honesty."

Isaac blushed and gasped, and with his free hand, he pushed me away. "Carter," he hissed at me. "We have company. Now go start the grill or we'll never eat."

Smiling, I shrugged at Joshua and winked at Hannah. She laughed and handed me a bowl of sliced onion. "Here. We'll need these cooked first," she said, piling some tongs and the bottle of oil on top of the onions.

"Do you always have lunch together?" I heard Joshua ask as I walked out of the kitchen.

"Most of the time," Hannah answered. "Most weekends, anyway."

I left them to it and set about starting the grill. Waiting for it to heat up, I threw a ball for Missy a few times, while Brady watched on as though the concept was childish. He preferred the cool shade of the trees in the garden. It was a warm spring day, and I knew at some point I'd be getting into the pool.

It was a shame, I mused, the hickeys and scratches on my back and torso had faded. I didn't half mind the idea of Joshua seeing those again.

"What's got you smiling?" Hannah's voice startled me. She was standing under the patio, putting plates of salads on the table. "Grilling onions isn't that much fun."

I chuckled. "Sorry, I was a million miles away."

She walked over to me. "So, has Isaac been treating you okay?"

My smile widened. "He's been great."

Hannah hummed. "I'm really happy for both of you." Then she nodded pointedly back to the door. "What's that Joshua's story?"

I groaned quietly. "Not sure."

Her look became serious. "Is he trying to get between you?"

I looked back to the door, making sure we were still alone. I spoke quietly anyway. "I don't know what angle he's playing. Isaac swears he's a nice guy, but I'm not sure."

She frowned just as the back door opened and the others walked out, and our conversation about our guest was over for now.

Carlos walked out first, holding Ada, and Isaac and Joshua followed. Hannah walked over and collected the fussing baby and declared it was lunch time for Ada first. She sat at the outdoor table, unbuttoned her blouse and started to feed her baby. She draped a light baby-wrap over her shoulder, covering her exposed chest and fed her daughter. Carlos put a bottle of water in front of her, kissed the side of her head. "I'll just grab the tray of meat," he said, and disappeared inside.

Isaac ran his hand along the back of a chair, feeling it, then stepped beside it and sat himself down. Joshua, still looking a little out of place, pulled out the chair next to Isaac and sat down.

I turned back to the grill, trying not to give a shit that Joshua sat next to Isaac. It was only lunch. It meant nothing. It was just a seat at the table. No big deal. Jesus, I really had to stop letting this guy get under my skin.

"Here ya go, chef," Carlos said, handing me the tray of kebabs and sausages.

Scraping the onion to one side, I started cooking the meat while conversation steered toward Joshua. Hannah soon learned that, yes, he worked with Isaac. He spent his time contracted to various schools for the blind across the country. No, he wasn't a teacher. Yes, he could read Braille.

"You don't have a base?" Hannah asked. "No home to speak of?"

I stopped turning the kebabs to listen.

"No," Joshua answered. "I used to keep a place in San Diego, but I was never there. I'd only spend a few weeks there every couple of months, so it was a cost I couldn't justify."

The table was quiet as they processed this information. I presumed Isaac already knew this, but going by his silence, I started to wonder if he knew this about Joshua at all. The guy was literally homeless. Not in a can't-afford-it kind of way, but in an I-chose-to-live-like-this kind of way.

"Kind of a weird question," Hannah said, "but what about your mail?"

Joshua chuckled, a little embarrassed. "It's all mostly electronic and comes through to my email, but my head office in New York catches anything I need. I can spend up to three months working in any one place, so they can forward it to the hotel I'm staying at if needed."

I methodically plated the sausages and kebabs while this information turned in my head. I thought about the life he led, living out of a hotel room. The loneliness must be dreadful; no wonder he hung around so much. I almost felt sorry for him. Almost.

While we ate lunch, conversation turned to Hawkins School, and the upcoming summer break. It was hardly difficult; Isaac could talk about his work all day long. He told us of the new books he had his youngest students reading and how Joshua had helped implement new visual audio description players. "Like I use at the cinema, with the headphones," Isaac explained. "Only these are for the classroom. The kids loved it. The first DVD we played for them was Toy Story. It was incredible."

I loved it when Isaac spoke about what his students had done. His whole face would light up and he'd smile proudly. I did envy how Joshua got to share that with him. I mean, I shared everything else with him, in every sense of the word, but his one true passion, his job, was the one thing I had no part in.

I'd met everyone he worked with, and Isaac would tell me all about his day; what happened, what was gossip. I loved that we had that to talk about, his job and mine, because it paved the way for endless conversation. And sitting around the patio table on a Saturday afternoon was no different.

After we'd eaten, it was mid-afternoon and getting hot. Hannah had fed Ada again and put her to bed inside in the cool of the air conditioning and I'd put the sprinkler on the grass for Missy. She'd run through it, futilely chasing the water stream, having fun and cooling down at the same time. Brady preferred the cool grass of the shaded garden and Carlos and Joshua started discussing football.

I stood up and peeled off my t-shirt. "I'm going in for a swim," I declared to no one in particular. I walked behind Isaac, who was still sitting at the patio table, next to Joshua. I put my hand on his shoulder and leaned in to whisper. "Join me?"

"I um," he started. "I'm-"

Before he could come up with some poor excuse, I took his hand. "Come on, you're coming in with me."

"I wasn't expecting to go swimming-"

"Then why are you wearing board shorts?"

Isaac sighed. "I thought we'd go in later."

I gently pulled on his hand. "Don't make me throw you over my shoulder."

Hannah walked back outside and grinned at us. "You know he will, Isaac."

I led Isaac toward the pool. He hardly protested. In fact, he was smiling and I knew once we got in the water, I'd pay. I kicked off my flip-flops and turned to Isaac. I pulled his shirt carefully over his head, mindful of his glasses and threw his shirt over the pool fence.

"Jeez, Carlos," Hannah said. "Why don't you work out like those two?"

"Because I'm a married heterosexual man," Carlos defended himself. "No one gives a shit what I look like."

Hannah threw the lid off her water bottle at her husband. I laughed and Isaac chuckled beside me. I looked at him, at his pale, well-defined, trim torso and smiled. I deliberately didn't look at Joshua, though I knew he was watching us.

I took Isaac's hand as we walked down the steps into the shallow end of the pool and stood there, waiting for him to get his bearings. We'd done this a hundred times. Isaac was familiar with his own pool, he did laps all the time, but he was still cautious getting in and out. Once he was in, however, was a different story.

Knowing he wouldn't want to take his glasses off in front of Joshua, I waited for him to stand in front of me before I reached up and took his glasses off, carefully putting them on the side of the pool. But just two steps later he threw his arms around me and pushed me underwater, before swimming up the lap pool.

I came up for air, laughing and chased after him. He was faster than me in the pool, but I grabbed his foot and stopped him mid-stride. Isaac spun around, swiping the surface with his hand to give me a face full of water. We quite often roughhoused in the pool, though I never did anything that would frighten him or undermine his trust in me. We were never rough or serious. We just played.

He had hold of my arm and grabbed at my chest, so I slid one leg around the back of his thigh, trying to throw him off-balance, but he quickly grabbed me and dunked me, somehow managing to bring us both under. So I tweaked his nipple, making him laugh underwater.

He came up grinning and ran his fingers through his hair, shaking the water out, then he rubbed at his nipple. "That hurt."

I moved a little closer to him and ran my foot up his shin. "Oh, dear," I said quietly. "Then I best pay special attention to it later."

He splashed me again, so I took his hand and led him toward the steps in the shallow end. I only had to put his hand on the beginning of the edge of the pool at the first step and he was right to get out on his own, so I got out and picked up two towels off the sun chair. "Here's a towel," I said, handing it to him.

He started to dry himself. "I'll go in and get changed."

"Need some help?"

"No, because I know you too well, Carter," he said, running the towel over his hair. Black spikes stood up in its wake. Then he whispered, "We have guests."

I laughed, tied the towel around my waist and collected his glasses from the side of the pool. I slid his glasses onto his face and hooking my arm through his, I led him to the back door of the house. "Last chance for my help."

Ignoring my offer, Isaac swatted me and went inside while I went back over to the others at the patio table. Wearing only a towel over my board shorts, I fell heavily into the chair next to Joshua and smiled at the three faces watching me.

Hannah smiled at me. "Feel refreshed?"

"Oh, yeah. You should go put your feet in if you don't want to go all in. It'll cool you down."

Isaac's sister smiled and tilted her head, which told me she was about to say something a little unexpected. "Joshua thought it was different that you'd wrestle with Isaac in the pool."

I looked at Joshua. "Different?"

He was obviously thrown by Hannah repeating this. "I just thought it was unusual for someone to behave that way in a pool, with a blind man. I mean, Isaac's obviously okay with it—"

"Okay with it?" I asked, keeping my tone light. "He starts it. Why would I go easy on him? He's fitter than me, stronger than me." I patted my exposed stomach, "he's in better shape than me. God, he kicks my ass on the treadmill."

Joshua nodded and smiled, clearly embarrassed. "Yes, I um... I didn't mean anything by it. I just was surprised, that's all."

Hannah smiled at him. "Carter has never once treated Isaac as though he was any different."

I shrugged one shoulder. "Why would I? He's remarkable."

"Oh, I know," Joshua agreed, though it seemed it was to placate the conversation. "I've seen him at work."

"Don't let his inability to see fool you," I said to Joshua. It was a warning as much as a statement. Any possibility of me liking this guy just withered. I didn't like how he talked about Isaac's blindness for a few reasons. One, it was not his place to say any fucking thing. Two, it riled me that he, or anyone, would see Isaac as anything other than an equal, and three, as someone who worked with blind people on a daily basis, he should know—and think—differently. "Isaac's one of the most capable people I've ever met, sighted or not." Then I added, for Joshua's benefit alone. "One thing I've learned and love about people who are blind is they treat everyone equally. They don't judge people by skin color, or the clothes they wear, or by preconceived stereotypes, such as how a sighted person might judge someone who is blind."

I figured that would be enough to shut Joshua up. I raised one eyebrow at him, silently daring him to say one more thing about Isaac, and wisely, he chose to just nod in agreement. Hannah tried not to smile.

Carlos stood up, nervous at the sudden tension. "Can I get anyone a drink?"

"Did someone want something?" Isaac called out from inside. "I can grab it."

"More water, please," I called out. "If that's okay?"

Isaac walked out the back door carrying four bottles of water, mumbling about being a damn pack mule. I stood up and grabbed the bottles he carried, then pulled out his chair for him. As always, he ran his fingers along the arm of the chair before feeling for the second arm, then sitting down. I sat down beside him. Isaac turned his face toward me, and asked, "So what were you guys talking about?"

Before any of us could answer, Isaac's cell phone, which was on the table, rang. The mechanical voice programmed to tell Isaac who was calling told us Detective Zinberg was on the line.

Isaac frowned, and I handed him his phone.

He swiped his thumb over the bottom left of the touch screen and answered the call. "Hello?... yes, this is Isaac Brannigan..." there was quite a long silence while Isaac listened to whatever the policeman was saying while we watched on in silence. "Can you hold on for one second?"

Isaac turned to face me and held out his free hand. I took it immediately. "Carter, can you take me to the police station tomorrow?"

"Of course."

He then spoke into the phone, "Detective? Sure, tomorrow is fine... yes, ten o'clock... okay, that's fine, thanks. Okay, bye."

Isaac frowned again and slid his phone onto the table. We all waited for him to elaborate. "Um, they think they've found my uninvited guest."

"The man that broke into your house?" Hannah questioned.

Isaac nodded. "Yeah, him."

"WHAT ELSE DID THE DETECTIVE SAY?" I asked.

Isaac shrugged. "Um, well, he said there had been other people he'd robbed too, apparently, and they caught him trying to pawn off items reported stolen." He squeezed my hand. "They can only hold him for a certain time apparently. Detective Zinberg wants me to go down to the station tomorrow morning." Then he frowned. "He didn't exactly say what for."

"To help with identifying the guy," I said. "That's what for."

Isaac shook his head. "What? In a line up?" he asked incredulously. "Are you forgetting something?" He pointed to his eyes. "These don't work."

"Oh, please," I scoffed. "You gave him a better description than what any able-sighted person could."

Isaac sighed impatiently, never one to take a compliment, particularly when it comes to how he functioned without sight. "Anyway, I guess we'll find out tomorrow."

Hannah took a sip of her drink. "Well, I'm glad they nabbed the bastard."

"Yeah," Carlos agreed. "And if he's done the same to other people, I hope they sting him for everything. Get busted for one house and you can get off all charges, but get busted for a few houses and you're gone."

"I hope so," I said flatly. "I hope that son-of-a-bitch gets what he deserves."

"I agree," Hannah said.

"Yeah, people like that shouldn't be on the streets," Carlos added, a little more diplomatically.

Joshua was uncharacteristically quiet, until me staring at him prompted him to speak. "Yes, Isaac, it could have been much more serious. He could have been there to hurt you, or worse."

I looked at Joshua, not entirely sure how to take what he just said. He said it could have been more serious as though what happened to Isaac wasn't serious at all, and the guy *could* have hurt him, as though he didn't. "He did hurt him. He pushed him to the ground."

"Exactly," Joshua agreed with me, confusing me even more. "What if the next person gets more seriously hurt, or if he gets more desperate? People like that shouldn't be on the streets, I agree."

Isaac squeezed my hand again, in what I think was an attempt to stop me from replying to Joshua. "Yeah well," Isaac said, putting an end to this conversation, "like I said, I guess we'll find out more tomorrow."

"I might get my boots back," I said, changing the subject. "We could go hiking tomorrow afternoon if the weather's any good."

Isaac smiled with gritted teeth. "Or we could just go to the outdoors store and buy you a new pair, like I've suggested a dozen times."

"I don't need a new pair of boots. There was nothing wrong with my old pair."

Hannah chuckled. "I love it when you two argue. It makes me and Carlos look normal."

"This isn't arguing," I reassured her. "He hasn't called me any names yet."

Ignoring us both, Isaac sighed loudly. "See what I have to put up with, Josh?"

The blond man smiled. "Yeah." Then he cleared his throat. "I might leave you guys to it and head back to the hotel. I've intruded on your afternoon long enough."

"Oh," Isaac said. "Are you sure? You're more than welcome to stay."

Joshua deliberately didn't look at me. "No, it's fine, really," he said politely. He stood up. "I've had a lovely afternoon, but I should get going."

"Okay, I'll walk you out," Isaac said.

Joshua said goodbye, smiling at everyone and giving me a small nod. I told him I'd see him during the week sometime no doubt, and he nodded again. I watched him and Isaac disappear through the back door and walk through the sunroom, and when they were out of earshot, Hannah leaned across the table.

"What's the deal with him?" she whispered, still aware of Isaac's better than average hearing.

"I don't know," I admitted. "But I don't like him."

Hannah and Carlos both grinned. "I think I can tell," Hannah said with a chuckle.

"I've tried to like him," I told them quietly. "Because he's Isaac's friend, but he's weird."

Carlos nodded. "He is a bit weird."

"He'll be nice as pie, but it's like there's something

lurking underneath," I tried to explain. "I can't put my finger on what it is exactly. It's like he's pleasant, but then he's not."

"Yes!" Hannah agreed. "I got that impression."

"He's here all the time," I told them. "Well, two or three times a week."

"Jeez," Hannah said with a frown. "Is he gay? Does he have a thing for Isaac?"

"Jesus, Hannah," Carlos said. "Carter already doesn't like the guy, don't go adding fuel to the fire."

I laughed. "Well, he told us he's gay. But he definitely knows we're together." I smirked at them. "Last weekend when he was here, I made sure I took my shirt off in front of him so he could see love bites all over me."

Carlos shook his head, but Hannah laughed. "Really?"

I laughed and nodded. "I even had fingernail scratches down my back." Looking down at my still naked chest. "They're faded now. You can't see them."

Hannah laughed and clapped her hands. She seemed genuinely proud of her brother. "Oh, my God. Isaac's an animal."

Carlos was smiling now. "Lucky Carter's a vet."

Isaac's voice interrupted us laughing. "Hannah," he called out. "Someone in here is awake and fussing."

Hannah stood up. "Okay," she yelled out to Isaac. She looked at the mess on the table, but before she could start packing up plates and empty dishes, I stopped her.

"Leave it. You guys go and take care of your little one. I'll take care of this."

"You sure?" Hannah asked. "It'll only take a second for me to help before we leave."

"I'm sure," I told her. "You guys have enough to do."

Hannah rolled her eyes and Carlos smiled at me, but they went inside. I could hear them talking with Isaac while

I packed up the table. When I walked inside with my hands full, they were getting ready to leave. Carlos was putting the baby's things in the car.

Hannah kissed Isaac's cheek and made him promise to call her after we left the police station tomorrow.

"Of course," he reassured her.

When she leaned in to kiss my cheek, I whispered, "Don't tell Isaac you know," I finished by pointing to my neck and chest.

"Don't tell Isaac you know what?" Isaac asked. He had the hearing of a hawk.

Shit.

Hannah giggled. "About the love bites and scratches you left on poor Carter here."

Isaac's mouth fell open and he turned to face me. "Jesus, Carter, I left you alone for a minute and you told them that!"

"Well, I..."

"Do I even want to know how that conversation came up?" he asked.

"Aw, don't be mad, little brother," Hannah said. "I have to say, I'm a little proud."

Isaac groaned and turned away from her. "Thanks a lot, Carter."

I wrapped my arms around him and gave him a fierce hug. "Don't be mad, baby. I didn't tell them about the ones on you."

Isaac sighed, resigned, and Hannah laughed as she turned toward the car. "Ooh," she said, turning around. "Joshua left the cake, didn't he?" Her eyes were big and hopeful.

I laughed at her. "I'll just get it for you."

"DON'T BE NERVOUS," I told him, taking his hand. "I'll be right there with you."

We were sitting in the Jeep in front of the police station.

"It's just a little daunting," he admitted quietly. "I don't like not knowing what's going to happen, ya know?"

I squeezed his hand. "I'm sure the detective will step you through it. He might just want to ask some more questions, or he might even have your stuff to give back to you."

Isaac frowned. "I'm sure if it were either of those two things, he'd have come to the house."

"Well, maybe," I conceded. "But the only way we're going to find out is if we actually walk inside. Remember, you don't have to do anything you're not comfortable in doing." I ran my thumb over the back of his hand. "Once the detective tells you what he wants you for, you can say yes or no. You don't have to do anything. You can withdraw all charges if you want."

He shook his head. "No, it'll be okay," he said. He took his hand back from mine and undid his seatbelt. "Let's get this over with." Once Brady was harnessed, Isaac took a deep breath and stood up straight.

I smiled and gently put his hand on my arm. "Come on. This way."

The front desk at the police station was just like you see on TV. There was a high counter with a glass partition, which a uniformed officer attended. He looked us both up and down and his eyes finally landed on mine. "Can I help you?"

Isaac answered. "My name is Isaac Brannigan. I have an appointment with Detective Zinberg at ten o'clock."

We were led down a corridor, which opened into a

waiting room with rows of offices along the far wall and a row of seats along the other wall. We were asked to sit there and wait, apparently the detective wouldn't be long.

I sat next to Isaac, and Brady sat between his feet. Isaac fidgeted with the harness in his hand. There was a lot of noise; voices, radios, phones, people walking. Sounds I doubt I'd have even noticed before I'd met Isaac.

"You okay?" I asked.

He nodded. "Yeah. Just wondering what I'm here for."

I patted his leg just as Detective Zinberg walked around the corner. "Mr Brannigan, Dr Reece, please come this way," he said, waving his hand toward one office in particular.

We sat in the two chairs across from his at his desk, and he fell into his chair with a sigh. The detective opened a file and basically recapped everything Isaac had told him in his statement the day it happened.

"You phoned two days later and reported financial documents had also been taken," Zinberg stated. "Is there anything else you've noticed missing?"

Isaac shook his head. "Not that I've found, no."

Then the detective explained the reason for our visit. "We have a person of interest that's helping with our enquiries. As I told you on the phone, he was caught trying to sell stolen items; items he claims he found."

Realizing it was not my place to speak unless spoken to, I looked at Isaac. His eyebrow creased. "Not just things stolen from me? Did he take things from other people?"

It was weird Isaac asked this. He knew the offender stole from other people. Maybe he just needed to hear it. The detective nodded. "Yes."

Isaac nodded slowly. "We're the others... blind?"

I turned to face the detective and waited for him to answer. I hadn't even thought of that.

The detective looked at me, then to Isaac. "They were all physically impaired in some way, yes."

"Jesus," I said out loud without meaning to.

The detective looked at me and nodded. "There've been three other incidents in the last two weeks."

Isaac cleared his throat. "Was anyone hurt?" he asked quietly. I put my hand over Isaac's and gave it a squeeze.

"Not seriously," Zinberg answered. "Much like yourself, the intruder pushed them as they were walking into their homes, eliminating the need to break in."

Isaac nodded again and chewed on his lip. "Makes sense, I guess."

"The other victims didn't get a great visual of the attacker either," the detective went on to say. "Although they aren't blind like yourself, they were either too scared to look, or in shock."

Isaac interrupted him. "What are their impediments?"

Zinberg raised an eyebrow at the question, but answered, "One was deaf, one elderly lady with a walking cane, one guy with Down Syndrome, all living independently."

Isaac's jaw clenched and his nostrils flared as he took a deep breath, his hold on my hand tightened.

Then the detective smiled at him. "It was your description of the intruder that led us to him, Mr Brannigan."

"Isaac," Isaac corrected him. "Please call me Isaac."

Zinberg continued, "Isaac, it was your description that helped us. The other victims—that we know of—didn't see much, but the second victim, the older lady, said she thought the man smelled familiar. She said her brother, when he was alive, rolled his own cigarettes with a port-wine tobacco."

Isaac nodded. "Yes, it's a distinct smell."

The detective smiled and nodded. "There were other connecting factors, but given you told us he smelled of port-wine tobacco, we knew then it could be the same guy."

Isaac sat back in his seat and seemed to breathe in relief. "And you have him now? He can't hurt anyone else?"

"We're holding him, yes."

Isaac tilted his head. "Holding him? What does that mean?"

"It means we need more proof," the policeman said. "We can get him for selling stolen goods, but unless we can place him at the scenes, that's all we've got."

"No fingerprints?" I asked. They dusted for them. I should know; I had to clean up the mess of black dusting powder.

The detective shook his head. "We've got possible partials. We're running them again."

Isaac shrugged and shook his head. "I don't know if he wore gloves, or if he touched anything else, sorry."

"Don't apologize," Zinberg said. "You've told us more than anyone else has been able to. This guy is smart."

"I did say he spoke as though he was well-educated," Isaac reminded him.

Zinberg smiled again. "Yes, you did."

"I even told you his accent dialect," Isaac said. "Does that match with this man you're holding?"

"Yes, it does," Zinberg said. "He's from the New York district."

Isaac nodded as though he finally understood something. "What you're saying is, it doesn't matter what I can tell you about this man—how he walks, talks, smells—the fact I can't give you a visual description, physically place him at my house, means my statement is useless. I'm sorry Detective Zinberg," Isaac said his name as though it tasted bad, "yes, it's unfortunate for you that I can't see. It has made your job *less easy*. But if you were any good at your job, you'd take the information I've given you, and use it."

Isaac stood up, apparently declaring this meeting over. I smiled at the detective. It had been a little while since I'd seen Isaac's temper and his well-aimed words. He was like a firecracker when he was mad, and it was empowering to watch him give someone else a piece of his mind. And to be honest, I was just pleased his stinging words were aimed at someone who wasn't me.

I stood up, took Isaac's arm and led him to the door.

"Mr Brannigan," Zinberg called out.

"I'd like to go home now," Isaac said, just for me. So I opened the office door and led us out to the waiting room.

"Isaac, stop." Zinberg followed us. "Please."

Isaac did stop and turned to the sound of Zinberg's voice. "Detective Zinberg, if you're going to treat me like a second-class citizen and disregard anything I might say because I'm blind—"

"I don't, no," he defended himself. "To be completely honest, the information you've given us is outstanding. Better than most people *with* eyesight could give. But it would only take a half-decent lawyer to put this case in the can because we can't place him at the scene—"

Detective Zinberg kept talking, but my attention was drawn to something else.

First to Isaac. His hand grabbed my arm, the hand that wasn't holding onto Brady's harness, gripped my forearm and his hold was squeezing. Wondering what on earth was wrong, I looked from his hand on my arm, back to Isaac.

Then I heard it.

Brady.

Brady was growling.

I'd heard him bark once or twice, but never had I ever heard him growl.

By now the detective had stopped talking and was looking at the dog at Isaac's feet, and together we both followed the dog's gaze.

I hadn't noticed the two uniformed police officers with a third man walk into the waiting room. Brady certainly had. He was staring at them; his fur was bristled at his neck and a low, low growl rumbled in his throat.

Zinberg looked at the offending man with the two officers, then looked to Isaac and his stronghold grip on my arm. "Loretto, Young," Zinberg called out, I realized, to the two police officers. "Take him to interview room four. I have more questions."

The man in question, the man Brady was growling at, looked at the detective beside us and rolled his eyes. "More questions!" He almost sneered. "You're gonna take the testimony of a blind man? Or his dog?"

Isaac's reaction to the sound of his voice was immediate. He gasped quietly and took a reflexive step closer to me, away from the man who just spoke. He pulled on Brady's harness, pulling him away from the man as well, and whispered, "That's him! I know that voice."

The man spoke across the room to Zinberg again. "If you're not going to charge me with anything, then I think I'm entitled to leave."

Detective Zinberg looked at Isaac, how he was holding on to me and then he looked again at Brady, who was still standing defensively. "Isaac, are you sure?"

Isaac nodded quickly and answered softly. "Yes."

Then the detective looked over at the man and smiled. "I don't think you're going anywhere." Then with a small nod to the two policemen, he said, "Take him into custody.

Charge him with four counts of assault, unlawful entry, theft, intimidation, possession of stolen goods, selling stolen goods, and whatever else you can think of. I'll be right in."

I watched in disbelief and shock at what had just happened, as the two uniformed officers led the man away. "You can let go of my arm now. He's gone," I said quietly, and Isaac's fingers peeled from their hold. I slid my arm around his waist and stood a little closer to him.

Detective Zinberg put a reassuring hand on Isaac's arm. "I think that was proof enough. Now, I believe the term was —how did you put it—if I was any good at my job, I'd take the information you'd given me and use it. Well, I'd better go use it."

Isaac opened his mouth to speak, but the detective cut him off. "I'm sorry you had to go through that just now, Isaac," he said sincerely. "I certainly didn't mean for you to run into him. But in an unfortunate sense, I'm glad you did. I'm glad your dog was here too."

He told us we were free to wait, though he'd understand if we wanted to go home, either way he'd let us know what happened.

"I think I'll go home," Isaac said. "You can phone me any time." He was quieter, more subdued and the detective noticed.

"That's perfectly fine, Isaac. I'll be in touch." Zinberg took a step in the direction of the officers and their suspect, then stopped and turned back to us. "Isaac, can I ask you something?"

"Yes."

"Does the name Max, or Maxwell Krabanski mean anything to you?"

Isaac stood silent for a moment, then shook his head. "No."

Zinberg nodded. "You don't know the name, through work, or through an associate?"

"No, I've never met anyone by the name of Max, or Maxwell, or Krabanski," Isaac repeated.

Zinberg looked at me. "Familiar with that name, Dr Reece?"

I shook my head. "No."

Isaac swallowed loudly. "Is that him? Is that his name?"

"Yes, it is," the detective answered. "I just wanted to know if you knew him in any way, before I go back in there. I'll be in touch this afternoon," he said, clapped his hand again on Isaac's arm, and disappeared down the hall.

It was clear Isaac was upset, so I pulled him against me and after a long moment of silence, he leaned into me. "Carter?"

"Yeah?"

"Please take me home."

CHAPTER TEN

ISAAC WAS QUIET ALL AFTERNOON. I suggested going to the outdoor store and letting him buy me new boots, hoping it would cheer him up, so we could go hiking, but he shook his head. "Another time," he said softly.

He was on the sofa reading through what looked like the papers Joshua had given him. I fed the dogs, tidied up after dinner and finally sat down beside him. "Are you okay?"

His fingers stilled on the page. "Yeah, I'm okay."

"It was a little confronting at the police station today, wasn't it?"

Isaac nodded. "In more ways than one."

"What do you mean?"

"Well, firstly, I wasn't expecting that man to be there, that Maxwell Krabanski. As soon as I heard Brady growling, I knew something was wrong... and then he spoke. I remembered his voice," he said quietly. "I won't ever forget it."

I slid my hand onto Isaac's leg. "Brady was incredible today."

He nodded, and quietly agreed. "Yeah, he was."

"You know, that Maxwell guy didn't look like how I'd pictured him," I said. "He was tall and thin, and older than what I thought. That's what surprised me the most. He'd have to be in his late-forties. I don't know why I envisaged some young asshole."

Isaac shrugged indifferently. "Oh, was he?"

He was quiet for a while again, seemingly distracted, so I prompted him. "Babe, you said 'firstly'. Was there a secondly?"

"Detective Zinberg," he replied with a sigh. "How he said in the beginning that everything I told them before was basically useless because I can't see. That my account of what happened doesn't count because I'm blind." He shrugged indifferently. "That kind of stigma really gets me down."

I rubbed his back and pulled him against my chest and lay back against the armrest of the sofa. "I know it does. Though it wasn't his personal opinion, more of how he knew some lawyer would twist it around in the legal system."

His voice was quiet. "Does that make it any better? Does that make it right?"

"No. No, it doesn't."

He nodded, took his sunglasses off and scrubbed his hands over his face. "I just hate having to defend myself like I'm some second-rate citizen, like my opinions don't count because I'm fucking blind. I'm a fucking human being with rights like everyone else."

I tightened my hold on him. "You're an amazing *fucking human being*, Isaac. Don't let those assholes get you down. They don't know you like I do."

He sat up, looking suddenly nervous. He fidgeted in his seat and turned his face toward me. "I want to see, Carter."

I blinked, surprised. Not that what he said was surprising, just how he said it. "I know you do."

"No, I really want to see."

I shook my head. "Isaac..."

"What if I told you there might be a way?"

"Might be a way for what?"

"For me to see."

His phone buzzed, making me jump. The caller ID voice activation told us it was Hannah calling.

Isaac sat unmoving for a long second, obviously not wanting to stop this conversation.

Hannah, Hannah... the phone's synthetic speech said until Isaac growled and answered. "Yes?... sorry," he said, I presumed to Hannah for the tone in which he answered the phone. "It went okay," he said next. "Well, probably better than okay. The guy's been charged."

His tone simmered once he started talking to his sister. She must have asked him for all the details of what happened at the police station because he started to relay the entire event.

I maneuvered myself around Isaac and got off the couch. Knowing he'd be on the phone for some time, I kissed the side of his head and gave him some privacy. He and Hannah could talk for hours, and sometimes they did.

By the time I showered and rejoined him on the couch, he was telling her how Detective Zinberg had called us this afternoon to tell us Maxwell Krabanski had officially been charged with four counts of assault, four counts of unlawfully entering a property, selling stolen goods and four counts of intimidation, and how he was an ex-executive who had a leg injury, which led to a pain meds addiction, which led to him being fired and broke, hence the need for quick cash and any bathroom cabinet medicine he could steal.

Isaac told Hannah everything, to all of which Hannah still had a slew of questions.

As Isaac talked, I settled in beside him, turned on the TV and switched it to mute, flicking through channels looking for something remotely interesting. My mind kept wandering to what he'd said about there being a way for him to see again. From what I understood, retinal detachment only had a small window of opportunity to be fixed, which was up to a week after the initial detachment, and even then it wasn't always successful.

Certainly not nineteen years after the accident.

But Isaac was no fool. He knew this about his sight, better than anyone.

So I wondered what on earth had happened to change his mind.

"Okay, love you too," Isaac said and disconnected the call. He put his phone on the coffee table and sighed. "Jesus, she can talk."

I laughed. "I think it's a family trait."

He pushed me playfully, but then settled himself against me again with another sigh.

"Is she okay?"

"Oh, yeah. I just got twenty questions. Next time maybe she should come with us. It'd save me all that time."

I rubbed his arm and was just about to ask him what he meant by his earlier comment about seeing again, but then he yawned. "Come on," I said, sitting us up. "Bedtime for you."

"Hmm," he agreed. "Sorry, I've not been very sociable today."

I took his face in my hands and kissed him softly. "Don't apologize. It's been a very trying day." I stood up and taking

Isaac's hand, I pulled him to his feet. "You go shower, it'll make you feel better. I'll lock up."

I was already in bed by the time Isaac walked out of the bathroom. He was naked. I threw back the covers for him to climb in bed. He was warm and smelled of soap. I smiled and kissed the top of his head as he snuggled into me.

"Babe?"

He hummed into my chest. "Mmm?"

I wanted to ask him what he meant about being able to see again, but figured with the day he'd had maybe he was just a little stressed out, so I left it alone. "You okay?"

"Mmm mmm," he hummed again. "Tired."

I traced circles on his back, which he loved. I felt him smile against me. I kissed the top of his head one more time and murmured, "Sleep."

And he did. Though it was fitful at best. He tossed and turned all night, even wrapping my arms around him didn't calm him down like it normally did. Usually if he was restless while he slept, I would cuddle into him or pull him against me, and it would somehow relax him, even in his sleep. But not this time.

Something was definitely on his mind.

It wasn't until the following night I got to ask him what it was. I'd picked him up from work and we spent the drive home taking turns, talking about our day. When we got home, I asked him the question that had been burning in my brain all day.

"Isaac," I asked as I poured us both a drink of iced tea. "What did you mean yesterday when you said there might be a way for you to see again?"

He swallowed hard. "Um, there have been some medical advances in retinal nerve damage..." he trailed off, as though he was uncertain of my reaction.

"Really?" I asked, excited at the possibility.

He smiled at my tone and nodded. "I've been reading about it. It's all very new, but there's been some success."

"How new?"

"Well, it's all just in the last twelve months."

"Oh." It was starting to sound not so good.

"They have to start somewhere, right?"

"Sure," I conceded, trying to sound keen for his sake. "They sure do."

"There've been some medical journal reports I've read about what this could mean for people like me."

"That is really good," I told him. "How far off are medical trials? I'd imagine they're still a while away yet if it's all so new?"

"No, they're past the trial stage."

Now it was sounding better. "Really? That means the American Medical Association has approved clinical tests."

His smile faltered. "It's not through the AMA," he said quietly.

"What do you mean it's not?" I didn't understand. All medical surgeries in America had to be approved by the AMA.

"It's not done here in America yet."

"Oh."

"There's a doctor in Argentina who has performed this surgery and—"

I cut him off. "Argentina?"

He nodded and kind of shrugged. "Yeah, in Buenos Aires, there's a doctor—"

"Isaac, stop."

"What?"

"You realize how this sounds, right?" I asked. "Having a surgery as risky as that, in a different country, with different medical and health standards, with a doctor who may not even be qualified—"

"Jesus, Carter!" he cried, throwing up his hands.

"What?" I snapped back at him. "Where did you even hear about this?"

He paused for a second, obviously deciding as to whether he should tell me. His voice was calmer, more composed and very defensive. "Josh gave me the medical journals and research papers."

I groaned and rolled my eyes. "Of course he did."

"What's that supposed to mean?"

"Ugh, Josh this, Josh that," I said petulantly. "God, he just breezes in and offers the world."

"Oh, for God's sake," Isaac said, holding up his hands. "Really, Carter? Is that what this is? Are you fucking jealous?"

"Of him?" I spat out. "No." I pulled at my hair. "Ugh, yes, okay. Yes, I am."

"What for?"

"He's like your new best friend. He's nice as pie to you, then glares at me, but I can't say anything because you think I'm being jealous."

"Don't be ridiculous." Isaac disregarded that comment completely. "He's been nothing but nice to you."

"Yeah, while you're there."

"Oh, for fuck's sake, Carter." He exhaled slowly, composing his temper. Then his face fell. "Can you at least try to be excited for me? This could change my life forever."

My mouth fell open. "What? Isaac, of course I am."

"No, you're not."

"Well, maybe I would be if I knew more," I told him honestly. "But it's not sounding very legitimate."

Isaac turned as if to walk out, but he stopped. "Josh was

right. He said you wouldn't like it. That's why I've not mentioned it before now."

"See? He's talking crap about me to you, making stuff up."

"Is he?" Isaac asked quietly. "Sounds pretty spot on to me. Do you think I should have the procedure done?"

"That's not fair. I don't know enough about it to comment objectively."

"It's a simple question, Carter. You either want me to see again, or you don't. Which is it?"

"No, no I don't. Not by some butcher in South America!"

Isaac swallowed hard and he lifted his chin defiantly. He walked from the kitchen through the living room to the hall.

"Isaac, please..."

"I'll be on the treadmill," he said coldly. "I won't be eating dinner tonight. Don't feel much like company either."

And with that, he walked out. A few minutes later, I heard the thud-thud-thud of feet hitting the treadmill, so I stripped off, threw on some board shorts and did lap after lap of the pool. Then I sat on the back patio and threw the ball to Missy until she got bored of it, so I changed into my running gear and took her for a run.

He was in the living room reading when I got back. I took Missy straight out to the yard, walked back inside, past Isaac without saying a word and flipped the light switch off as I went, leaving him in the dark.

I showered and got into bed.

I stared at the wall, waiting for him to come to bed, so I could pretend I was already asleep.

He never did.

THE NEXT MORNING WAS AWKWARD. The sound of the shower woke me, seeing Isaac's side of the bed untouched, I got up and found the spare bed rumpled.

Fuck.

I didn't know what to say. I knew he could be stubborn, but fuck! What did he want me to say? I wasn't backing down on this. This was about his health and his safety, not to mention his hope and heartache when it all went bad.

And it would.

I made coffee and waited for him to walk out before I went in to get ready for work. "Coffee's on the counter," I told him as I walked past.

I didn't wait for a reply.

After a quick shower and shave, I walked into the kitchen. Isaac was there, with an already harnessed Brady. "I can cab it if you'd rather not drive me."

I sighed. "Isaac, I can drive you. I don't mind at all."

He gave me a nod. "Thank you."

We didn't speak the entire way to his work, until he was getting out and re-clipping Brady's harness. "Will I book a cab home?"

"I'll be here," I told him quietly. Then I added, "Isaac, I don't want to fight with you."

He stood up straight by the side of the Jeep, and lifted his chin proudly. "Then don't," he said simply, before walking down the concrete path to the school's front doors.

This was the old Isaac. The Isaac from twelve months ago.

This was the impossible Isaac, who wouldn't listen to reason, or anyone else's point of view. The man who would put defensive walls up and push people away.

I wanted to bang my head on the steering wheel, I wanted to yell and scream and kick something. He was so infuriating.

I got through my day, being professional and polite, but my assistant, Rani, wasn't fooled. I didn't have to explain anything, it must have been written on my face. She asked how Isaac was. I said he was fine, but she gave me a smile, a kind pat on the arm and some distance, taking care of more than her share of work. She was worth her weight in gold.

I picked Isaac up from work, like I said I would, and I'd hoped the day at work would have cleared the air between us and we'd start over. But we didn't.

He was standing on the path where I'd been collecting him from, talking to another teacher. His head turned at the sound of my Jeep coming in through the gates and I could almost see the mask being put into place; he stood taller, his shoulders straightened like he was steeling himself, and his smile died.

I got out and walked over to him as he was saying goodbye to his colleague. "Hey," I said softly.

"Hey."

We walked back to the Jeep in silence, and remained that way for the entire drive home. I knew if this was going to be a battle of wills, about who could be the most stubborn, he'd win hands down. But I'd never backed down to him in an argument. I never made concessions for him because he was blind. I'd never treated him any different than the way I'd treated anyone else.

I wasn't about to start now.

But the silence was killing me. So when we got back to his house, I asked him how his day was, to which he replied, "Fine."

I asked him what he wanted for dinner, and he

answered with, "There's a pre-packed salad in the fridge. I'll just have that." Which, translated, meant *I won't be eating with you.*

I sighed, and then he announced he'd be doing his usual treadmill run then spending the evening going through class work. And he was doing this, according to him, because that's what he did every Monday night before I moved in. It had nothing to do with me, apparently. Or so he said.

I was used to his stinging words, though it'd been a while since he'd aimed them at me. It was a trait of his to lash out with hurtful words, to hurt those around him. He rarely missed his mark.

Tuesday night wasn't much better.

He still only answered questions or attempts at conversation with a short, closed response. I cooked dinner, which he did eat, but the only thing he said was a quiet, "thank you." He busied himself tidying up the kitchen, then declared he had reports to get started before the end of the school year in three weeks. Again, I spent the night walking Missy, on a longer route than normal, avoiding going back to Isaac's.

I mean home.

It occurred to me I'd never thought of it as home, not even after I'd moved in. I'd only been there for a few weeks, but it was still *Isaac's* place. Sure I lived there, but it wasn't my home. I tried not to dwell on that realization or what it meant.

I got back to Isaac's, fed the dogs and showered, then crawled into bed. I was exhausted; body weary and emotionally spent. I had a heavy lump in my chest and a sick feeling in my stomach. My mind was turning and I couldn't sleep.

He was still up reading, or avoiding me, when I got out

of bed to grab a drink. He was on the sofa, his fingers skimming the pages in front of him. After a glass of tap water, I walked back out and stopped at the hall door. "Isaac, I don't want to fight with you. I want you to be happy. So maybe if you showed me the medical journals you mentioned, I might be able to read up on what you're talking about."

He tilted his head and his voice was quiet. "Okay."

He slept in our bed that night. He was up before me, but it was a start.

On Wednesday afternoon, I thought things might have been getting better. I talked about my day as I was getting dinner ready. Whether he was listening, or whether he cared, I don't know. He nodded and smiled politely, but it was a one-sided conversation at best.

He sat at the kitchen counter while I stood on the kitchen side prepping a quick stir-fry. I figured it was progress, considering he was in the same room as me, but it was obvious he was trying to work up the courage to say something. I plated up dinner just as I'd finished my story of the pregnant beagle who was booked in for a caesarian birthing next week. She'd had complications with the last litter, so it was a mutual decision with the owner not to chance it this time. It wasn't riveting conversation, but I thought Isaac might say something at least. But he just sat there.

I put the plate of dinner in front of him and put a fork to his left. "Isaac?"

"I brought home those journals," he said abruptly.

Oh.

"Oh." I said quietly. I was glad he did, I wanted to read them. But I also dreaded bringing the subject matter back up again. We were just starting to talk again. Kind of. "Where are they?"

"In my satchel."

He was anxious again, as though he wasn't entirely sure he wanted me to read them. Maybe it was something he now didn't want me to see or be a part of. "If you don't want me to read them..."

"I want you to read it, but I don't want you to, in case you don't agree with it."

"It's up to you, Isaac." I didn't want to ask what would happen if I didn't.

Then he whispered, "I don't want you to tell me you think I'm stupid—"

"I would never think that."

He shrugged sadly. "I just want this. So bad. I can't help it, Carter, regardless of what that makes me?"

What did it make him? Scared. Lost. Hopeful. Yearning. "It makes you human, Isaac."

He put down his fork and pushed his plate away. His shoulders fell. "A blind human."

"A perfect human."

He shook his head. "You need to stop pretending I'm something I'm not. I'm blind. There will always be things I can't do. There will always be things you'll need to do for me."

"I don't care about that."

"I do!" he said. "Every day. It bothers me, every day."

"We've been through this, Isaac," I said. "I thought we were past this."

"I'll never get past this," he said, shaking his head. "I don't understand why you're so against this. I don't want you to read those reports if you'll just pick out the negative aspects and tell me not to do it."

"I'm capable of reading medical journals objectively, Isaac. I read veterinarian journals all the time."

"Are you capable of understanding what it's like for me? Because I don't think you can. You'll read it from Carter's perspective, where you think I'm wonderful and don't care if I'm blind." He frowned and his voice was quiet, but there was an underlying anger in every word. "Try reading it from my point of view, from a blind person's perspective, where *I* care if I'm blind, where life isn't all rosy and perfect, Carter."

I didn't know what to say. His words stung, and as always they were said with perfect aim. I know I told him he was perfect all the time. Because he is perfect. He's perfect for me. I didn't *not* care he was blind, it just didn't bother me. I've told him this a hundred times, and he was now using it against me.

"I don't know what you want me to say," I said quietly. I picked up my still-full plate and put it in the sink. I couldn't even look at food. "Leave your plate. I'll clean up later," I told him. "I'll um, I need to take Missy for a walk." I grabbed the lead, to which Missy pounced over to me excitedly. I hooked her lead to her collar and looked back to Isaac. "I don't know what you expect me to say, Isaac. If you want me to apologize for loving you just the way you are, then I'm sorry. I'm sorry I put you on a pedestal. I'm sorry if I think you're amazing. And I'm sorry for being honest. I've always told you the truth, or if I thought you were making the wrong decision, so why would this be any different?"

He didn't answer, not that I expected him to. I got to the door and said, "If you want me to read those documents, leave them out for me when I get back. If you don't, I'll understand."

I walked, and walked and walked some more. It was hardly a work out. It was more mechanical steps, one foot after the other, trying to make sense of the thoughts in my head.

My heart was heavy, my stomach was in knots. I felt awful, heartsick that we'd been fighting, and I felt lonely. I loved Isaac, wholly and completely. But the further I walked, the more I thought about what he said. Could I look at this whole mess from his perspective?

If I were blind, if I'd never seen his face, if I'd never seen his smile, would I be willing to risk everything to change that?

Of course I would.

Fuck.

When I got back to the house, the house was dark except for the kitchen light. Brady came out to meet us in the hallway, padding sleepily across the floor. I gave him a pat and Missy licked the side of his mouth. I re-entered the alarm code and, needing to pee, walked to the bathroom first. On the way back, I stopped at the bedroom door, surprised to see a sleeping Isaac in our bed. I smiled to myself, in what felt like the first time in days, and walked into the kitchen.

There on the counter was a neatly-stacked, two-inch high pile of papers and files.

All the information Isaac had from Joshua was there.

In Braille.

Fuck.

Sure, I'd learned some words. Isaac had taught me the basics, but trying to read medical research... Jesus, it may as well have been written in Russian, or Morse Code or invisible fucking ink.

I thumbed through the pages looking for anything printed in words. Of course there wasn't anything. Why would there be? It was for Isaac to read, it would only be in Braille.

With a loud sigh, I picked up the pile of papers and files and collapsed into the sofa, and putting my fingertip to the paper, I started to read.

The first page took me about half an hour and I still couldn't make head or tails of it. I wasn't even sure if I was doing it right, or if I was reading the right thing. I could make out the occasional word but it was pointless.

So I grabbed a notepad and pen and started writing down what I think were headings. I flipped through pages and just read the titles and sub titles. I was looking for key points or points of reference, and I wrote them down.

My laptop was at work, and I wouldn't use Isaac's laptop and screen reader without his permission. Things were already strained between us, I didn't want him to think I was snooping behind his back. So I figured I'd write down any points of origin, any references I could find, and look them up online tomorrow.

It was methodical, looking for shorter lines at the beginning or tops of paragraphs, for anything that might be a heading, a name or an address and wrote everything down.

God knows how long it took. I don't even know how far I got through that pile of papers. But my eyes were heavy, and I was fairly sure I wasn't 'reading' anything properly. I remembered thinking I really should get up and go to bed, but I wanted to get this done. I wanted to show Isaac I was serious about this.

I must have fallen asleep on the sofa, because Isaac woke me up in the morning. He gently shook my shoulder. "Carter?"

I sat up, startled. And groaned. "Ugh, my neck." I'd obviously slept with my head bent at an angle because the pain in my neck was sharp and pinching. "Shit. I didn't mean to fall asleep."

"You're lucky you snore," Isaac said, walking back to the kitchen. "Or else I might not have found you."

I scrubbed my hands over my face and stretched my neck, feeling the stabbing pain from my skull down my spine. "I really didn't mean to sleep out here," I said. I didn't want him to think it was deliberate, considering our sleeping arrangements over the last few days. "Sorry."

"It's fine," he replied from the kitchen. "Coffee's on. Go shower."

Well, at least it was unprompted conversation. I stood up and felt every vertebrae in my spine protest. "Ugh, Jesus..." I groaned, gently rotating my torso trying to stretch out the kinks. "I must have slept like a pretzel."

Isaac chuckled. "Go. Or you'll be late."

One extremely hot shower later, one not-so-hot coffee and we were on our way. We'd driven in silence for most of the trip, and as we neared his work, Isaac said, "So, how'd you go with those papers?"

He'd no doubt found them sprawled all over the coffee table, so he knew I'd attempted to read them. And, it was pretty obvious he wanted me to read them in Braille so I would know how hard he had it, every day. "Um, slow. I'm not very good at Braille. I kept losing my place and I did a lot of letter-guessing. It was very slow."

I pulled into the parking lot and found a spot close to the path. Isaac sat there with his hands in his lap, fiddling with his fingers. "If you want, maybe I could read them to you?"

And for the first time in what felt like forever, I grinned. "I'd like that."

He gave a nod and got out of the Jeep. I unlatched

Brady's harness and ruffled the fur on his forehead. He smiled at me with a slobbery tongue before jumping out on Isaac's side. I walked around to where Isaac was fixing Brady's harness. "I'll see you when I get home. It's Thursday, so I've got house calls this afternoon."

"No problem," he said with a smile.

I picked up his satchel and put the strap over his shoulder. It was the closest I'd been to him in four days. "Have a good day."

"You too." And with that, he gave Brady the command to go and they walked off toward the front doors of the school.

Things weren't great between us, but at least we were now talking. I smiled all the way to work.

"SOMEONE'S IN A BETTER MOOD TODAY," Rani said with a wiggle of her eyebrow. "I take it Isaac stopped giving you grief?"

I smiled for her and pushed my sandwich wrapper in the bin. I dusted the crumbs off my desk and swallowed down the last of my lunch. My assistant had come to know me well over the last twelve months, and that included my relationship with Isaac. "I don't think he'll ever stop," I said.

Her eyes glanced at my laptop open on my desk. "Working during your lunch break?"

"Uh, no, not really," I said. "Just looking something up for Isaac. Remind me to take my laptop home. If I walk out the door this afternoon without it, hit me over the head with it."

"For real?"

I smiled at her. "Well, no. But a reminder would be good."

"Deal."

Lucky she did remind me, because as I was running late for my house calls, I almost forgot it. I was tripping over myself with my bag and a box of different products for my house call patients when Rani called out, "Laptop!"

I stopped halfway through the door, and in front of a waiting room full of somewhat amused clients waiting to see one of the other vets, I had to hold the door with my foot, shuffle everything in my hands as she slipped my laptop bag over my shoulder.

"Thanks," I said with a grin, and made my way out to my Jeep.

I was down to three house visits now, given that I'd taken Isaac off the official house call list. They were all patients my predecessor, Dr Fields, had seen and although it wasn't something I'd done as a vet anywhere else, I kept the appointments out of professional courtesy. It was, after all, how I met Isaac.

The first two appointments weren't on my standard visits list. They called me to come only when needed. One was a breeder of Burmese cats, so it really was easier and more cost effective for me to visit her, rather than her trying to bring in several cats or kittens at one time. The second was a guy who kept pythons. His three year old diamond python had an inflamed eye. Not my favorite type of patient, but I took a swab for testing, flushed the eye with a saline solution, told him to keep the snake isolated from his other snakes, and told him I'd be in touch.

I chuckled to myself on the way to Mrs Yeo's, imagining her reaction when I tell her I'd just treated a snake. Her no-nonsense, tell-it-like-it-is attitude was often hilarious. I grabbed the bag of dried cat foot from the front seat and knocked on her door.

A short, older Chinese man opened the door. "What you want?" he barked gruffly at me in the same broken English Mrs Yeo spoke in.

I blinked in surprise at his rudeness. "My name is Doctor Carter Reece. I'm the vet that looks after Mrs Yeo's cat."

The man stared at me with his eyebrows furrowed, then looked at the cat food and my bag, then back to my face. "Good. You can catch that stupid animal." He stepped aside, letting me in. "You take it with you."

I hesitantly walked inside, but turned back to the grumpy old man. "I'm sorry, is Mrs Yeo here?"

He stood with a blank look to his face for a moment. "She die last week. I clean out her place. So much stuff, rubbish. I take most of it to trash."

I stood in the little living room, not sure I understood, and at a complete loss for words. "I'm sorry," I whispered. "She passed away?"

"Yes," he answered curtly. "Last week. Friday... no, Saturday..." He shook his head. "I can't remember."

I slowly looked around the room I was standing in. It was almost empty. The lounges were still there, but strewn in papers. The small kitchen counter was filled with empty containers and boxes, the cupboard doors were open, the shelves bare.

"The cat," the man said loudly, startling me. "You take the cat. Or I just kick it out. Someone else feed it."

I still hadn't moved. I couldn't speak. I just stood there, helplessly lost, holding a bag of cat food and my bag.

The rude little man stood in front of me. He waved his hand to get my attention. "Mr? You find the cat. You take it."

I nodded, and swallowed so I could speak. "Yes, I'll take it."

I found poor Mr Tiddles hiding, frightened, under the one remaining dresser in one of the bedrooms. He looked like he'd not been fed in a week. Then it dawned on me that he probably hadn't.

I picked him up and held him to my chest, cuddling him and whispering calmly to him, "It'll be okay," over and over. I placed him in one of the boxes, and put him on the front seat of my Jeep.

I fought back tears the whole way home.

CHAPTER ELEVEN

I PULLED into the drive and groaned when I saw Joshua's car parked out front.

This was not how I was expecting this afternoon to go. I was looking forward to spending some time with Isaac, having him read to me. I thought maybe we could lay on the sofa together while he read those medical journals to me, and I'd tell him I was sorry for fighting, and he'd say he was sorry too, and we'd make out, make love and everything would be back to good.

But now Joshua was here, and Mrs Yeo...

I walked through the internal door, carrying Mr Tiddles in the box. Both dogs greeted me eagerly, then curiously, as they caught scent of the cat. I walked through the back sunroom toward the kitchen and the sound of Isaac laughing added weight to the lump in my throat.

I hadn't heard him laugh in days.

Isaac was sitting at the kitchen counter with Joshua and turned to the sound of my approaching. "You're earlier today," he said cheerfully. "Did Mrs Yeo run out of green tea?"

I set the box down on the floor, against the wall out of the way. Joshua looked at me, and his smile died. I must have looked exactly how I felt.

"Carter is everything okay?" Isaac asked.

Just then, Mr Tiddles meowed from inside the box.

Isaac's face jolted to the sound. "What was that?"

I cleared my throat. "That's Mr Tiddles," I said quietly. "Isaac, Mrs Yeo passed away."

And as soon as I said the words out loud, the tears I'd been trying to hold back couldn't be stopped. I wiped my hands at my face. "I'm sorry," I said weakly. "I didn't mean to—"

Isaac pushed off his chair, and in three quick strides, had his arms around me, cutting me off mid-sentence. "Don't be sorry." His hands quickly sought my face and wiped away the tears. He put his forehead to mine and wrapped his arms around me again. "Don't apologize."

I buried my face into his neck and slid my hands around his back, and he held me while I cried.

Joshua's voice was quiet. "I'll get going."

I released my hold on Isaac, thinking he'd want to say goodbye, but he didn't. He pulled me in tighter. "Thanks, Josh. I'll speak to you tomorrow," was all Isaac said. And just like that, when I needed him most, he chose me.

I didn't wait for Joshua to leave. I just didn't care.

I fisted Isaac's shirt and held him as tight as he held me. I breathed in his scent, letting it invade my senses. "I've missed you," I murmured into his neck.

"I've missed you too."

His words bought on a fresh wave of tears. "Her nephew was there," I told him through my tears. "He was awful. He was just throwing her things away like her life meant nothing. I had to take the cat, Isaac, he was just going to let him starve."

"Shh, baby," he said soothingly. "It's okay." He leaned against the kitchen counter and pulled me against him.

After a long moment, I pulled back and taking some deep breaths, wiped my face. "I'm sorry, I didn't mean to lose it."

His hands held my face and his thumbs wiped my cheeks. "It hasn't been a good week, has it?"

I shook my head. "No."

He brushed his nose to mine and I could taste his breath on my tongue. He lifted his chin, ever so slightly, and kissed me, the softest of touches. He held his lips there, barely touching mine—for the sweetest moment, an almost kiss—then with his hands on my face, he pulled my lips to his. Open-mouthed and deep, warm and consuming; he kissed me.

His lips, his tongue, his taste. His hands, his body, his warmth. He owned me with his kiss. I pulled my mouth away to breathe, and then kissed him just how he'd kissed me. I wanted him. I needed him. I needed to be close, I needed to feel wanted, desired.

Loved.

Alive.

I held his face and our tongues met in his mouth. His hands were now on my back, holding me against him. His hands slid down to my ass, and he pulled me into him, grinding his erection against mine, making me groan.

"God, Carter," he moaned my name into my mouth.

With my hands still at his face, I pulled back and softly kissed his swollen lips. "Isaac..."

And then the cat meowed.

Isaac jumped at the noise. "Jesus."

We both chuckled, easing the sexual tension, the urgency between us. I took a small step back from him, though he kept his hands on my waist and after a few thought-collecting breaths, Isaac said, "Tell me what happened."

I told him how Mrs Yeo's nephew was abrupt and rude, very uncaring. "He didn't give a shit. He was just tossing everything away, as though everything in her house was an inconvenience to him." I shook my head. "That poor little old lady, Isaac. She had no one in her life that cared for her."

Isaac shook his head. "She had you. You didn't need to keep calling in to see her once her old cat died, but you did. And you'd stay while she made tea and ranted about how crazy the world was." He ran his hands up my sides to my face. "You lost a friend today, Carter."

I nodded, feeling the burn of more tears in my eyes. "Her nephew couldn't even remember which day she died, Friday or Saturday. He just didn't care."

"That's awful."

"And poor Mr Tiddles," I said. "He was so scared when I picked him up, and starving hungry. I put some food in the box with him. I'll set him up in the laundry for tonight and figure out what to do with him tomorrow."

Isaac nodded. "Okay."

I didn't move. I just stood there, against him, with my hands now resting on his collarbones, my fingers gently resting on his neck. I didn't want to let him go. I didn't want to be *not* touching him.

Isaac smiled. "Today?"

"Yeah." I nodded and kissed him softly. "I just don't want to let you go."

His voice was quiet, but unwavering. "I'm not going anywhere."

He wasn't talking about right then, he meant he wasn't going anywhere from me. After the shitty week we'd had, after the fighting and the silence, he still wasn't going anywhere.

I took his face in my hands again and lifted his lips to mine. "I'm not going anywhere either."

The cat meowed *again* from inside the box, making Isaac jump *again*. He put his hands on my chest and pushed me away a little. "Yes, you are. Please do something with that cat before it gives me heart failure."

"Don't go anywhere," I said, pecking his lips again. "I won't be a second."

I picked up the box and gently put it down in the laundry. I set up a dish of the dried cat food I'd taken to Mrs Yeo's and one of water. I opened the box and lifted the cat out, keeping hold of him while I tipped the box on the side, threw in an old towel for a bed, and a makeshift litter box. I gave him a good cuddle, told him he didn't need to be scared, he wasn't alone anymore and then I put him to bed, closing the door behind me.

Isaac was still standing against the kitchen counter, though he'd taken his sunglasses off. He put his hand out, which I took immediately, and he lifted my hand to his face, leaning his cheek into the palm of my hand.

He didn't speak. He didn't have to.

He kissed the palm of my hand and sighed. His other hand sat on my hip and pulled me against him. Then he nuzzled his nose into my neck. The hand that was on my face, slid down my chest to wrap around my lower back. His fingers were digging into my skin and he was moving, subtly writhing against me. He trailed soft kisses along the skin at my neck, below my ear, my jaw.

Jesus.

He took my earlobe between his lips, then whispered breathily in my ear. "Carter?"

I knew what he was asking. I nodded. "Please."

I led him to the bedroom, where he took care of me, so gentle, so confident with my body. He touched every part of me, every inch of my skin was savored. His hands, his mouth, knew every part of me.

Then he made love to me.

He sat on the bed with his legs in front of him. I straddled him, facing him with my legs wrapped around him, taking him deep in my body. He held me while I rocked us, he kissed me softly, he told me he loved me.

I didn't realize just how disconnected I'd felt, how splintered and off-kilter I'd been this week, until he put me back together. Until he validated me. Until he set fire to my blood and held me while I unraveled in his arms.

I'd never felt so alive. So loved.

Later that night, after a bath for two, and an ordered-in dinner, we lay in bed. Isaac was resting his back against the headboard while I lay with my head on his chest. Using one hand to hold the papers and the other to read with, he somehow, rather awkwardly, started to read the Braille reports out loud to me.

I had every intention of listening, but the sound of his heartbeat and the deep rumble of his voice through his chest as he read, lulled me to sleep.

I TOOK coffee in to him, while he was still in bed. "What's that for?" he asked rather sleepily.

"I thought we could try reading those reports this morning. I'm sorry I fell asleep last night."

He sat up and took the coffee cup. "What time is it?"

"It's early."

"Couldn't this wait until tonight?"

"Mark will be here tonight, remember? You and he were going to share your bed and kick me to the spare room?"

Isaac grinned as he sipped his coffee. "That's right. I forgot about that."

"Well, you two better not be serious about those sleeping arrangements," I said jokingly. Isaac and Mark always flirted with each other. My best friend would flirt with a rock if he thought it'd put out.

Isaac took another sip of the coffee and went to put it on the side table. I took it for him and set it down. "How are you feeling this morning?" he asked quietly.

"I'm okay. Still a little sad that Mrs Yeo's gone, but I'm just happy we're okay. Thank you for knowing what I needed last night."

"I needed that too."

I smiled, and leaned in, kissing his cheek. "Now, we've got about an hour. Did you want to start reading to me?"

"If you want."

"I want to be involved," I told him. "If it's something you want to investigate further, then I'll do it with you." Then I added, "I'll even try to be objective."

He smiled at my poor attempt to be funny. "Pass the reports over," he said. "They're on the dresser."

I WAS JUST FINISHING up in my office, and could hear the other staff laughing at the receptionist desk. I'd called a small meeting first thing this morning to tell my crew about Mrs Yeo, and it had been a rather somber morning. But something had amused Rani, Kate and Luke, my fourth year grad student. Correction. Not something, but some*one*. I smiled as I walked from my office to the waiting room.

"Hey!" Mark cried when he saw me. Grinning, he lifted his arms out wide and quickly crossed the room to embrace me. "I was just telling these guys stories about you from college."

I glanced over at my staff, who were all grinning. "He tells lies," I told them.

Mark guffawed. "And I hadn't even got to the part where you were dressed up as Ann Darrow, King Kong's buxom blond toy thing, and got arrested for solicitation."

"That wasn't me," I said quickly, then looking at my staff, I said it again. "That wasn't me." They laughed, so I turned back to Mark. "You were Ann Darrow, I was King Kong. *You* were picked up for solicitation. I just got dragged to the station in a gorilla suit."

Mark chuckled. "Oh, yeah."

I shook my head at him, thankful for the empty waiting room. "It might not have been a good idea to ask the police-woman if she was interested. Or the police*man*."

"Yeah, she didn't have a sense of humor," he said with a frown. Then he looked at me, "But you made a great King Kong."

I turned back to my staff, who were still grinning at us. "See what I have to put up with?"

Mark slung one arm around my shoulder. "You love me."

"That's a matter of opinion."

He picked up his bag. "Shut up, and take me home."

"Have a great weekend, guys," I said to the three still standing at the receptionist desk. "I apologize if he offended you with any... propositions."

Mark pretended to be insulted. "I resemble that remark."

I rolled my eyes and Rani laughed. I groaned, "Don't encourage him."

Mark pouted. "Come on, let's go get Isaac. At least I know he loves me." He smiled at his audience and walked to the door. "And I'm sleeping in Isaac's bed tonight."

I pushed him out the door. "No you're not, and don't say things like that in front of my staff!"

"Why? Would they be jealous?"

"Mark!" I hissed at him. "They can hear you!" We were only a few feet from the door.

"Good," Mark said loudly. "Cause that Rani's a babe."

I sighed. "Sorry, Rani," I called out.

Rani stuck her head out the door and smiled. "Bye, Mark."

Mark stopped walking and beamed at her. "No," I said, grabbing his arm. "Not with anyone I work with." God, it was going to be a very trying weekend. I pushed him toward my Jeep. "Get in the car and shut up."

He laughed, threw his bag in the back of the Jeep and climbed in. Without the audience, he was much more subdued. "So, how's Isaac? More importantly, how's living together going?"

"It's good," I told him, as I pulled out into traffic. "Well, this last week has been less than stellar. We had a big fight..."

"What about?"

I considered not going into detail, but knew I couldn't keep any secrets from him. So I told him about Isaac's new-found desire to have his sight restored. I told him about what Isaac had read to me this morning, about the 'research' and medical journals.

"So what's the problem?" he asked.

I sighed. "I don't know, this Joshua's a slimebag and I just don't trust him. It just doesn't add up somehow."

"Like the saying goes, if it looks like bullshit and smells like bullshit..."

I laughed. "I don't think that's quite how the saying goes, but yes, exactly."

"But Isaac's not stupid."

"I know he's not," I said quickly. "But I think the possibility of seeing again is clouding his judgment."

Mark shrugged. "That's fair enough, isn't it?" he asked. "I mean, if it were you, wouldn't you try anything?"

I sighed and pulled into the parking lot at Isaac's work. "Please don't say anything to him. Don't let on you know anything unless he brings it up."

Mark nodded, then looked over to the front of the school and smiled. "There he is." Then he asked, "Who's that guy with him?"

"Ugh. That's Joshua. He's like a rash that won't go away."

Isaac started to walk toward the Jeep, whether just because he heard it or because Joshua told him, I wasn't sure. Mark got out and walked over to him before me, and mindful of Brady, threw his arms around him. "Here he is! My best friend's husband."

At first, I cringed at what he just said, but the look on Joshua's face was priceless and I couldn't help but smile.

"Oh, Mark," Isaac said, pulling out of Mark's hold. "And I thought I missed you."

I snorted. "He just traumatized my staff."

Isaac turned toward me and smiled kind of shyly. "Hey."

"Hey."

Mark rolled his eyes at us, but then held his hand out to

Joshua. "Mark Gattison. Best friend extraordinaire of Carter and weekend bed-buddy of Isaac."

"Mark!" Isaac gasped. "Oh, Josh, I'm sorry. Mark has no filter."

"And no social skills," I added. I didn't correct Mark's comment about sleeping arrangements in front of Joshua. I hoped he wondered if it was true.

Joshua shook Mark's hand. "Nice to meet you." Then he looked at me. "Carter, I'm sorry to hear of the loss of your friend yesterday. And I'm sorry if I imposed."

"It's fine," I told him.

Mark spun around to look at me. "What happened, Car?"

I gave him a weak smile. "I'll explain later. Let's go home, huh?"

Mark gave me a quizzical look. "Okay," he said, then sliding in between Isaac and Joshua, he took Isaac's hand and led him toward the Jeep.

I followed them, smiling. Isaac called over his shoulder, "Bye, Josh."

I turned so Joshua could see my smile. He was looking at the three of us a little stunned, I think. Then again, Mark managed to stun most people he met. Isaac opened the passenger door and dropped Brady's harness.

"You're in the back with Brady," I told Mark.

"Cool," he said, giving the dog a ruffle on the face. "You and me buddy, we get the backseat all to ourselves."

Isaac gave the command and Brady jumped into the backseat. Mark followed him and buckled the dog into the car harness. "Da-a-a-d," Mark whined. "Are we there yet?"

Isaac laughed as he did up his seatbelt. "It's going to be a long weekend, isn't it?"

I got in and shut my door. "Yep. It sure is."

CHAPTER TWELVE

MARK WAS A GOOD DISTRACTION. He made us both laugh, and it was good to focus on someone else that wasn't us for a while. Mark declared it was pizza and beer for dinner, and while we ate, he asked all about the man who followed Isaac and came into the house uninvited. Isaac told him everything; from the incident itself to the morning at the police station when it was Brady growling at some stranger that gave the man away.

"As soon as the man spoke, I recognized his voice," Isaac told him. "But it was Brady who recognized him first."

"That must have been scary as hell," Mark said.

Isaac swallowed his mouthful, and nodded. "It was, yeah."

"I would've shat myself," Mark announced crudely.

I looked at the slice of pizza in my hand, then to Mark. "Nice, Mark," I said flatly. "Real nice."

Isaac chuckled. "Yeah, it wasn't *that* scary."

Then Mark asked me what Joshua meant when he said he was sorry for the loss of my friend yesterday.

I took a mouthful of beer and nodded. "You know Mrs Yeo, who I visited every other Thursday?"

"The one you both got the cat for when her old cat died?" he asked.

"Yeah, well she passed away," I told him. "I found out yesterday."

He frowned. "That's so sad."

"Yes, it was," I agreed. "She was a sweet little old dear."

Isaac snorted. "Well, she wasn't really," he said. Mark and I both stared at him and he smiled. "She was ninety-three and cranky. She hated the kids in the street, she'd yell at them, and would think it was funny if she made them cry. She ranted about technology, cars, the news, the state of the world. You name it, she hated it. She was hardly a sweet little old dear."

Mark put his hand to his mouth to cover his smile. "Really?"

I stared at Isaac with my mouth open. He put his arm around my shoulder and nuzzled his nose into the side of my face. "Except Carter. She adored him," Isaac said softly. "The one bright light in her life."

I smiled sadly at his words. "Well, me and Mr Tiddles."

"Ah, the cat that's giving both your dogs the evil eye," Mark said, pointing his beer bottle to the window sill.

I'd left the laundry door open this morning for the cat to venture out into the house. I put Missy out in the back yard for the day, so I figured it would give the cat some time to acclimate to a new house while it was free of inhabitants. The cat however, had ventured out to find the sun on the front window sill, and hadn't got much further.

Isaac took another mouthful of his beer. "Is it still on the window sill?"

"Yep, poor little guy," I told him. "I think he'll be fine, but if he doesn't get on with the dogs, then I can put a sign up at work to see if someone wants him." Then I realized I hadn't even really asked if it was okay with Isaac. "That's only if it's all right with you, Isaac?" I said, putting my hand on his leg. "I didn't even ask, I just brought him here."

Isaac shook his head. "It's okay," he said. "You didn't have much choice. It'll just take some getting used to. Cats are very quiet, and if I can't hear it, it might startle me if it's suddenly in front of me or something."

"I can get a collar with a bell on it," I said.

Isaac relaxed into my side, put his feet up on the coffee table and his hand on my thigh. He smiled and took another mouthful of beer. He rarely drank alcohol. He said the dulling of his other senses and loss of proper balance wasn't a good thing for him. But the way he smiled lazily and chuckled to himself was very cute.

"Oh, no," Mark said. "No, no, no. You two don't start acting all lovey-dovey on me now. No fondling in front of me." He got up off the other sofa and put one hand on Isaac's knee and took the beer bottle from his hand.

Isaac smiled. "Carter, what's he doing?"

Mark laughed. "You, Mr-Sexy-in-a-suit, are going to dance with me."

"I'm what?"

"Sexy in a suit," Mark repeated.

"No, not that," Isaac said with a laugh as Mark pulled him to his feet. "The other part."

Mark gently pulled him by both hands to the middle of the living room. "You're gonna get your groove on."

"I've only ever danced with Carter," Isaac told him. "And I can assure you, you and I are not dancing like *that*."

Mark threw his head back and laughed. "Give me the details, please," he said excitedly.

"Well," Isaac started. "We started out here, slow dancing, but we finished in bed-"

"Right," I called out, cutting him off. "No more beer for Isaac."

Both of them laughed, and Mark told me to go be Mr Maestro and play them some music. I got off the lounge and walked over to the iPod dock. "What kind of playlist?"

"Something funky," Mark answered.

I pressed play on Isaac's workout playlist. I figured it would help if he knew the songs, and I started to clean up after dinner. Putting the empty pizza boxes and beer bottles on the kitchen counter, I laughed as Mark tried to teach Isaac how to dance to fast music.

Mark was his usual flirtatious self, dancing with his hips and wandering hands, and Isaac was having a blast. I sat on the sofa with my bare feet on the coffee table, giving Missy a rub on the forehead while Mark and Isaac joked around and made me laugh.

Even as the music kept tempo, their dancing slowed down, and I still smiled at them. Isaac was still dressed in his work suit, sans the jacket, but he looked sharp in his gray pants and white shirt. He'd taken his tie off when he got home and undid the top button, and Mark undid the next button, and the next, then looked at me with a raised eyebrow. "Jesus, Carter. He's like sex in a suit."

I smiled, and Isaac stopped swaying his hips and pulled back his hands.

"No," Mark said, taking Isaac's hands and putting them back on his waist. "We're just getting to the good part."

"Um," Isaac stalled, and turned his face toward me. "Carter..."

"Carter's grinning like an idiot watching you," Mark reassured him, then slid his hand over Isaac's ass.

"Hands," I said lightly, knowing Mark only did it to get a reaction from me.

Mark laughed. "Right. Rules are... dancing is fine, groping of ass is not."

Isaac chuckled and slid his hand over Mark's ass and so I cleared my throat and called out, "Hands."

Isaac snorted. "Not just my ass. Yours too, apparently."

Mark wrapped his arms around Isaac and loudly smooched into his neck, tickling him, making him wriggle and laugh. Then Mark pulled away from Isaac, looked at me and grinned. "Your turn, Carter, baby," he said loudly. "I've warmed him up for you. Now show me how you two slow-dance."

I finished the last of my beer and stood up, quickly taking Mark's place. I stood in close to Isaac and put his hands on my hips. He leaned in, inhaled deeply and hummed, "Mmm, I know that scent."

Mark swallowed, loud enough for us to hear. "He never commented on the way I smell."

I glanced back at Mark and smiled, then ran my nose along Isaac's neck where Mark had opened his shirt collar. Knowing Mark was still watching, I deliberately ran my hands up Isaac's sides, around his back then slowly down and over his ass and pulled our hips together. "He likes the way I smell."

Isaac hummed again, this time swaying his hips into mine, wiggling his ass under my hands. "And he can put his hands on my ass all he likes," Isaac added.

"Jesus," Mark groaned.

Jesus was right. Three or four beers and Isaac's inhibitions had all but disappeared. Fuck, he was killing me. Just when I thought I'd have to put a stop to our little display, Mark shook his head. "I'm leaving you two to it," he told us. "Keep the sex noises down tonight, too. It's bad enough I have to jerk off alone."

Isaac smiled into my neck. "Goodnight, Mark."

"Night, Mark," I said. Then I added, "There's Kleenex on your bedside table and lube in the bathroom."

Mark laughed as he walked down the hallway. "Nah, it's okay. Brought my own."

Isaac laughed, and pulled my hips hard into his. "Shall we go and work on those sex noises?

IT WAS EARLY when I left a still-sleeping Isaac, and went out to the store. Mark hadn't surfaced either, so I tried to be quick. I called into the local market for an array of things, collected three coffees on my way, and headed home, to find Mark foraging for food and Isaac still in bed. I yelled out to Isaac, telling him to get out of bed. His response was a muffled moan.

"I brought breakfast and coffee," I called out.

Mark was quick to rifle through the paper bags, pulling out croissants and bagels, as Isaac walked into the kitchen, shirtless. At least he'd put on some sleep pants. "My head hurts," he mumbled.

I picked up his coffee, and lifting his hand, wrapped his fingers around the hot drink. "Thought you might be a little hung over. That's why I ordered you a double shot of coffee."

Isaac moaned as he put the take away cup to his lips and took a small sip. "I knew I kept you around for a reason."

I smiled and kissed the side of his head. "Thanks."

He put his coffee down on the kitchen counter, then with his hands flat on the bench, he let his head fall forward and took some deep breaths. "I feel awful."

Mark laughed through a mouthful of bagel. "Hangovers suck."

I rubbed Isaac's back. "It was all Mark's idea. Blame him."

Isaac mumbled, "I do blame him."

Mark chuckled and put the bag of pastries under Isaac's nose. "Eat food, drink coffee, hot shower. You'll be good as new."

I picked up the bag of breads. "Did you want croissants, bagels or a Danish pastry?"

Isaac screwed up his nose. "Coffee, then shower. Maybe food later." He took another sip of his coffee just as Mr Tiddles meowed from the kitchen floor. Isaac almost spilled his drink. "Jesus!"

Mark pressed his lips together so he didn't laugh out loud, and I picked the cat up. Lifting Isaac's hand, I gently ran his hand over Mr Tiddles' head. "He didn't mean to scare you."

Isaac grumbled and took back his hand. "Damn thing's too quiet."

"I'll get him a bell for his collar from work on Monday," I told him.

"Hmm," Isaac hummed, still not impressed. "I'm going to have a shower."

"Don't forget Hannah's coming for lunch today," I called out after him. I gave the cat a quick scratch behind the ear and gently put him on the floor.

He stopped at the hall door. "Do I have to be alive for that?"

Mark laughed. "I better get some more beer."

Isaac groaned. "You can shove your beer."

"Then I thought we could go into the city tonight," I added. "Take Mark in, show him around, do something fun. How does that sound?"

Isaac smiled and half shrugged. "As long as it doesn't involve beer, anything loud, or being upright for too long, I don't care."

"I can help you with the not being upright for too long," Mark joked. I pushed his arm and grinning, he stood up straight and stretched his arms above his head. "I'm gonna go do some laps of the pool."

"I'm gonna have a shower and go back to bed," Isaac mumbled, his voice fading as he walked down the hall.

"Well, I'm gonna..." I said, looking around, not sure what I was going to do.

Mark pushed me in the direction Isaac just disappeared. "You're gonna go make him feel better," he said with a laugh. "Jeez Carter, your half-naked, gorgeous boyfriend just said 'shower and bed' in the same sentence... do the math."

I laughed at him, looked at the hallway, then back to Mark. "How many laps are you doing?"

Mark grinned. "About twenty minutes worth."

"Do me a favor," I said, walking toward the hall door. "Make it thirty."

LUNCH WITH HANNAH and Carlos was as it always was; good food, good conversation and lots of laughs. Mark had met Isaac's sister and brother-in-law a few times over the last year and of course, he charmed them both.

Isaac had come back to life, with a little help from me

giving him a soapy handjob in the shower and then sleeping his hangover off for another hour. He woke up, helped me prep salads and get everything ready, and then he laughed with everyone around the back patio table at lunch.

I told Hannah and Carlos that Mrs Yeo had passed away, and Isaac was quiet while I retold a much shorter version of meeting her horrible nephew. But then out of the blue, Isaac called Brady over, hooked up his harness and asked, "Carter, can I borrow your car keys?"

I had to admit, I was stunned. "Um..."

"Not for me, obviously," he went on to say. "Mark? Could you be my driver?"

Mark's eyes shot to mine, but he answered Isaac brightly. "Of course I can."

"Sure," I said. "Is it a mystery trip?"

"Yep," Isaac said, standing up.

Mark joined him, oblivious as to where he was going with Isaac, but happy to go regardless. He slid his hand into Isaac's and smiled smugly. "Don't wait up."

I rolled my eyes, and taking the keys out of my pocket, I threw them to Mark. "Behave." I caught myself smiling as I watched them walk out, hand in hand.

Hannah was grinning at me when I finally looked at her. "So, how're things with Joshua?"

My nostrils flared at the mention of his name, and Hannah laughed, making a sleeping Ada stir.

"I just have to mention that name and you almost growl," she said, highly amused. "You can watch Isaac and Mark being all flirty and handsy and you smile, yet one mention of Joshua and you bristle."

I sighed, suddenly finding the lid to my water bottle very intriguing. "It's different."

"Of course it is," she agreed. "You know Mark. You know, as much as Mark plays it up and says the most outrageous things, he'd never cross a line with Isaac."

I looked at her then. "No, he wouldn't."

"But Joshua?"

I shrugged. "I don't know him. I don't know what he's after."

"You don't trust him," Carlos he said. It wasn't a question.

"No. Not at all," I admitted. "I've tried to like him. I'm nice enough to him, for Isaac's sake. But no, I don't trust him."

Hannah sighed and nodded. "Isaac was very quiet this week. He wouldn't tell me what was wrong, I figured Joshua was involved somehow. I thought maybe Isaac realized what a douche he was."

I shook my head. "Um, well, no this last week, Isaac and I had a big fight. We hardly spoke for four days."

Hannah's eyes almost popped. News of Isaac and me fighting was an obvious shock to her. "What? What on earth was it all about?"

"Hannah, look," I started. "I'm not sure I should say anything, I mean, I'm surprised he didn't tell you."

She was concerned now. "Tell me what?"

I knew they talked every day, and they talked about everything, but then I remembered how he didn't really want to tell me about this new radical eye surgery either. But I wasn't sure if it was my place to say anything now.

"Carter," Hannah said sternly. "If Isaac says anything to you about telling me, you tell him I threatened physical bodily harm. To both of you."

I smiled at her, and after a deep breath, I put the bottle

cap on the table. "Isaac thinks he might have found some doctor who can fix his eyesight."

Hannah stared at me, not moving a muscle as she processed what I said. Then she blinked, twice. She and Carlos spoke in unison. "What?"

I told them all I knew. I told her how Joshua had some information on research and case studies on a doctor in Argentina who had success in restoring sight in cases similar to Isaac's. I told them how I'd tried to read the information in Braille, but had Isaac read it to me instead. I explained that I'd found some information online about the clinic and doctor in question, but it was dodgy at best. Then I told them, even though with everything Isaac had read to me, knowing all the information he knew, I still wasn't sold.

Hannah listened intently, and after everything I'd just told her, her first question wasn't about anything to do with the ton of information I'd just dumped on her. "Is that what you fought about?" she asked.

"Yeah, he thought I was being negative and didn't want him to pursue it. But, I'm not being negative, honestly," I said to her, shaking my head. "I'm just thinking rationally, logically. He was so upset with me. He was really nervous about telling me, which is, I presume, the same reason he's not mentioned it to you yet."

Hannah nodded thoughtfully. "Yeah, maybe... Or maybe he knows he'd get the same reaction. I know you're only concerned about him, Carter, you don't have to justify that to me," she said.

I smiled sadly at them both. "Hannah, if it is available, if it's legitimate, and if it's safe—and if it's what he really wants —then I'm all for it. But, until then..." I sighed.

Carlos watched Hannah as she nodded slowly and was quiet for a long moment. "Why?" she asked. "Why now?"

"Well, there've been a few things in the last few weeks that have really affected him. First was Ada," I told her. As hard as it was to bring up the birth of her daughter as a negative thing, I had to tell her. "That first time he held her, he told me afterwards there'd only been a few times in his life when he'd *truly* wished for his sight back, and that was one of them."

Hannah frowned and nodded.

"Then there was the whole home invasion thing. I know he acted all brave and okay, but Hannah it *really* frightened him, and understandably so. He had nightmares..."

Hannah's eyes welled with tears. "He never told me that."

"Then there were the police reports. I know it worked out in the end, but at first they basically told him his statement, his testimony as a victim, would be rendered useless because he couldn't see. Like he was being punished for being blind." I shook my head. "God, Hannah, he was so angry."

Hannah was quiet while she gathered her thoughts. "There've always been a few incidents over the years that would set him back."

I nodded. "It just seems these last few weeks have really hit him hard. Has he ever been *so* serious about getting his sight back?"

She shook her head. "It's never been an option before."

"It's not an option now."

"Not a sensible one."

"Mmm, yeah well, I don't think it's an option at all."

"What do you mean?" Carlos asked.

"I just... look, I'm not a doctor. I'm a vet. There are a lot of things I don't understand medically in the human body, but I have a pretty good understanding of the nervous system. I know there are new developments with stem cell research, and they're working medical miracles every day, but," I looked at them both and shook my head, "not this. Not yet."

She nodded. "All the doctors over the years have always said it's not reversible. The damage was done after the accident." Then she frowned. "Anyway, if it is so great, why aren't they doing it here, in the States? If it's such a breakthrough, why are they not doing it here?"

"Exactly!" I said adamantly. "I'll email the link to the online info, you can have a look yourself. Anyone can set up a website and say they're legitimate, can't they? It's not that difficult, is it?" I asked.

Carlos shook his head. "No, not really."

"I mean there were testimonials which could all be fake," I continued. "There were histories on developments and trials, but any half-educated jerk can set up pages of information that only has to sound half-credible. People like Isaac are going to believe it, because they *want* it."

"In Argentina?" she asked with a frown, obviously stuck on the location.

"Yeah," I said with a nod. "I mean, I'm not saying anything against the Argentinean medical practices, but if this is so cutting-edge—so state of the art..."

Carlos finished for me, "Then why isn't it done at the best ophthalmologist hospitals, here in the States, or in London or Melbourne?"

I nodded. "Well, apparently Joshua claims the Argentinean Health Authority has approved it. He told Isaac the AMA won't approve certain procedures without the clinical research and funding proven by our regulators, not some Argentinean private research company and funder. That is kind of true, but not exactly, but he says that's why it can't be done here legally. I mean, different countries have different statutes and medical guidelines, which means *they* can perform procedures not approved here. That's not unusual. Joshua told Isaac the international clinical trials would get bogged down in US legislation for years before this surgery can be performed here, with all the studies and further research it could take even longer.

"Not to mention how much cheaper surgeries are in Argentina than in the US..." I shook my head. "It wouldn't matter anyway, because all Isaac heard was there's a doctor who's willing to do it, and he's done it before with success. That's all Isaac needed to know."

Hannah sighed. "Mmm, that Joshua claims to know an awful lot, doesn't he?"

I huffed. "Don't even get me started on him. He's been an issue between me and Isaac from day one."

"Exactly."

"What are you saying?" Carlos asked, looking at Hannah.

"We can analyze the 'whys' and the 'whats' behind this change in Isaac, and all the bullshit he's being fed, but I think we should be looking more to the 'whos'."

"You think Joshua is behind all this?"

Hannah nodded. "Think about it. He's always hanging around, he's caused nothing but problems between you and Isaac. You've never fought until he showed up."

"We've had our disagreements."

"Nothing like what it's been like lately," she said. "Every problem in your lives in the last two months has a common denominator."

Joshua.

"Do you think he's after Isaac?" Carlos pressed on. "Is that why he's doing this?"

I felt sick at the thought. "I don't know."

We were all quiet for a moment, trying to understand what was just brought to light.

Then Hannah said, "You know what's weird? There he is, feeding Isaac all this information about this new, revolutionary surgery to restore his eyesight. Why would he do that?"

I shrugged. "I don't know. To help him?"

Hannah laughed sarcastically. "Do you think so?"

"No."

Her smile faded. "What does he gain from it?" she asked. "Why does anyone do anything for anyone these days?"

I looked at her, not sure where she was going with this.

"Financial gain," Carlos said.

My eyes widened. "You think he's after money?"

She smiled. "How much is this 'amazing surgery' going to cost Isaac?"

"I don't know. I didn't think to ask, to be honest. He never mentioned it. Isaac rarely mentions money."

"Mmm, it makes you wonder..." She trailed off, and was silent a while, seemingly lost in her thoughts.

"Hannah, what are you thinking?"

"Joshua travels the country selling and setting up technology in schools for the blind, yes?"

"Yeah."

"So what if he lined up one blind person for this surgery at every place he stops at, and takes a commission from the doctor's fee?"

My stomach twisted at the thought. "You think he'd do that?"

"Do you?" she asked, staring at me. "Do you think he seems the type?"

She knew I did.

"He'd just need to single out one blind person who was either rich enough or depressed..."

Rich enough.

Isaac was rich enough.

I shrugged one shoulder, half agreeing. "I guess he could tell from Isaac's suits that he has money, but it's not like he's seen bank statements or anything..." my words trailed away. I knew as soon as I'd said the words.

That mother fucker.

"The bank statements that were stolen!"

Hannah's eyes widened. "No," she breathed the word. "They caught the guy who stole all that stuff."

"But the financial documents never fit in. That Krabanski guy who was charged always said he was paid to take those papers."

Hannah stared at me. "Oh. My. God."

I pulled my cell out of my pocket and scrolled through my call history. I'd have his number from when he called me about my boots. I found the number I was looking for and hit call. I looked at Hannah while I waited for the phone to pick up. "Isaac's gonna kill me for this."

"Hello?"

"Detective Zinberg? It's Carter Reece. I'm the boyfriend of Isaac Brannigan. I came with him to the station the day you charged Maxwell Krabanski for the four home invasions."

"Yeah, I remember you."

"I think I have some information on the financial records that were stolen from Isaac's house."

"Mr Reece, Max Krabanski has been charged with those crimes."

"He always claimed he took those papers on behalf of someone else, and we didn't believe him because, well because... well, because he's a thief and a liar."

"What's your point?"

"I think I might know who wanted that information."

"And who would that be?"

"Joshua Lindstrom."

Zinberg was quiet for a moment. "He was questioned in the beginning, yes? A colleague of Mr Brannigan's?"

"Yes. He travels the country setting up computer equipment in schools for the blind."

"Ah yes," he said as though it jogged his memory. "And what makes you think he's involved? He was cleared of any possible involvement for the break-in. We had witnesses that put him arriving at his hotel at the time of the incident."

"No, not the break-in," I repeated. "The financial documents. Is it possible for you to make some phone calls to the last places he's been, say in the last twelve months, and see if any other blind person has had money taken from their accounts?"

"Mr Brannigan said no money has been stolen."

"No, none has. Yet," I said. I think Zinberg's patience was wearing thin. "See, I think Joshua Lindstrom might be coercing blind people to part with large sums of money for the promise of surgery in Argentina to restore sight."

There was silence on the line for a long moment. "Do you have any proof?"

I sighed. "Well, no."

"That's a pretty big statement to make."

Ignoring his comment completely, I said, "I know it's an outlandish thing to say, but it's all starting to make sense.

Joshua's pushing for Isaac to have this surgery, which may or may not even exist, for God-only-knows how much money. He would have had to have known the financial position of a potential victim before he spent the next six weeks convincing them they could have their sight restored."

"Mmm," the detective hummed.

I just kept talking, "I can give you the name and details of the so-called doctor and anything else this Joshua guy is trying to spiel off to Isaac. Could you make some phone calls? Just ask if anyone had been propositioned, had financial documents stolen, or even if they met with this doctor in Buenos Aires. Lindstrom was in New York before now, there were two schools there, and before that I'm sure he said he was in Philadelphia. He spends at least six weeks at each school. I don't think it has anything to do with what he does at the schools themselves. I think that side of his job is legit, but I think he uses his position and the trust these people put in him, to weed out possible victims."

Zinberg sighed. "And Mr Brannigan agrees with you?"

"Um, Isaac doesn't know I'm speaking to you. I'd like to keep it that way, for now..."

The detective groaned into the phone. "Jesus."

"Just a few phone calls," I urged him. "That's all I'm asking."

"I can make some phone calls," he said with a sigh. "I'll go back as far as six months and see if anything comes up. If I find anything, I'll hand the information over to fraud. I'm not making any promises."

"Thank you. Thank you so much."

The phone call clicked off in my ear, and I slowly put my phone back in my pocket. I looked at Hannah and Carlos and took a steadying breath, wondering what on earth I'd just done.

"Isaac's gonna hate me for that."

WE WENT into the living room, and while Carlos tried to settle little Ada, Hannah spent the next ten minutes trying to convince me I'd done the right thing by asking the police to re-check Joshua's past.

"Isaac might not ever have to know," she said. "The detective could call you in a week or so and say there's nothing to it, and it will all be fine. Isaac will be the none the wiser."

"Maybe," I conceded. "Or Joshua could get taken in for further questioning and the police might tell him it was me."

Hannah rolled her eyes at me. "Or you could fall apart under the guilt of it, and tell him yourself."

"I've never kept anything from him."

"Neither have I. But you love him, and you're trying to protect him," she said, patting my arm.

"I just don't think he'll see it that way," I mumbled, as the Jeep pulled into the drive and the garage door went up. I sighed. "Hannah, don't say anything to him. Let's just see how it works out."

"Okay, but if he asks..."

"If he asks, tell him," I said to them both. "Don't lie to him."

"If he asks you?"

"If he asks me, then I'll tell him," I said. "I can't lie to him either."

Except I was.

Fuck.

I could hear Isaac's and Mark's voices, and I looked at

Hannah and whispered, "Am I lying to him by not telling him?"

She opened her mouth to say something, but they walked in through the kitchen from the sunroom. She looked at them instead. "Here they are? Where did you two get to?"

Mark had his arm linked through Isaac's, and Isaac had one hand behind his back. They stopped in the kitchen, and Isaac asked, "Carter?"

"Yeah, I'm here," I told him from the living room. It was an open space, but it was a big room. "What's up?"

He turned his face to the sound of my voice. "I wanted to get you something," he said with a shy smile. Then he brought his hand around from behind his back. He was holding a small tree, maybe ten inches high, in a small pot. "It's a Chinese blossom tree."

"Oh." I was a little confused.

Isaac explained, "I thought because you bought a tree for Mrs Yeo when Mr Whiskers died, you might like to plant one for Mrs Yeo." He shrugged, my silence obviously had him worried. "I thought the Chinese blossom tree would be appropriate..." his words faded to quiet.

I quickly crossed the floor and put my hands to his face and kissed him softly. "It's perfect," I whispered, knowing he'd hear the emotion in my voice. "Really, Isaac, it's perfect."

He smiled and leaned forward to peck his lips to mine. "I wanted to do something for you."

And the guilt of what I'd done just a half hour before—telling the police to investigate his friend—lay heavy in my chest.

"Is everything okay?" Isaac asked. He was always so perceptive to my silences.

"Sure," I fibbed. "Just caught me off-guard, that's all."

He smiled and handed me the small tree, then pulled a white paper bag from his cargos pocket. "And this, too."

"What is it?"

"A collar with a bell on it for that damn cat."

Mark laughed. "I picked it."

Isaac handed the bag over. "I didn't care what it looked like," he said. "Just as long as it made a noise every time the thing moves."

I put the little tree on the counter and opened the bag. The collar Mark had chosen was a blue, sparkly leopard print with a diamante buckle. I looked at my grinning friend. "Really?"

"What?" he scoffed. "It has two bells?"

Isaac chuckled. "Is it bad?"

"It's... very pretty," I answered.

Mark snorted. "I was gonna get the pink one with rhinestones."

Hannah stuck her head over Mark's shoulder to take a look. "Well, I like it."

"Oh," Isaac said. "Then I know it's bad."

Hannah gently whacked her brother's arm, but she was smiling. "Okay, boys," she said. "We need to get going. We need to get this little baby girl home."

She did the rounds of kisses and goodbyes, Carlos followed with handshakes, and I said I'd help them take the baby's gear out to her car. Carlos fastened tiny Ada into the car seat, and Hannah took the baby-bag from me. "Carter," she said. "I know you're worried about this whole Joshua thing, but it'll blow over soon."

"I hope so."

"Isaac loves you."

"I know he does," I told her. "I just hope Joshua's not

involved in any way. It would devastate Isaac to have a friend betray him like that."

Hannah nodded and after she'd gone, I stood in the front of the house, wondering if Isaac would include me in that betrayal.

I turned and walked back inside, hoping to God I never found out.

CHAPTER THIRTEEN

ISAAC WAS DOZING on the sofa, so I kissed him on the cheek and told him I wouldn't be long. Then Mark kissed him on the cheek and told him not to get up, he needed all the beauty sleep he could get.

Isaac mumbled, "Fuck you."

"Love you, Isaac," Mark sing-songed.

Isaac smirked, still pretending to be half-asleep. "Love you, too."

"Come on," I said, throwing his overnight bag into his chest. "Or you'll miss your train, and as much as I love you, you're not staying here another night. Isaac's liver can't handle you staying here any longer."

We'd gone into the city as suggested, had a beautiful dinner at some overpriced restaurant, then had agreed on one or two drinks at a cocktail lounge before moving on. But then they started playing jazz music and one or two cocktails turned into one or two cocktails too many and we never made it any further.

Hence the reason why Isaac was dozing on the sofa and not coming to the train station to say goodbye to Mark.

Isaac groaned, and pushed at Mark's face. "Carter," he whined. "Take him away."

Mark laughed and told me, "I think I broke your boyfriend."

I dragged him by the arm toward the door. "Leave him alone and get in the car."

On the way to the train station, Mark said, "You know, Isaac knows you don't like his friend."

I snorted. "Well, I never exactly hid it. And Isaac's very perceptive with me. He picks up on the slightest nuances in my voice."

"Yeah, I know," Mark said with a smile. "He doesn't miss much."

I wondered where he was going with this. "Did he say anything else about it? Did he say it bothered him? I mean, I haven't been out and out rude to Joshua."

"Nah, he just said it in conversation."

I slowed to a stop at a red light. "What else did he say about Joshua?"

Mark smirked at me. "He talked about you, mostly. Just how you call Joshua, Joshua. Not Josh. And how you don't call the house, home. He said you still refer to it as his place, not yours, even though you live there."

I was caught staring at Mark when the car behind me honked its horn at me. I slipped the Jeep into first and looking to the road, I pretended to concentrate on driving while I collected my thoughts. "He said that?"

Mark laughed. "Jesus, Carter. You just said before he's perceptive with you, and you're surprised he noticed things like that?"

"Well, I..." I stopped talking and just shook my head.

"You wanna tell me what that's about?"

"Um," I started. "Well, I call Joshua, Joshua, because that's his name and I don't like him."

Mark chuckled. "Okay, fair enough." Then he was serious. "And Isaac's house?"

"It's where I live, and I love it. I love living with him. I love the everyday things. But it's his house," I admitted. "It's all his things, mine are in storage."

"Carter..."

"I know, I know," I mumbled.

"He likes having you there," Mark said with a smile. "He might whine and bitch about it, like he does, but he loves it." Then he added, "Except for last week, when you and he fought."

"He told you about that?"

"Of course he did."

Jeez. They only went shopping to get the little tree and were gone for an hour. "Is there anything he didn't tell you?"

"Nope," Mark said with a grin. "He told me how you like to think of yourself as some kind of masterful top in bed, but how you really just love nothing more than a good fucking."

My mouth fell open. Isaac wouldn't say that. He just wouldn't. Surely. "He did *not* say that."

Mark roared laughing. "No, he didn't, but the way you blushed right now told me all I need to know."

I whacked him in the arm. "Fuck you."

"Not if you're suddenly the big, burly bottom."

I pulled the Jeep into a drop-off zone at the train station parking lot. I wasn't going to validate him with a comment, but I couldn't help myself. "We switch it up, okay?" I said, getting out of the Jeep.

Mark laughed and got out of the Jeep, pulling his bag from the backseat. I got out of the driver's seat, but stood, leaning against my Jeep. Mark dropped his bag at my feet. "So, you gonna tell me what's really eating at you?"

"What do you mean?"

He shook his head. "You can't fool me, Car. I know when you've done something that's eating at you. Isaac might not see it, but I can."

Shit.

"I um..." I exhaled loudly. "I ah..."

"Oh, shit, Carter. What did you do?"

"I asked the police to run more checks on Joshua."

"You *what?*"

I took a deep breath and told him my reasoning. I explained how I thought it was just all too coincidental that Isaac had financial statements stolen at the same time this guy waltzes into his life, with promises of restoring his sight.

He could have lectured me for going behind Isaac's back, or he could have told me I was fucking stupid, and I wouldn't have argued. He'd have been right.

But he didn't. He was quiet. I could see a parking security guy looking at us, more than likely irritated that I was still parked where I shouldn't have been parked at all. Then Mark sighed. "It does sound coincidental when you say it like that. But is that what you really think?" he asked. "Or is your dislike for the man clouding your judgment?"

"I had to do something," I said defensively. "If he's trying to hurt Isaac in any way..."

He nodded. "I get it, Carter. I understand that. Just don't expect Isaac to take the news well when he finds out you were the one who ratted on his friend."

"If Joshua is in any way involved, then I don't care. It'll be worth it."

"And if he's not?" Mark pressed. "If you've gone behind Isaac's back... Do you not remember the first six months of your relationship? You spent the entire time getting him to trust you, trust your judgment, getting him to trust Brady, and you could blow it in one go."

Fuck.

"I know," I whispered with a sigh. I ran my hands through my hair. "Fuck, Mark. What have I done?"

Before he could answer, the parking guy yelled out for us to move on. He hugged me, hard. "You're a good man, Carter. You'll be fine." He pulled back and kept his hands on my arms and smiled. "Now go home, spend the afternoon *switching it up*, or whatever you called it."

He grinned hugely. I told him it was good to see him, that it was good to have some laughs with him. He told me he couldn't believe he came to Boston and never got laid. I told him the men and women of Boston would call me later to thank me. He laughed, got on the train, and I watched it pull away. Mark had been a welcome distraction for Isaac and myself. We'd had such a good weekend, and I was a little hesitant to go back, in case things between us had gone back as well.

My phone beeped in my pocket, telling me I had a message. It was Mark. *Don't just stand there. You look like an idiot.*

I smiled at my phone.

When I got in my Jeep, it beeped again. *It's not like you to lie, Carter. You need to tell him the truth.*

I sighed. Fuck. Hannah said not to tell him unless he asks, Mark says to tell him. I wanted to reply to him, saying I didn't lie. I didn't blatantly tell him an untruth. But, I didn't divulge information that involved him, and to me, that was basically the same thing.

Mark was right. It wasn't like me to lie. I didn't want to tell Isaac because I knew he'd be so mad at me, and that was something I just didn't want. I didn't want to go back to fighting with him.

I didn't have a fucking clue what I was supposed to do.

Unfortunately, I didn't get to be the one to decide if Isaac knew or not.

ISAAC WAS fine on Sunday night. Hungover, but happy. Too tired to read, he plugged in his screen reader, popped in one earphone and had his laptop read to him. More research, he said.

The perfect opportunity for me to bring up the conversation about what I'd done, how I'd told the police to investigate his friend, but I didn't.

I chickened out.

And again on the Monday. I picked Isaac up after work and he said Joshua had taken a call at work from a school he'd spent time with in New York. It wasn't uncommon for him to take follow-up calls from previous schools, but this sounded different, Isaac said.

"He sounded, I don't know, worried about it," Isaac said. "I asked him if everything was okay, and he said it was, but it didn't sound like it."

Shit. I tried to keep my tone as indifferent as possible. "Did he say what they were calling about?"

"From what I could make out, someone had called asking questions about him," Isaac told me. "In some official capacity. So the school called him to tell him they'd passed the caller on to Josh's head office to answer on his behalf and they were just calling to let him know."

"Oh."

"Yeah, anyway then his head office calls the school

and spoke to them," Isaac went on to say. "I asked him what it was all about and he said there'd been a change to his next job or something about a new schedule or something to now include Chicago, he said he thought it was. Anyway, he won't be at school for the next two days."

"Isn't he nearly finished with your school anyway?" I asked. "Didn't he say that last time he was here?"

"He's tenured until we break for vacation, so this week and then next week," Isaac explained. "There's a lot involved in what he does. Setting all the equipment up is the easy part, but the integration software and teaching us all how to use it is a long process."

I had no doubt these phone calls were from the police, questioning the staff and even students of his previous schools to see if there were any others. This was the perfect time to bring up my involvement in it, but again, I couldn't do it.

I didn't want to upset Isaac. I didn't want to have him yell at me and hate me because of what I'd done. Like he'd said, Joshua wouldn't even be there for the next two days, and then next week would be his last at the school before he disappeared to Chicago and we never heard from him again.

I even thought if he was prepping for his next stint at another school for two days, and with only a week to go at Hawkins, he might finish up early. I was hoping he'd announce his work at Hawkins was done, and he'd be gone from our lives forever.

Which is why I was surprised to see his car parked in the front of Isaac's on Thursday. Isaac had said he'd cab it home if he had to, but he obviously didn't have to. Which meant Joshua was back at Hawkins. I wondered if he knew anything, if he somehow found out just who had pointed the finger at him.

Not knowing what kind of reception I'd get, I walked in to find them sitting in the living room. Over the back of the sofa, I put my hand on Isaac's shoulder and leaned down to kiss the top of his head. "Hey," I said.

"Hey."

I looked over at Joshua, and keeping it polite, I smiled and said, "Hi."

"Hello," he said, a little too nicely.

I turned my attention back to Isaac, and looking down over his shoulder, I saw Mr Tiddles curled up on his lap. I walked around the sofa and sat down beside Isaac, and gave the cat a scratch under the ear. "How was your day?"

"Good," he answered. "Yours?"

"Yeah, good," I replied. "That little bulldog bitch I told you about came in. We're expecting her to birth in the next day or so."

Isaac smiled. "Oh, that's good!"

"I might do some laps," I told Isaac. "Then maybe after dinner I thought we could take the dogs for a walk."

Isaac snorted. "Well, you can walk Missy, but Brady and I will come with you." Isaac turned to face the direction Joshua was sitting and chuckled. "Carter thinks me taking Brady on his harness is 'walking the dog'."

I rolled my eyes for Joshua's benefit and playfully pinched Isaac in the ribs where he was ticklish. "I do not, and you know it."

Isaac jerked away from my hand, startling the cat. Isaac chuckled, petting the not-amused feline. "Don't. You'll upset Mr Tiddles. My job as the human heated seat for his royal highness is very important."

I laughed. "Yes, I can see he's found a use for you."

"Go swim," Isaac dismissed me, waving his hand in the general direction of the pool.

I smiled, a little pleased that Joshua bore witness to our silly banter. I stood up and put my wallet, phone and keys on the kitchen counter. "I feel like steak for dinner. How does that sound?"

"Sounds good," Isaac answered.

I walked toward the hall door to go get changed, and whether it was guilt or manners that got the best of me, I looked over to the man I couldn't stand. "Joshua, will you be staying for dinner?"

My invitation threw him. "Oh, um..."

Isaac smiled. "You can stay for dinner, Josh."

"Oh, well. Okay, if it won't be a problem."

I smiled at him, then walked down the hall to get changed, not sure what on earth just possessed me to ask a man I didn't like, to stay longer than he had to.

A few laps of the pool cleared my head a little, until Isaac walked out the back holding my ringing phone. "Carter?"

I stood up and ran my hands through my wet hair. Thinking it could be work calling about the bulldog whelping. "Can you answer it for me?"

"Um..." Isaac hesitated. It was a phone like his, he knew what to do to take the call. He put the phone to his ear. "Hello? Isaac Brannigan speaking."

I climbed out of the pool, roughed the towel over my hair then wrapped it around my waist and walked over to him. Isaac said, "No, he's here now. I'll just get him for you." He hesitated, looking a little confused, and handed me the phone. "It's Detective Zinberg."

Shit.

I took the phone. "Carter Reece speaking."

Isaac turned and walked back inside, so I sat down at the back patio table. "What can I do for you?" I asked, more for Isaac's benefit than the detective's.

"I wanted to inform you that we believe there's enough information for a preliminary investigation into Mr Lindstrom," he said. "We've made some phone calls to the last few schools he's been to, and there has been some... activity... with regards to other blind people having appointments with a doctor in South America. One person parted with money..."

"Oh, Jesus..." So it was the police who had called the school in New York asking for information on Joshua, a *minor* detail he neglected to tell Isaac. Then it really hit home that he'd done this to someone else. "Is that person okay? I mean, did they go to Argentina?"

"We're still looking into it at the moment," the detective said. "I'll be looking into any activity here in Boston, but it's out of my hands in New York State. But they're handling it. If we can prove anything illegal actually happened overseas, it'll be a matter for the FBI."

Jesus Christ.

"He's here, at Isaac's house, right now," I whispered into the phone.

"Dr Reece," the detective said into the phone. "I don't need to remind you this is an on-going investigation. As it stands right now, Mr Lindstrom has done nothing wrong, he simply works at a range of different schools for the blind, and offers information on outside services some people might find helpful. We have no records of financial transactions, and as such, Mr Lindstrom is innocent until proven otherwise." His tone was sharp and clear. "Do you understand what I'm saying to you?"

"Yes," I said softly. My head was spinning. "Don't say anything to anyone."

"That's correct."

I nodded, though he couldn't see. "Okay."

"We'll be in touch," Zinberg said. "I'll let you know if we find anything."

"Okay," I mumbled. "Thanks."

I sat out the back for a while with Missy's head resting on my thigh, absently scratching the top of her head, thinking about what the police were now looking into. How it was my phone call that started it, how I was now implicated in it.

How I'd just taken any possible chance of Isaac having his sight restored—no matter how unlikely it seemed—and threw it away like it was nothing.

I knew right then I had to tell him.

I knew I had to man up and come clean, no matter how mad he was at me, I couldn't lie to him anymore.

Taking a deep breath, I walked back inside to find Joshua was just leaving. "Oh, are you not staying for dinner?"

Joshua looked at right at me. "I'd rather not," he said coldly. And with that, he walked out. I looked at the door he walked out of, shocked. Then I looked at Isaac who sat on the sofa, unmoving and silent. From the stoic look on his face, the way his jaw was set, I knew it wouldn't end well.

His voice was calm and quiet. "What did Detective Zinberg want?"

Walking over to the sofa, I sat down beside him and took his hand. And with a lump in my stomach and a pounding heart, I said, "Isaac, I have something to tell you."

He lifted his chin defiantly. "Does it have something to

do with the police wanting to know about Josh and the work he did in New York?"

"You knew about that?"

"Yes, he told me." He kept his face away from mine. "Exactly why did Detective Zinberg need to talk to you about that?"

"Isaac, I phoned him the other day and asked him to look further into Joshua's past."

He jerked his face toward mine. "You what?" he asked, his voice so low I barely heard him.

"I wanted the police to see if there were any other people Joshua might have dealt with who were considering having this retinal regeneration surgery."

"You *what?*" he asked, louder this time.

"Isaac, I don't think Joshua is what he seems."

Isaac slowly pulled his hand from mine. "Do you realize what you've done?"

"I might have stopped someone else from being misled—"

"No," Isaac spat out, cutting me off. "You've more than likely just cost him his job."

"If he has nothing to hide—"

He stood up and took a few steps away from the sofa, he turned back to face me. "Carter, he works with kids for fuck's sake!" Isaac cried. "Do you know what that means, Carter? Do you even give a fuck? If the police so much as *look* like they're investigating him, for anything, his career is over."

His abrupt anger surprised me. "Isaac, please," I said, trying to keep my tone calm, rational. "Do you not think it's convenient that he comes into your life, you have financial documents stolen, and then he tries to convince you to pay to have a surgery done that might not even work?"

"No! I don't think that's convenient," he almost yelled at me. "What I think, is you can't stand to see me have friends aside from you."

"That's not true," I told him. "Isaac, Detective Zinberg said there's someone in New York who Joshua's also been trying to get to have this surgery."

"Of course there is," he cried, throwing his hands up and walking to the kitchen counter. "Josh told me about them. So someone else wants their vision back too, Carter." Then he yelled, "Is that a fucking crime?"

I stood up and faced him. "No, of course not," I yelled back at him. "But taking money from them for a product they can't deliver is."

"What the hell would you know?" he cried. He was really fucking mad. "You're a vet, not a doctor, you haven't read half the research this doctor has done."

"*Claims* to have done," I argued. "He claims. Anyone can get on the internet and claim to be anything!"

"You wouldn't understand—"

"And Joshua does?"

"His mother was blind!" Isaac spat back at me. "He understands more than you could possibly ever know."

Fuck. "I didn't know that," I said quietly.

"You don't know a lot of things," he sneered at me.

"Maybe if you told me everything..."

"Why?" he cried. "Why do you think I've *not* told you everything? Because you've been against this from the very beginning. I knew you'd hate the idea. I didn't even want to tell you at all, but Josh convinced me I should."

"What?" I asked, stunned. "Why would you *not* want to tell me?"

Isaac laughed, but it wasn't a happy sound. "You don't want me to have any surgery, because you like me blind.

You like the fact you can be the hero and think you're the amazing, compassionate guy for pitying the blind man."

I took automatic steps toward him. "That's not true," I said softly. "You know damn well it's never bothered me."

"Well, it bothers me!" he yelled again, thumping his hand to his chest. "It fucking bothers me."

I shook my head and quickly walked over to him, and took his hand. "Isaac."

"Don't touch me," he said coldly, taking a small step back. He shook his head and his face paled. "It doesn't matter now."

I didn't understand. "What doesn't matter, baby? Of course it matters."

He shook his head and took another small step away from me. "No, it doesn't. Not anymore. It's over."

Was he talking about Joshua? "It *is* over, Isaac, because if he's involved in this, if he's gone out of our lives for good, then it's over."

"No... I mean us."

"What?"

"You heard."

"Isaac..."

His voice was soft, and very resigned. "No. No, Carter. You lied to me. You went behind my back. I can't trust you. And if we don't have trust..."

"Isaac, please. It's not about you and me. Joshua was up to no good since the day you met him. I wish you could see that."

"I'm blind, Carter! I can't *see* it!" he yelled. "All I can see is how he's been friendly, and honest with me, which is more than I can say for you. He's offering ways to help me, while you've been nothing but jealous! Jealous over every little thing."

"I am not!"

"You are! You can't stand that I have a guy friend that isn't you. It's suffocating!"

"That's not true," I said weakly.

"It is so, Carter. You know, just because I'm blind doesn't mean I'll tolerate you trying to control who I can and can't have as friends, Carter. You never liked Josh and you couldn't stand to see me with him."

"You know what?" I asked. My own anger surprised me. "No, I didn't like him. He'd be as nice as pie to you, then sneer at me. He was an asshole when you weren't around, and I'm not fucking sorry he's gone."

Isaac's jaw clenched. And the infamous Isaac Brannigan temper flared. I hadn't seen his true, hurtful temper in almost a year. He squared his shoulders and smiled. "Is that why Paul ended up in bed with another man?"

His question floored me. It hit me like a fucking truck. Isaac knew all about my ex, and he knew exactly how hurt I was by what Paul did. It felt like the air had been sucked out of the room. I could barely talk. "What?"

Isaac sneered at me. "Is that why he cheated on you? Because you suffocated him? You were trying to control who his friends were, who he could talk to? So he fucked someone else in your bed?"

My stomach fell through my feet. Isaac always had a way with hurtful words, to aim for the heart, to aim to kill.

He didn't miss with me.

I couldn't speak. I could barely think. Without another word, I took my wallet and keys off the counter and picked up Missy's lead. My dog bounded over to me, like she always does, and I hooked the lead to her collar.

"Good. Go," Isaac said coldly. "I don't want you here."

I couldn't even reply. The words wouldn't come. I took

Missy, got into my Jeep and left. I was too angry to cry, though his words tore at me. I knew he was mad, and I knew he had every right to be, but the words that came out of his mouth crossed a very real fucking line for me.

I had no idea where I was going. I had no idea where I *could* go. All my belongings were in storage, save my clothes and a few things I had at Isaac's. The truth was, I didn't have anywhere else to go.

So I wasn't surprised when I found myself in a familiar driveway. I stared at the house for a little while, not sure of what to do. I was so fucking angry, and my eyes burned with tears I refused to cry.

I opened my car door, and Missy and I got out. I walked hesitantly to the front door, wondering what on earth I'd say.

Hannah opened the door, looked at me, down to my dog then back to me. "Carter?"

I nodded, as the first of my tears fell. "I don't have anywhere else to go."

CHAPTER FOURTEEN

HANNAH USHERED ME INSIDE. "CARLOS?" she called out, and her husband came around the corner to see who'd arrived. He took one look at me and his face softened. Hannah lifted the baby she was holding, "Here, can you take her?"

Carlos quickly took little Ada, and Hannah threw her arms around me.

"I'm sorry," I said through my tears. "I know you've got a lot happening with Ada."

"Never mind that," she said, pulling me and Missy into the living room. "Tell me what happened." We sat down and she looked at me softly. "You told him you'd spoken to the police?"

"I didn't have to," I said, wiping my face. "My phone rang, it was Detective Zinberg. Joshua was there, and I think he might have pieced it together; that there'd been renewed police interest in his involvement, and then I get a phone call from the same detective?" I took a steadying breath. "Anyway, Joshua left in a hurry, and Isaac just sat there. He asked me outright if I was involved. I couldn't lie to him."

Hannah nodded sadly. "Shit, Carter. I'm sorry."

I shrugged. "And we had a big fight, it was so bad. He told me he didn't want me there. That we were over. He couldn't trust me." Fresh tears started to fall. "Fuck, Hannah, then he was so awful... you know how he says cruel things to hurt people?"

"Oh, God," she whispered. "What did he say?"

"He told me it wasn't surprising my ex cheated on me," I said, wiping my eyes on the sleeve of my tee-shirt. "He said I was suffocating him and maybe that's why Paul fucked someone else in my bed." I shook my head, digging the heels of my hands into my eyes, trying to stem off fresh tears. "He said I was suffocating him."

Hannah pulled me in for a hug. "God, he can be such a prick."

"He thinks I'm trying to control who he's friends with, who he can talk to," I mumbled to her through my tears. "Honestly, Hannah, I'm not! I don't care who he's friends with."

"I know you don't," she said soothingly. "As long as they're not some lying asshole like Joshua, trying to swindle money out of him."

"Isaac blames me," I told her. "He's not wrong, you know. I am to blame. It's my fault Joshua's under investigation. But I'm not sorry. I hope they pin him for everything."

Hannah asked me what else Detective Zinberg had said, and after I told her, she then asked me what other horrible things Isaac had shot at me. I told her everything.

Then she asked me about my ex, Paul, and why Isaac would bring that up.

I shrugged. "Just to hurt me. He knows everything that happened between him and me, and it was over a year before I even met Isaac. But I loved him," I told her, then I corrected myself. "Well, I thought I did, but then I met Isaac." I shook my head and took a deep breath. "I'd moved in with Paul; it was my idea. I wanted it and I think he just agreed to shut me up."

Then something occurred to me.

"Oh, God. How could I've been so stupid?" I said, as my head fell into my hands. "Just like Isaac. God, I pressured him into moving in with me too, didn't I?" I looked at Hannah then. "Am I that bad? Am I that needy? Suffocating?"

She shook her head. "No, Carter. Not at all. Isaac asked you to move in, remember?"

"Yeah, only because I pestered him for so long." Fuck. How could I have not seen that? "He said no for months. Oh God, I *am* suffocating."

"No, you're not!" Hannah said sternly, using the same tone she quite often used with Isaac when he was being a dick. "Isaac loves you. He does, with everything he is. He'll come around," she said. "He just needs time to cool down and see things for what they really are."

I shook my head. "I'm not sure he ever will. He was so mad. I've never seen him that pissed off. He was yelling... And we both know how stubborn he is."

Hannah frowned and let out a long sigh. "Maybe I should go visit him. See if he's okay. Or call him at least."

"I'm sorry for involving you," I told her. "I had nowhere else to go. I couldn't take Missy to a motel."

"I'm glad you came here," she said, patting my hand. "You're always welcome here."

Carlos stuck his head around the door. "Dinner's ready. It's only spaghetti bolognaise. Nothing fancy."

My stomach turned at the thought of food. I shook my head. "No, thank you. I'm not hungry."

Hannah looked at me, and put her hand on my knee. "You should eat."

I pushed my hand against my stomach, trying to quell the nausea at the mere mention of food. "Not tonight. I couldn't." Hannah frowned again, so I tried to smile for her. It was watery at best. "I'll go sit out back, at the patio table while you guys eat."

"Carter—"

"I could do with some time," I said quietly. Then I realized I hadn't even asked if I could stay here. "Is it okay if I crash on your couch? I can look for somewhere to live tomorrow..." My eyes welled with fresh tears.

"Oh, Carter," Hannah whispered. "Of course you can. But don't give up on him yet."

"It's not me who's giving up, Hannah..." was all I could get out before my emotions got the better of me. I shook my head, took a deep breath and walked through the house with Missy at my heels, to the back patio.

It was early evening, the sun had not long set. I sat at the table, Missy sat by my side like she knew something was wrong. I'd have emotions—tears, anger, hurt—come at me in waves, but I just sat there. I don't know for how long. Hours, I think.

I heard Hannah on the phone; it was a conversation that started out softly-spoken, but ended with Hannah yelling down the phone to Isaac that he was a stubborn ass, who's inability to see what was in front of him had absolutely nothing to do with his blindness.

She stomped out through the back door and threw herself into the chair next to mine. "That man... fucking arrogant sonofabitch... ugh... I love him, but I swear, some days I could punch the ever-loving shit out of him."

I gave her half a smile. "I take it that was Isaac."

She huffed. "He's impossible."

I took a deep breath, and asked the dreaded question. "Do I want to know what he said?"

Hannah shook her head. "He's really mad."

I knew what that meant. He told her he didn't want me back, he didn't want me at the house. He didn't want me. I nodded and swallowed so I could speak. "It's okay, Hannah. I understand."

"Carter, I'll try talking to him again tomorrow."

"It's okay," I whispered. I cleared my throat and stood up. "I might turn in, if that's okay? Could you show me where a blanket is? I'll crash on the sofa."

Hannah led me inside and down the hall to the first door. "It's the spare room, but it's not that organized. We just shoved everything in here when we set up the nursery for Ada, it's not too fancy, but it's a bed."

"It's perfect," I told her.

She stood in the doorway for a long moment. "Carter..."

"I'll be okay," I answered, without hearing the question. I looked at her then. "Thanks for this. I'm sorry to impose. Missy will be fine in the back yard for a day, she won't cause you any trouble."

Hannah frowned then, and her eyes welled with tears. "You're welcome to stay here for as long as it takes for..." she stopped herself from saying his name. "For as long as it takes." Then she said, "Oh, I'll just grab you a towel. Have a shower. It'll make you feel better."

She disappeared and came back half a minute later with

a towel and some sleep pants. "They're Carlos'. They'll fit you." She smiled. "Get some sleep. We have a four week old alarm clock that chimes every three hours. And by chimes, I mean screams." She gave me a tired smile and left me to it.

I showered, dressed and climbed into the strange bed. The bed was queen size, cold and quiet. There was no body to lie next to, no soft chuckles, no tender finger tracing patterns up my spine. There were no arms wrapped around me, no whispered words in my ear. No soft snores, no one to tangle his feet in the sheets, no one to hog the blanket, no one to sleep on the diagonal, taking up most of the bed.

No one.

I stared at the wall until Ada cried at midnight, then again at three. I considered getting up to feed her, or burp her or even to walk with her. But then she was quiet, and somehow I slept until she woke up again at six.

I went through the morning, feeling detached. Carlos gave me a pile of clothes to wear, and I took them, too tired, or too emotionally wrecked to feel ashamed or embarrassed. I just took them with a nod for a thank you, showered and dressed. My stomach rumbled at the smell of coffee, but then promptly churned when it came to drinking it. I gave Missy a pat, then a cuddle, telling her not to worry, we'd sort out somewhere to live today.

When I stood up and turned around, Hannah was standing at the back door, holding her little bundle of pink, watching me with my dog. She was teary. "Carter, you know you can stay here."

"I know, and thank you," I said quietly.

"But you don't want to impose..."

I couldn't look at her, so I stared at the ground and nodded. "I just... I don't want him to think you're on my side, ya know? He really needs you."

"He needs you, too," she said.

I bit the inside of my lip, welcoming the pain instead of tears. I tried to talk but couldn't get the words out, so I kissed Hannah on the forehead, then Ada, and left for work.

I got to the animal hospital early, praying for a busy day. When Rani got in, she took one look at me and shut my office door behind her. "What did he do this time?"

I shook my head. "It wasn't him. It was me this time."

She blinked back her surprise. "Well, you look terrible."

"Thanks," I said flatly. I scrubbed my hands over my face. "I didn't sleep."

"I can tell."

"I'll need to duck out during lunch, but I shouldn't be too long," I told her. "Oh, and I know it's not exactly in your job description, but I was wondering if you could check out some real estate sites for rentals."

Rani's mouth dropped open. Then she whispered, "You moved out?"

I nodded and my voice cracked when I spoke. "But I can't talk about it yet." Not without crying, or without the urge to punch something, I thought to myself.

She nodded. "That's cool. Now stand up, come with me," she said, dragging me out of my chair. "We have a shit-load of work to do today, and you're doing it. No time for thinking, just work, work, work."

I smiled at my assistant, grateful for the distraction, and dived headfirst into work. She kept me busy all morning. She never let me stop. She fed me coffee, and literally stood in front of me until I drank and ate something. Then she gently reminded me at lunchtime, I'd mentioned needing to go somewhere.

I looked at my watch. Shit. "Thanks, Rani," I said. "I won't be long."

She eyed me cautiously, but said nothing, just giving me a nod. I didn't tell her where I was going because she'd want to come with me, to keep an eye on me or something. But I needed to do this alone.

I pulled up at the front of Isaac's. It was Friday lunchtime, so I knew he'd be at work. I wasn't up to facing him, and from his conversation with Hannah last night, I was certain he didn't want to see me either.

I used the key to the front door, thankful he'd not changed the security code on the alarm, and I walked into his house. It was quiet, eerily so. It looked exactly the same, like nothing had changed. When the truth was, everything had changed. There was no sign of him being upset or unable to function like me. His coffee cup was sitting in the kitchen sink, just like always. He'd even pulled up his side of the bed where he'd slept.

Like my leaving hadn't affected him one bit.

I walked into the wardrobe, pulled out my bag and stuffed what clothes I could into it. I took my toiletries from the bathroom and then walked into the living room to look for anything of mine.

There wasn't anything.

It was like I'd never lived there to begin with.

The soft jingle of Mr Tiddles' bell sounded as the cat uncurled itself from his spot in the sun. He stood up and meowed at me, so I scooped him up and gave him a pat. I checked his food bowl, wondering if Isaac remembered to feed him, but he had. There was fresh dry food put out either last night or this morning.

And it hit me.

Everything was as it should be. The house was in perfect order, like all was right with his world. Isaac didn't seem to care that we'd broken up. Like our fight, or my leaving, hadn't affected him at all.

I gently put the cat down, picked up my bag, reset the alarm, locked the door and numbly drove back to work.

Numb.

Numb just about summed it up. I was in a fucking daze.

I somehow shuffled through the afternoon, thankful for my assistant, Rani, who managed to keep everyone, clients and staff alike, away from me. She kept me busy with doing check-ups on the animal patients that were staying overnight, and then with inventory. Though I had no idea what the hell I'd counted, what I'd noted, or what needed to be ordered. I didn't have a clue.

I hadn't realized the time until she followed me into the storeroom and closed the door behind her. "It's after five," she said softly. Then she pulled out a piece of paper. "Here's a list of rentals in the area that allow dogs, starting from cheapest to the most expensive."

"Oh," I said quietly. I cleared my throat and spoke louder. "Thank you, Rani. For this, for everything."

"You're welcome," she replied with a kind smile. She hesitated for a moment, like she wanted to ask something but wasn't sure she should. She asked anyway. "Can I ask where you're staying?"

"Um," I started, putting the clipboard down. "I stayed at Hannah's last night. She said I'm welcome to stay as long as I need, but they don't need me there, with the baby and all."

Rani nodded. "As long as you have somewhere. I was gonna offer my couch if you needed."

I smiled for her. "Thanks, Rani, really. I'll be okay."

"Good," she said brightly. "Then go, so I can get finished up."

I walked to my office, grabbed my keys and picked up

my phone. No missed calls. No messages. I pocketed the phone, plastered a smile on my face to say goodbye to Rani, then sat in my Jeep for a minute or two before turning the key.

I needed to get my shit together. I needed to act like I was on top of this. No, it wasn't what I wanted, but I was a grown man and I needed to deal with it. People dealt with heartbreak every day. From what I saw at Isaac's house, he seemed to be managing just fine.

So I took out my phone and called Hannah. She answered cautiously. "Carter?"

"Just putting in a Friday night pizza call," I said, trying to be cheerful.

Hannah was surprised. "Oh."

"Is that okay?"

She laughed. "Stupid question," she said, then covered the phone, though I could hear her muffled voice. "Carlos, pizza for dinner?"

There was a distant, muffled response from Carlos, then Hannah returned. "Carter?"

"Yeah?"

"Carlos said any pizza is fine, as long as it comes with beer."

I smiled, for what seemed like the first time in forever. "Deal."

By the time the sun had gone down, we'd polished off the pizza, and even had a few beers sitting at the back patio table. Someone's name very deliberately didn't get mentioned, and I was grateful. I ignored the feeling that Hannah and Carlos were babysitting me, or pitying me, or both. I didn't doubt they were, but I ignored it and just tried to act like I wasn't falling apart.

NEEDLESS TO SAY, I didn't sleep much, and when the sun was finally up, I hovered my thumb over his number a hundred times before I plucked up the courage to call him. I had no clue as to what I would say if he answered, though truthfully I was more worried about him telling me, again, that we were really over.

But I had to do something, and I figured a phone call would be a good place to start. My call went through to voicemail, where I said, "Isaac, please. We need to talk." He never called me back. Part of me never expected him to, but it hurt nonetheless.

And I was back to square one.

I spent the rest of the morning looking at the rentals list Rani had given me, and made some phone calls. I even went to have a look at one. It wasn't great, and a little too far from work, so I told the realtor thanks, but no thanks.

I got back to Hannah's and Carlos' place to find Carlos folding laundry and Ada in her bouncer. "How was the house?" he asked as I sat down.

"Ugh. Dark and cold inside, back fencing needed work to be dog-proof."

"So, no good?"

I shook my head. "Nah. Where's Hannah?"

Carlos sighed, long and loud. "She went to see Isaac."

"Oh."

"Well, she spoke to him on the phone first," he said. "And that didn't end well, so she got in the car and went to see him. I'm thinking she'll be home soon."

And about ten minutes later, she walked through the door. She didn't look mad. She wasn't angry. She looked... sad.

"Everything okay?" Carlos asked. Then he sighed. "Did he say something to upset you?"

"No more than usual," she answered. She looked at me and my stomach knotted. "Carter, I tried to talk to him. I tried to get him to listen, and it was all rather civil..." she shook her head. "But then Joshua turned up."

My throat squeezed shut. My voice croaked. "Joshua?"

She nodded. "I asked him if the police had been in touch."

Carlos sighed. "Oh, Hannah."

"What?" she cried. "You know what? Fuck him. He had the audacity to smile at me, and said it was all a miscommunication and had all been sorted out."

"What?" my voice was just a whisper.

Hannah nodded. "That's what he said. So I asked him why he was doing this. I asked him what he got out of it, ruining two perfectly happy lives, and that's when Isaac got mad."

Joshua was there. With Isaac. While I... wasn't.

I tried not to think about what they might be doing. Alone. The two of them. "Hannah," I whispered. "What were... are they... what was he..."

Hannah's face fell. "Oh, Carter. I'm sorry. I'm so sorry."

My chest tightened. Even putting my hand against my sternum didn't help. "Are they... togeth..." I couldn't even finish the word.

"He said they had plans," she offered quietly. "That was all he said."

I nodded. I tried to swallow, but I suddenly didn't feel very well. "Did he look okay? Was he okay?"

"Carter, don't, sweetheart. Don't do that to yourself."

"I might just go..." I mumbled, "just go lie down. I don't feel very well." I walked quietly down the hall.

So that was it. He'd moved on. Already. I truly meant nothing to him. It was really over. They had plans. Him and Joshua. Together.

I crawled into the bed and waited for the numbness to dull the ache in my chest. But it never came.

CHAPTER FIFTEEN

HANNAH DRAGGED my sorry ass out of bed before dinner. I didn't feel like eating, I didn't feel like talking to anyone, looking at anyone, or even being around anyone. But Hannah wouldn't have an ounce of my self-pity.

Fucking stubborn Brannigans.

She was trying to get something cooked, but Ada was fussing. Carlos had mysteriously disappeared, and when I thought she was gonna give me cooking instructions, she didn't. Instead, she handed me Ada.

"There's expressed milk in bottles in the fridge," she said, stirring two different pots at once. "Take the teat off and microwave it for twenty-eight seconds." I stared at her, not too sure what I was doing, holding a baby and trying to heat milk up. Hannah raised an eyebrow at me, in true Brannigan style. "Go on," she urged me. "You can do it. You must have bottle fed all sorts of baby animals."

Trying to hold and soothe a still-fussing Ada, I heated the milk, put the teat back on and handed it to Hannah to test. By this time, Ada was crying and squirming, and I was bouncing her in my arms.

Hannah swirled the bottle, splashed a few drops on her wrist and smiled. She must have had the milk-heating procedure down to a science because she said, "It's good." So I tucked Ada into my arm like a football and stuck the bottle into her open, crying mouth.

The silence was immediate, and I let out a huge sigh of relief.

Hannah smiled. "See? Nothing to it."

I almost smiled as I walked into the living room and sat down with a now feeding, much happier Ada.

"She'll need burping and changing afterwards," Hannah said from the kitchen.

"Oh. Okay."

Hannah was the master in the art of distraction. She just wasn't very subtle about it. She made me burp Ada, clean up spit, change what was thankfully only a wet diaper and then redress her into pajamas.

I was trying to settle Ada and get her to sleep by walking a path into the living room carpet when Carlos got home. Even as he came in, juggling bags of groceries, and then on his second trip to the trunk of the car, a carton of beer, I was still relegated to Ada-duties.

Not that I minded. She was a cute little thing. But I knew what Hannah was doing; if she kept me busy enough, I couldn't think about Isaac. And if I had Ada, as opposed to standing at the stove stirring the large pot, I had to stay focused on what I was doing, and multi-task at the same time.

Hannah made this look easy.

By the time Ada finally went down to sleep, it was dinnertime. Not that I was particularly hungry, but Hannah put a plate in front of me anyway.

She certainly wasn't about to let me wallow. I pushed

the food around my plate, but when Hannah gave me a none-too-pleased look, I managed a few mouthfuls. She was strictly a take-no-crap person, a trait I assumed came from years of looking after Isaac.

We ate at the back patio table again. It was, Hannah had said, where they ate most meals in the warmer months. Carlos took the empty plates inside and came back out with two beers. He handed me one, sat in his seat with a sigh, patted his belly and took a swig of his beer. "All I'm missing is the baseball on TV."

Hannah rolled her eyes and went inside, leaving Carlos and I alone to drink beer. It was either a deliberate move to give us some guy time, or to avoid listening to us talk crap.

We talked about baseball, which morphed into football, which turned into talk of childhood idols to movie stars, and the later it got, the more beer we drank, and the more shit we talked. I even laughed at his impersonation of 80's big hair rock bands with his air guitar.

I knew it was a deliberate ploy for me to forget about things, if only for a little while. And it worked, kind of. Until long after we *should* have stopped drinking, but didn't, Carlos started talking again about Ada.

He talked of the wonders of creating life and how he never thought it was possible to love someone so much. He never expected the love, he said.

Even as drunk as I was, I knew I should say something. That's how conversations go; one person talks, then the second person responds.

But I couldn't.

I never expected the love, either.

"Carter..."

"It's okay, Carlos," I said. "You're allowed to talk about your baby girl and the wonders of kids and family and love.

I'm not *that* fragile." He smiled sadly at me, so I added, "She's the most amazing smelling creature in the world, after all."

It was supposed to be funny, but the mere mention of something Isaac would frequently say, brought the weight of the last three days back with a dull thud.

Carlos sighed, knowing our conversation had just taken a nosedive. "I'm sorry," he said. "For what it's worth, I thought you'd make a good brother-in-law."

I took a deep breath, my heart squeezed tight in my chest. "I thought he was it for me," I admitted quietly. "I thought he was my family."

"Give him some time," Carlos said. "Wait until this Joshua douche leaves and maybe then Isaac will have some perspective."

I shook my head. "I went to the house the other day. When I picked up a few things? I figured it'd be better if he wasn't there."

Carlos stopped picking at the label of his beer and looked at me. "And?"

"And it was like I never lived there." I took a mouthful of beer. "Not a thing out of place, the bed was made. He'd even fed the cat."

Carlos stared at me, like what I said didn't make sense to him. "So?"

"It's just life as usual for him, like he doesn't even care," I explained. "And here I am, I can't even fucking function properly." I took another mouthful of beer. "You know what I've learned?"

"What's that?"

"I've learned a lot of things about myself in the last few days," I told him. "I've learned what I thought was being attentive and thoughtful, wanting to give him the world, as it turns out, is suffocating. So all this time I thought I was showing him how much I adored him, I was just pushing him a little bit further away."

Carlos looked at me for a long moment then he pointed his beer bottle at me. "You know what? I'm gonna tell you a story about Isaac." He drained his beer bottle and swallowed it down before he spoke again. "You see, when I first met Hannah, their dad had not long died, and she was doing everything she could to protect her brother. He was young and dealing with not only the death of his father, but also his training to be a teacher, being gay, then his guide dog Rosie died... It was a hard time for him.

But he had Hannah. She wasn't much older than him, you know. She'd been his caregiver for a long time. She was all he really had," Carlos said quietly. Then he smiled. "Things between me and Hannah got serious, and I can tell you, Isaac was not impressed."

I nodded. "I could imagine."

Carlos sighed. "God, he was an arrogant prick."

I snorted at that and Carlos smiled and shook his head. "Jesus, he wouldn't budge an inch. I was more than nice to him, I was obliging, cooperative, you name it, I did it. And he *still* hated me."

"He hated you?" I asked. "No, Isaac thinks the world of you."

Carlos laughed. "Now, maybe. But not then. God, every time Hannah and I had something planned, he'd call her up and tell her he needed her. It got to the point where Hannah told me she couldn't see me anymore, because it was her responsibility to look after Isaac."

I frowned. "What happened?"

"I paid Isaac a little visit and told him to grow the fuck up."

I scoffed out a laugh. "Really?"

Carlos nodded. "Yep. I told him it was unreasonable for him expect Hannah not to live her life because of him. I told him if he kept pushing, pushing, pushing for her to choose, that one day—maybe not then, but *one* day—maybe she wouldn't choose him, because he'd pushed too much. I told him I loved her and I wasn't going to go away just because he didn't like me." He smiled at me. "I told him if he thought by making it so difficult that I'd just give up, he was very wrong. I told him it was the opposite for me. I'd just fight harder for her."

"What did he say?" I asked.

Carlos smiled. "Not much he could say, really. But his attitude changed, that's for sure. He started being nice to me after that. He told me later that he knew I was an okay guy, because if I'd fallen at the first hurdle, then I wasn't the one for her."

I took another mouthful of my beer. I knew where he was going with this. I shook my head. "Isaac doesn't want me. I blew it."

"Have you spoken to him?" Carlos asked. "Have you asked him?"

"No. He won't take my calls."

"So that's it? You're just walking away without a fight?"

"I um... I..."

"Didn't think you were the quitting type."

"I didn't quit," I said weakly. "He asked me to leave."

"Let me tell you something about these bloody Brannigans, Carter," he said. "They're fucking stubborn. I should know, I married one. Tell him you're not going anywhere."

"See, Carlos, I can't," I told him. "I can't *fight* for him, I can't push him. He already thinks I smother him, suffocate him, so if walk back in there and tell him I'm not going anywhere, I'm just suffocating him even more."

Carlos shook his head. "That's bullshit and you know it. You've never suffocated him, ever. He's just being an ass because he knew he'd hurt you when he said that. So you're just gonna wait around until it all falls to shit and he realizes he was wrong?"

I nodded. "It's all I *can* do."

"And you die slowly of a broken heart while he takes his time being a stubborn ass, pretending to get on with life when he's too pigheaded to admit he's wrong?"

I didn't answer. I didn't have to.

Carlos put his empty bottle on the table and stood up. He clapped his hand on my shoulder before walking inside. "That's what I thought."

I sat there by myself, drunk and depressed for I don't know how long. I pulled out my phone to check the time. 11:27 pm. Fuck. I scrolled through my contact list, knowing I shouldn't be calling at this time, let alone drunk, but found the name I was after and hit dial.

"Carter?"

As soon as I heard his voice, my eyes pricked with tears. "Yeah, Mark," I said, sucking back a breath. "It's me."

———

IT WAS AROUND two o'clock in the morning by the time I got into bed. I spent over two hours on the phone to Mark. He listened while I told him what happened, how Isaac asked me if I was involved in pointing the finger at Joshua, how I couldn't lie to him.

I told him what Isaac had said, about me suffocating him, about how I must have suffocated Paul to make him cheat on me. Mark had threatened to walk to Boston to punch Isaac in the mouth for saying that, his voice was shaking with anger, but it was an empty threat.

I still defended Isaac, of course, reminding Mark that Isaac's method of self-preservation was to strike out with hurtful words. And that just pissed Mark off even more. I spent the entire conversation see-sawing between hurt and anger, wiping away tears with the hem of my shirt one minute, then speaking through clenched teeth the next.

Then I told him how Joshua was at Isaac's today, and how they had plans tonight. For all I knew he was still there. Maybe they were in bed, maybe Isaac was being un-suffocated by Joshua as we spoke.

Mark was quiet then as he listened to me cry.

I told him I was sick of the tears, I was sick of feeling lost. I loved Isaac, I loved him still. I probably always would. And then I told him, very profoundly, that having your heart broken sucked.

He asked me if I wanted him to come visit, he'd be there in the morning if I just said the word. But I explained to him that as much as I would love to have him here, I didn't exactly have a 'here' for him to stay at.

He told me to go to bed, that he loved me, that Isaac had lost his fucking mind, and that he'd call me tomorrow, or today rather, he corrected himself. It was a quarter to two.

I didn't hear Hannah get up with Ada at midnight, and if she heard me talking to Mark or heard me crying, she never said. I staggered out of bed around nine in search of strong coffee, and Hannah just smiled and patted my arm. "I know you're about to apologize," she said. "You don't need to."

I smiled into the coffee cup as I sipped the hot drink. "Sorry."

She leaned against the kitchen counter. "So, what's on your agenda for today?"

"I need to shower," I started. "Because I stink. And then I need to take finding somewhere to live a little more seriously."

Her brow pinched. "What do you mean?"

I shrugged and inhaled the smell of coffee. "I guess I kind of hoped I wouldn't need to find somewhere. I hoped Isaac would..." I stopped short, and started again. "Considering he and Joshua are..." I put the coffee cup down. "I just need to find my own place."

"I'm really sorry," Hannah said quietly.

"Don't apologize for him. Please."

She huffed. "For what it's worth, I don't think there's anything going on between them. Isaac just said it because he's pissed off at both of us, and he knew I'd tell you." Then she sighed quietly. "Isaac loves you, Carter. Not Joshua. I know he does."

"I think he's shown us who he'd prefer, yes?"

Hannah shook her head. "No."

I didn't want to argue with Hannah. It was the last thing I wanted. "It doesn't really matter anymore." I tipped my coffee down the sink. "I'm gonna get showered, get organized. Busy day."

I spent the day, even a Sunday, checking out real estate office windows, looking at rental lists. I wrote down addresses, and drove past the houses, making notes of the ones that looked half decent.

I could have done most of the work from a computer, but figured the day out would do Missy and I the world of good. And when I got back to Hannah's, I took Missy for a long walk, trying to keep occupied and not sitting around thinking. And as a way to show my appreciation to Hannah and Carlos for giving me place to stay, I offered to babysit Ada while they had dinner out.

It'd been five weeks since they'd had a night off, or any kind of break, so it was the least I could do.

Hannah almost tackled me, jumping excitedly, and then ran down the hall to get ready. I guessed she thought it was a good idea. She gave instructions as they were walking out the door, but considering Ada had not long been fed and changed, I was confident we'd be just fine.

She started to fuss a little, so I picked her up and walked the floor with her. I told her, in the sweetest, softest voice, that her uncle was a wonderful man, that I loved him with every fiber of my body, and that he was a complete and utter ass.

I whispered that her uncle took my breath away, and that she'd grow up to know a remarkable man. He was brilliant, in everything he did, how he faced the world head on, how his blindness certainly wasn't his downfall. No, his downfall was his stubbornness, his spitefulness. That was his downfall.

The more I walked, rocking little Ada gently in my arms and the more I talked soothingly, the quieter she became. Soon enough she was sound asleep in my arms. I sat on the sofa with Ada cocooned on my chest and it wasn't long before Hannah was waking me up, taking her still-sleeping daughter and telling me softly to go to bed.

Monday morning was weird. I woke up, and for one split second, I woke up refreshed and even happy. But then I rolled over, and I was in a strange bed, in a strange room. And then I remembered.

I got to work and was met by Rani, who offered me coffee and a smile. And I somehow made it through the day.

I forced myself to deal with people, with their pets. I didn't hide in the storeroom or in my office.

I needed to pull my shit together and deal with it.

I made some phone calls to real estate agents regarding the rentals I was interested in, and had made appointments to see them later in the week.

I cooked dinner for Hannah and Carlos, admittedly it was grilled meat and salad, but I told them I had three places to look at. It made it real, telling them, that it was actually happening.

I had no doubt Hannah had spoken to Isaac; they talked every day. But I didn't ask what was said, and she didn't say. I felt bad for putting her in the middle of this whole mess, she looked genuinely upset, as though I'd added more stress to her already stressed life.

I walked Missy until it was late, giving them some privacy, and avoiding Hannah's saddened face.

On Tuesday after work, I told them I'd go out for dinner and take Missy with me, and Hannah stopped me. "You don't have to distance yourself from us," she said. "You're very welcome here."

I smiled and rubbed her arm. "Thanks, Hannah. I really appreciate everything."

"But?"

"But I need to get my shit together," I told her. "I need to move on."

Her eyes welled with tears. "From me?"

I gave her a hug. "No, Hannah, not from you, or Carlos, or gorgeous little Ada."

"From Isaac," she said softly.

I gave her a small nod. "I've left messages on his phone, Hannah. He doesn't reply. I think it's pretty clear he doesn't want me."

"But he loves you."

I shook my head and swallowed hard. "No, he doesn't." I took Missy's lead and walked out the front door. I didn't even cry.

It was Wednesday afternoon, after work, and I was looking through the second place on my rental list when my cell phone rang.

Isaac's name flashed on the screen, and I froze. The realtor looked at me, looking at the ringing phone in my hand, and smiled. "Are you going to answer?"

"Um..." I wasn't prepared for this. But the shrill sound of the phone cut through me, and I took the call. "Hello?"

There was a long beat of silence. "Carter..."

"Isaac..."

I swear I could hear him breathe. "Hannah called me," he said quietly. "She said you were looking for a place..."

"I can't stay with her forever," I answered just as softly. There was more silence, so I asked, "Isaac, are you okay?"

He was quiet for a moment, and then he whispered, "Sure."

I don't know what on earth possessed me to say it, maybe it was morbid curiosity, maybe I just needed to hear it from him directly. "So, does Joshua treat you well?"

"What?"

"I was just curious, that's all," I said, trying to sound casual. "Hannah said you told her that you and Joshua had plans, or a date, or something." I couldn't keep the sting out of my voice. "You didn't wait long. What was it? Two days?"

His voice was louder now. "Is that what you think?"

"It's what you said." Then something occurred to me, and I swallowed thickly. "Unless you were *with* him while we were still together." I pushed down the sudden urge to vomit. "Oh, Jesus... were you?"

"Carter, I..." and he stopped talking. "You know what? Never mind," he said coldly. And the line clicked off in my ear.

I ran my hands through my hair, took some deep breaths and ignored the nauseous feeling in my stomach.

"Uh..." the real estate lady's voice broke the silence.

I turned to her, and taking a last look around at the empty room, I shrugged and could barely form the words. "I guess I'll take it."

I TOLD Hannah I'd agreed to take on a lease for the house and to say she was less than pleased was an understatement. She was royally pissed. Not at me, but at her brother.

"He told me he was going to call you!" she cried. "I went and saw him. He said he would."

"He did call me."

"No," she clarified. "To sort out this godforsaken mess."

"Look, Hannah, I appreciate everything," I told her again. "But you should probably be mad at me. I was the one who got angry on the phone."

"Don't worry," she said with pursed lips. "I'm mad at you too.

"Well, I'm mad too," I told her. "I'm really pissed off, actually."

"Good," she said back at me. "Then call him back and let him have it."

I laughed at the ridiculousness of this conversation. "Hannah..."

She sighed dramatically. "What is it with you freakin' men? You're freakin' hopeless."

Carlos walked into the kitchen where we were, and

kissed her cheek. "It's in our DNA, darling."

She grumbled at him, but eventually smiled. "I just wish you and Isaac would talk. I swear, he's not with that douche bag Joshua. He's not." She folded her arms and huffed. "That man... he either sneers or smiles too fake. Ugh. He's a slimebag."

I nodded. "So... Joshua was there again?"

Her shoulders fell and she sighed. "Carter..."

Well, that answered that. Of course he was there. "Anyway," I said, changing the subject. "The house is kinda nice. Big yard, Missy will love it. It's not too far away. Close to work."

We didn't talk about Isaac again that night, but when I finished work on Thursday, Hannah was rather upset. She'd called Isaac like usual, but this time they fought.

She told him, apparently, he was making the biggest mistake of his life and if he thought for one moment Joshua's intentions were good, he was very, very wrong. She told him he was a fool for letting me walk away, for pushing me away.

Then he told her, apparently, to mind her own fucking business. That he could live his life how he wanted to. He blamed her for siding with me, that we were against him, that we wanted him blind. He told her we had no idea how much he wanted to see.

"Do you believe that?" Hannah asked. She was still upset. "Can you believe he still thinks that?"

"Yeah, I can," I told her. "God only knows what that asshole Joshua has told him."

Hannah started to cry. "That guy would have no idea what Isaac's been through."

Carlos hugged his wife. "He's going soon, isn't he?" he asked. "Then this will all be over?"

I nodded. But seeing Hannah upset over this, over me and Isaac, just broke my heart. It wasn't fair. I walked out the back door, and took out my phone. I called Isaac's cell phone, but of course he didn't answer.

So, I left message after message after message.

I told him he could be mad at me all he fucking wanted. He could yell and rant at me, hate me if he wanted, but he couldn't do that to Hannah.

He might think he doesn't need anyone, but if he pulled his head out of his ass long enough, he'd realize that Hannah needed him. He could say all the hurtful things he wanted to me, but he had no right to treat his sister that way. It wasn't fair. It wasn't fair at all.

But by the time I'd waited for his phone to ring out and voicemail to kick in on the fourth time, the fight in me was gone. All that was left, was a very raw hurt. I took a couple of breaths to stop any more tears, and I exhaled shakily into the phone. Before the message cut off, I said the only thing that was left to say.

"Isaac... I love you. Please."

***

FRIDAY MORNING WAS BUSY, and I told Rani I had to go out after lunch to sign the lease for my new place. So when I collected my phone and keys from my office before I left, I saw I had one missed call, one message.

Isaac.

I almost didn't listen to it. I almost hit delete. My thumb hovered over the delete button, but the masochist in me had to know. So I pressed the message to listen to it, and lifted the phone to my ear.

His voice was quiet. Sad. "Carter... this whole mess, this

whole thing... I never meant to hurt you, or Hannah..." his voice trailed away. "Anyway, I'm going away for a week or so. I need some time away to think and I can't do that here, my house is just... But when I come back, I'll be different, you'll see. Can you just give me that? Please? Because this is all for nothing without you."

Rani opened my office door. "I thought you were going?"

I was sitting at my desk and must have listened to Isaac's message four or five times. "Here, listen to this," I said to her. "Tell me what you think of it."

Rani sat down across from me, took my phone, and listened to Isaac's message. She frowned and handed it back to me. "What does that mean?"

I shook my head. "I don't know."

"You don't think he'd do something stupid, do you?"

I almost laughed. "Isaac? Of course he would."

"No," she said. "I mean, with his eyesight. He said he was going away for a while and when he came back he'd be different."

"I think he was speaking metaphorically. That he'd be in a different headspace," I said. "We told him that half concocted surgery wouldn't work." I realized as I said the words, like a penny dropping. "He's not that stupid, is he?"

Rani raised one eyebrow. "Stupid, no. Desperate, yes."

I pressed his number and listened to it ring out in my ear. So I pressed it again, my knee bouncing. "Come on, Isaac. Answer your damn phone." The call clicked over to voicemail, again, but I didn't leave a message. I just hit redial. Nothing.

"Fuck."

Rani looked at her watch. "Call his work. He's still there, yeah?"

It was twelve-thirty. "Today's the last day before

summer break," I said, scrolling through my contact list. I found Hawkins, and hit call.

I asked for Isaac, and was put on hold. But when the line picked up, it wasn't Isaac at all. It was Marianna, his boss. I'd met her quite a few times, and it was clear she adored Isaac.

"Marianna? It's Carter. Can I speak to Isaac, or if he's in class, could you pass on a message to him for me?" I was met with silence. "Marianna?"

"Yes, Carter, it's just that..." her voice faded away. "I'm confused. Isaac's not here. I thought he was with you."

"What?"

"He only had an end of year party on with his students this morning, and he said he needed to leave early today. He said he was going on vacation. With you."

With me?

On vacation?

Oh, Jesus.

"Marianna, did he say where we were going?"

"Carter, is something wrong?"

"Marianna, I'll explain everything later, but right now I need to know where he said he was going?"

"He said you were taking him on some hiking tour," she said. "He's always talking about how you both go hiking."

"Where?" I asked, a little too loudly. "Marianna, I need to know. Please."

"You're starting to scare me, Carter."

"Please," I begged. "Where did he say he was going?"

"Carter, I—"

"Marianna! Please. Where? Where did he say he was going?"

Her voice was distant. Her answer stopped my heart.

"Argentina. He said he was going to Argentina."

CHAPTER SIXTEEN

MY HEART STOPPED BEATING. My stomach lurched. I think I swayed in my seat.

Marianna's voice echoed through the phone. "Carter? Can you please tell me what's going on?"

I shook my head. "I'll call you as soon as I can," I spoke quietly. "I need to go..."

I stood up. "He's leaving for Argentina. That's where he's going. He's not going away to think. He's going to let that butcher operate on his eyes."

Rani picked up my keys from my desk and pushed them into my chest. "Go!" she said. "You need to go."

"I um, I don't even know what flight..."

"It doesn't matter, you just need to get your ass to Logan International Airport, now. I'll call the terminal and see which airlines are going to Argentina today. I'll call you, but you need to leave right now."

I pulled the Jeep out into traffic, with one hand on the wheel, one hand with the phone to my ear.

"Carter?"

"Yeah, Hannah, look. I don't want you to panic, but I'm on my way to the airport."

Her reply was quiet. "What do you mean, 'don't panic, I'm going to the airport'?" Then she got louder. "What the fuck does that mean?"

Trying to drive a stick shift and talk on the phone was proving a pain. I almost dropped the phone. "Hannah, I think Isaac's going to Argentina."

There was only silence, followed by a very quiet, "What?"

I explained the voicemail from Isaac, then the phone call to Marianna and Hannah sobbed. "Oh, my God."

"I don't even know where I'm going. I'm just going to the airport to see if I can find him," I told her, just as my phone beeped with another incoming call. "This could be Isaac, I have to go."

"Oh, Carter, hurry," Hannah said quickly. It sounded like she said, "I'll meet you there," before she clicked off the call, but I couldn't be sure.

"Hello?" I said, answering the incoming call.

"Carter? This is Detective Zinberg."

I stuck the phone between my ear and my shoulder and changed gears. "Yeah?"

"Are you driving?" he said. "Because I can call back."

"No!" I cried. "I mean, yes, I'm driving, but no, don't call me back. I'm glad you called actually."

He seemed to ignore me, because he acted like I hadn't spoken. "We've looked into Joshua Lindstrom, and while there's nothing definitive on him yet, but with the so-called ophthalmologist in Buenos Aires, we've handed the case over to the FBI. It looks like he's been preying on blind people for years. We've spoken to a few people from all over the country. This is not an isolated incident."

"That's great, Detective," I said, probably a little too rudely. "I need you to do me a favor." I didn't wait for him to ask. "I need you to stop a flight to Buenos Aires. I'm on my way to the airport right now. Isaac's getting on a plane."

"Shit," the detective said.

"I don't even know what flight it is yet," I told him. "Can you call them and get them to hold the plane?"

"I can't. This isn't the movies, Dr Reece."

"Then call Isaac, you can do that, can't you? He'll believe it if it comes from you. Tell him what you know. Tell him not to get on that plane."

The detective grumbled something that sounded like an agreement, so I ended the call. "Shit, shit, shit," I swore to no one in particular, threw my cell onto the passenger seat beside me, changed gears and put my foot down.

Just as I got to the airport, my phone rang again. It was Rani. I answered her call, and all she said was, "Gate six. Next flight to Buenos Aires is at one-thirty, the next one's not until four. It has to be this flight, Carter. You've got fifteen minutes."

Fuck.

I had to park a fucking mile from the terminal, ran through the parking lot and then I raced through the terminal like a fucking madman, looking for Gate six.

I noticed on the screens as I ran, that the flight to Buenos Aires was flashing 'final boarding call', and I ran through the lounge, up to the counter, startling the lady behind the computer. "The one-thirty flight to Argentina. I need to be on it."

"Oh," she said, with her hand to her heart.

"I know I'm late," I said, out of breath. I pulled out my wallet and handed over credit cards, telling her, "I don't care what it costs, I don't care where I sit, I just need to be on that plane."

She punched into the keyboard. "Final boarding call has been made," she said like I should care. "We only have one seat that might be available, sir. It's in business class."

"I'll take it."

"Well, the seat is technically taken," she said, typing into the computer. "But that person might not be taking it yet, sir," she said, just as it dawned on me, I didn't even have my passport.

Then she looked past me, around the terminal until she found who she was after. "Excuse me, sir?" she called out. She double-checked her screen. "Mr Brannigan?"

I spun on my heel.

And there he was. There they were.

Isaac and Brady.

My shoulders sagged, and I finally breathed in God-knows-how-long. I collected my belongings off the counter, and looked at the sales attendant. "Never mind."

Brady was pleased to see me, but it seemed Isaac was a million miles away. He was holding his cell phone, turning it over in his hand.

"Hey?" I said softly.

Isaac's head jerked up toward the sound of my voice. "Carter?"

I knelt in front of him, and rested my hands on his knees. "You scared me."

His reply was just a whisper. "I'm sorry..."

"Mr Brannigan," the sales attendant said beside us. "Final boarding call. If you're going to take the seat, you need to board now."

He shook his head. "No, thank you."

She hesitated, looking at me, then back to Isaac. "Our cancellation policy won't allow a refund—"

"I don't care," Isaac said softly. "It doesn't matter." The attendant stood there for a moment, then was gone. I didn't watch her leave.

I took Isaac's hand. "You're not leaving?"

He held up his cell phone. "Detective Zinberg called me... He said it was all some elaborate scam. He said you told him to stop me."

I sighed. "Isaac, I'm sorry."

He shook his head. "There wasn't any point in me going anyway." His voice was quiet. He looked... devastated.

"Isaac—"

"You were right. I was foolish to think he could fix me."

"You don't need fixing, Isaac. You never did."

He shrugged. "It wouldn't have mattered, even if he could have fixed me. There's no point in having eyesight if the reason for me wanting to get my vision back isn't in my life."

Oh, Isaac.

"You, Carter, I wanted to do it for you," Isaac whispered, his bottom lip trembled. "Of all the things I want to see the most, in all of my life, is you. I wanted my sight back so I could see you."

"You do see me."

He shook his head and spoke to his hands in his lap. "I'll never be able to see you."

I took his other hand, holding both his in mine. "You do see me. No one has ever seen me like you do." I lifted his hands to my face. "You know me, you see me, like no one else."

"Not through these eyes."

"No," I agreed quietly. "You see me with your heart."

He pulled his sunglasses off and threw them on the seat beside him, and then he started to cry. I slid my hand around his neck and pulled his face into my neck.

"I'm sorry," he sobbed, his hands fisted into my shirt. "I'm so sorry for everything."

I wanted to tell him it'd be okay, but the truth was I didn't know if it would be. But he was hurting, and it killed me. "Oh, Isaac."

He sobbed into my neck. "I have no one left. I've finally pushed everyone away." He cried harder. "I ruined everything. I always do. I spent so long trying to be something I'm not. I wanted to be perfect for you, that's all I wanted. I wanted to be perfect for you."

"But you *are* perfect."

"No, I'm not," he said, shaking his head. "I'll never be perfect."

"You're perfect for me."

He pulled back from me and wiped his nose with the back of his hand. "Why are you here, at the airport? Why did you come?"

"I couldn't let you get on that plane. I didn't know what would happen to you once you got there. But the plane was ready to leave, so I was trying to buy a ticket."

"You'd have come to get me?"

"Yes."

He shook his head again, disbelievingly, and fresh tears fell down his face. "Why would you do that? I've been horrible to you. I said such horrible things."

"Yes, you did," I told him. I shifted on my knees, resting back on my haunches. "And I can't lie, Isaac. What you said about why Paul cheated on me, hurt me very much."

He nodded, and his face contorted as though in physical pain. "I know. God, I'm so sorry. I didn't mean what I said.

You were never suffocating, you were always wonderful. You've always been so good to me, and I was so horrible to you and Paul was a jerk."

"Well, maybe I was a little suffocating," I conceded.

He shook his head vehemently. "No you weren't. You were wonderful. You put me first every day, I was the center of your world, and instead of telling you how special that was, I threw it back in your face." He scrubbed his hands over his face again. "I don't deserve you."

I nodded. "You're right, you don't."

He sucked back a ragged breath. "I know." He sat back in the seat, but buried his face in his hands. "Carter, I've made such a mess of everything." He shook his head and sagged, defeated. "I feel so embarrassed... humiliated."

"Don't. You have no reason to. The only person to blame here is Joshua and the bastard he worked for, not you."

Isaac wiped his face. "I thought he was my friend," he said quietly. "If it weren't for you and Hannah, *again*, God only knows what would have happened to me. Or Brady! What if I got to Buenos Aires and they did something to him? Or if they took him from me, or hurt him?" He shuddered at the thought. "I guess it just proves I'm useless on my own."

"No, it doesn't, Isaac. Joshua would have had no leverage with you, if you'd just believed in yourself. He preyed on you because he knew he could feed your insecurity. If you would just see how perfect you are. If you just *realized* how perfect you are, then he wouldn't have stood a chance."

"I do believe in myself," he offered weakly. "Well, I did. I did, up until I met him. He never told me I was... *not* perfect. He just told me I could be better. 'Wouldn't it be better?' he'd ask me. And I wanted to be better. I wanted to see. For you, for Hannah." A single tear rolled down his cheek. "You want to know the most awful thing?" he asked, crying harder. "The hardest, most horrible thing?"

"What's that?"

Tears ran down his cheeks, but his voice was quiet. "He gave me hope."

"Oh, Isaac. There's always hope."

He shook his head. "No, there wasn't. I was told from the day I woke up after the accident, when I was eight years old, there was never any hope. I was told I would never see again. Impossible, they said. Once the nerve dies, that's it, it's too late." He exhaled loudly. "And for the first time since I lost my sight, someone told me 'yes'."

I squeezed his hand. "You know what? One day there might be. They're working on new medical breakthroughs every day. I'm sure deaf people never dreamed of a bionic ear, and people with regenerative visual disorders are having sight restored. Isaac, who knows what will be available in two, five or ten years' time?"

"But not now."

"No, not now. Not yet. But soon. There is always hope. If there are new developments, by licensed, accredited doctors with the proper research, with the proper facilities and procedures to restore your sight, and if it's what you want, then I will be there with you, every step of the way."

He nodded and smiled sadly. "Do you think they will, one day?"

"Yes, I do," I said, putting my hand to his face, wiping away his tears. "Yes, I do."

"Isaac, what do you want?" I looked around the airport lounge, at the few people who were watching. "Do you want me to take you home?"

He shook his head. "I want you to move back in with

me," he said quietly. "I want you to forgive me. I want you to tell me you believe me when I say nothing happened with Josh, nothing at all. It wasn't like that. It was never like that with him," he said shaking his head. "It killed me to think you believed it, even though that's what I implied. I can't blame you, when it was my fault. But Carter, I couldn't have ever done anything with him, or anyone else, when I'm still in love with you."

I smiled, finally, and squeezed his hands. "I'm still in love with you, too."

Isaac took a deep, shaky breath. "Really? After everything I've done?"

I leaned up on my knees and put his hands back to my face. "Yes, really. But Isaac, I think we have some real issues to deal with. I want to move back in with you, but things have to be different."

Isaac nodded quickly. "They will be."

"No, I mean, not in your house."

His brow furrowed. "What?"

"I never lived there," I told him. "Well, I mean, technically I did, for about four weeks, but it was never my home. It was still your house, with your things and none of mine. I don't care about possessions, or whatever, but I just felt like everything was yours, like it was just where I lived, not my home..." I took a breath. "I'm not making any sense."

"That makes sense," Isaac murmured. "Why didn't you tell me?"

"I didn't realize until I moved out, and when I went back to grab a few things, it was like I'd never lived there."

He frowned. "I spent hours cleaning when you left. I could still smell you everywhere," he whispered. "It drove me insane."

"Oh, Isaac."

"But I don't care," he said, suddenly brighter. "If you want to move somewhere else, I'll move with you..." his words faded away. "If you want me to. If that's what you want. It's up to you."

"It is what I want," I told him, rubbing his hand with my thumb. "Maybe we could find a place together. Somewhere that's ours, not yours or mine."

Isaac's eyes welled with tears, but he smiled. "I'd really like that."

Then from the corner of my eye, I saw something, or some*one*, running. It was Hannah. She came running into the airport lounge, and stopped when she saw us. She put her hand to her mouth and started to cry.

"Isaac, Hannah's here."

He put his head up. "Where?"

I stood up and pulled him to his feet. Hannah was now walking over to us, tears running down her face and without breaking stride, she threw her arms around her brother.

"You scared me," she cried. "You fucking crazy bastard, what were you thinking? Have you lost your fucking mind?"

I think a few people stared, but I just smiled. This was a typical Brannigan apology.

"I'm sorry," Isaac said. He buried his face into her shoulder.

"You should be. You took ten years off me," she scolded him, as she hugged him tighter. "You almost killed poor Carter, he was a fucking mess because of you," she said, then she pulled back and took his face in her hands. "He loves you, for real, Isaac. Forever. Do you understand what that means?"

He nodded. "I do now."

"Good," she said, then she slid her arm around him and smiled through her tears.

"Can we go now?" Isaac said.

"No," Hannah added abruptly. "Carlos is coming with Ada. I ran ahead. I told him we'd be at Gate six." Then she softened. "I'm really glad you didn't get on that plane."

Isaac hugged Hannah again, and while they were getting reacquainted, I looked down at the ever-patient, always waiting Brady, and gave him a hug. "Oh, Brady, buddy. I've missed you too. Hey? So has Missy. She's missed you so much."

He thumped his tail on the ground, and when I let go of him, he licked my face. "Ugh," I said, wiping dog slobber from my cheek. "Brady just kissed me."

Hannah laughed at me, stepped from underneath Isaac's arm, and pulled my arm. "Here, swap you places."

I slid my arm around Isaac's lower back, and instantly felt... *relieved,* like my body melted into his. As soon as he knew it was me, he dropped Brady's harness and threw his arms around me for me a proper hug. I held him tight and buried my face into his neck. He mumbled over and over how sorry he was, how he loved me, how he missed me.

Carlos walked up to us, carrying a baby carrier, out of breath, but smiling. "Oh, thank God," he panted, handing over the carrier, with a wide-awake Ada, to Hannah.

Isaac turned to face him. "Carlos, I'm sorry..."

"Isaac, don't apologize," he said, giving Isaac a man-hug. "Just don't ever do that again. I can't be expected to run that far. I'm not fit. I'm a married, straight guy. I don't work out. I'm gonna have a heart-attack." He leaned his hands on his knees.

Hannah looked at her husband and gave him the death stare. "Did you run while you were carrying the baby carrier, *with Ada?*"

Carlos stood up, waved his hand at Isaac, then at her,

then back to Isaac before throwing both hands up. "Ugh. You know what? I'm not even gonna answer that." Then he looked at me. "You'll never win."

Isaac smiled and leaned into me. "Can we go now? I'd like to go now."

"Yep," Hannah said. "Let's go."

Carlos took Isaac's suitcase, I picked up Brady's harness and handed it to Isaac, picked up his sunglasses off the seat and slid them onto his face.

Hannah looked around and smiled. "Is that everything?"

I slipped my arm around Isaac's waist and whispered, "Yeah. It's everything."

THREE MONTHS LATER

JOSHUA LINDSTROM WAS NEVER CHARGED. Although he was undeniably linked to the whole case involving the Argentinean doctor, there were records of his numerous phone conversations with the office in Buenos Aires, but no trace of funds changing hands. It simply wasn't enough to have charges brought against him. He couldn't even be charged with paying Max Krabanski to steal the financial documents, because there was no proof, only hearsay.

There were, however, three other people willing to come forward to say Joshua had tried to coerce them into parting with money for a procedure that would never work and what would come of that, only time would tell.

It brought to light his string of lies. His name wasn't even actually Joshua Lindstrom. It was Joshua Van Pelt, Lindstrom was his mother's married name. It wasn't too uncommon for people to use different surnames through their lives, and he paid his taxes accordingly, so it was hardly a criminal offence.

It was a little shocking to hear Joshua Van Pelt wasn't

even gay, like he'd led us to believe, but that he had an ex-wife and kids in Oregon. He didn't lie about his blind mother; that much was true.

At the end of the day, Isaac didn't care. It was over. Joshua was fired from his job and couldn't hurt anymore people in the blind community. The so-called ophthalmologist in Buenos Aires was shut down, temporarily anyway. The guy wasn't even a doctor. His con was, that the blind person would be put under a general anesthetic in a mock clinic, and when they woke up the procedure would be simply deemed unsuccessful without anything actually being done. The money would have already been transferred, with no course of refund, and the patient goes home, penniless, sightless.

It was disgraceful.

But Isaac considered himself lucky, in more ways than one.

He never lost any money—the asking price, he told me, was a hefty forty-two thousand dollars—he never left the country, and against all odds, he never lost me.

It wasn't easy. I'll be the first to admit it. But dare I say it, we're now in a healthier place.

When we left the airport after his almost-trip-to-Argentina, I told him I was expected to sign a lease for my new house. While he didn't say anything, his grip on my hand squeezed to the point of pain. He nodded, as though he understood.

The truth was, I didn't want to live apart from him either, but we couldn't just go back to the way it was. So I made a deal. I told him I'd move back in until we found *our* place, if and only if, he agreed to counseling.

Therapy for him. And therapy for us, as a couple.

He lifted my hand to his face and after a quiet moment, he nodded.

So I moved back in, and he made himself an appointment with a therapist his doctor recommended. Sessions started the next week, and it was going well.

I think in the beginning, Isaac thought it was silly and a waste of everyone's time, but he wanted to show me he was willing to change. The more he went to his single sessions, the more he talked about the accident where he lost his sight, the loss of his parents, the home invasion, his fears, his insecurities, his accomplishments.

And although some nights were rough after some sessions, on the whole, he was much happier. He seemed... settled.

The couple's therapy was good too. We were growing, becoming stronger. It wasn't all wonderful, nor was it easy. But I loved it.

What I *did* love, was the new house.

We went house hunting, narrowed it down to two, then had Hannah help us decide. I think Isaac had Hannah's input because he was worried about my taste. He thought if my taste in music and movies was any indication...

See? Yes, he was doing well in therapy, but he was still Isaac.

The two houses we narrowed it down to, were similar. Both were big, stylish, had four bedrooms, and a pool—they were very similar to Isaac's house. We brought Hannah with us on a final inspection of the two, and she thought both were lovely, but it was Isaac who ultimately made the final decision.

I was taking Hannah through, showing her where Isaac's lounge suite would go and how mine would fit in the media room, when we lost Isaac. We soon found him though, on the back patio, listening. When he turned to face us, his smile was spectacular.

"Can you hear that?" he asked.

Of course we couldn't, but once we were quiet and concentrated hard enough, we could hear what he was listening to.

Birds. Lots of them.

The real estate lady looked at the three of us like we were mad, but told us the house backed onto a nature reserve.

Isaac said, "It sounds like the ponds down at Wompatuck."

I smiled at the real estate lady. "I think we found our house."

We worked out a finance payment deal between us, and had lawyers draw it up. Because Isaac could afford the house outright, it didn't make any sense to go through a bank and pay interest. So, he bought it, and I paid repayments like I would a home loan. I wasn't too happy about that in the beginning, but Isaac said any interest he made off my payments he'd donate to the local APSCA.

Sneaky bastard knew I'd never argue with that.

So we bought it, moved in and were having a little housewarming with people from my work and Isaac's school, due to arrive in about an hour, which was why I was trying to get everything organized. Mark had arrived the day before, and for some reason had decided he needed Isaac to help him grab a few last minute things before the party.

I didn't mind. I got more done without those two horsing around anyway. As I finished prepping the last of the fruit salad, I smiled as I remembered how Mark had taken it upon himself to visit after Isaac and I had broken up and got back together.

Mark had hugged me, long and hard, and told me he was truly sorry he couldn't have come when I really needed him.

Then he started on Isaac. He told him if he hurt me like that again, blind man or not, he'd kick his ass. Then he pulled him into his arms and hugged him fiercely, and they proceeded to slow dance around the living room while Isaac explained how sorry he was.

I only had to remind Mark to keep his hand off Isaac's ass once.

"What's got you smiling?" Hannah's voice startled me. She was holding a smiling little Ada on her hip.

"Oh, just thinking. You know," I said, and tipped the cut melon into the bowl. "I didn't hear you guys come in."

"Isaac and Mark pulled in before us. They let us in the through the garage," she explained. "Got everything done? Anything I can help with?"

"I've pretty much got it all organized," I told her. "That's if those two remembered the cheesecake."

Hannah smiled. "They were getting things out of the trunk. I left them to it." She gently poked Ada's tummy. "Your Uncle Isaac and Uncle Mark are silly, aren't they?"

I grinned and put the fruit salad in the fridge, just as Isaac walked in with his arms full, Mark was behind him. Isaac stopped walking, waiting for someone to unburden him, which I did. I took the cheesecake and bread rolls from him, and gave him a kiss on the cheek.

"Did Mark behave?"

"Mark always behaves himself," Mark said, sliding a carton of beer onto the kitchen counter.

"Mark tells fibs," Isaac said with a smile.

"Here," Hannah said to Isaac, handing Ada over. "Take her and I'll finish up in here, you boys go and sit down."

Isaac took his little niece against his chest and bounced her in his arms. I put the beer in the bottom of the fridge and when I stood up, Mark was taking Ada from Isaac. He whispered what sounded like, "Do it now."

Isaac wiped his hands on his cargos, as if he was nervous. "Um..."

I looked between them. "Isaac, what's going on?"

"Well," he said slowly. "I wanted to do something... well, I wanted to do it later, but Mark thought I should do it now."

"Do what now?"

The kitchen was quiet, everyone was watching Isaac. "I um, I wanted to do this in private..."

Carlos walked in from watching the big screen. Hannah shushed him before he could say anything.

I walked over to Isaac. "Babe, you okay?"

He nodded quickly, and smiled. "Can we have a moment alone?"

"Sure," I told him, and taking his hand, I led him to the front living room where Mr Tiddles was stretched out on the floor in the sun. "What's up?"

He swallowed hard. "I bought you something."

I smiled, but I was wary of how nervous he was. "Okay..."

He reached into his shorts pocket and pulled out a pouch. "I'd heard of these, and did some phoning around. Mark took me to get them," he said quietly, and handed me the pouch.

I pulled the strings apart to open the pouch and tipped the contents out onto my hand.

It was two silver rings.

Not just any rings, but rings with raised dots on them. Braille. They had Braille dots peppered on the surface. I was pretty sure what it said by looking at it, but I gently put my fingertip to the metal and read the words.

I love you.

Isaac bit his bottom lip. "I uh... I um..."

I kissed him to shut him up. "Isaac. It's beautiful."

"It says I love you."

"I know."

He lifted his hands and felt the rings before he took one of them. "This one's yours. It's one size bigger than mine." Then he took my right hand, and before he slid the ring on, he said, "I just thought we could have matching rings. But, you know, I wouldn't mind if this were to go on your left hand."

I was smiling and my heart was hammering. "I wouldn't mind either."

He was still holding my right hand, and when I thought he was about to slip the ring on my finger, he froze. I could have sworn he'd stopped breathing, but he took my left hand and ever-so slowly, lowered to one knee.

I gasped at the realization of what was happening, and movement at the corner of my eye made me look to the door. Mark was there, holding little Ada, grinning hugely, and Carlos and Hannah were there too. Both were wide eyed, and Hannah had his hand over her mouth.

"Carter," Isaac said gruffly, making me look back to him. "I'm not perfect, although you seem to think I am, I can tell you I'm not. But with everything I am, I am yours." He took a shaky breath. "I want to spend my life with you, and I was hoping you'd want that too. I need you to tell me when I'm being obnoxious, even when we're old and gray. Will you do that? Forever, Carter? Would you be my husband?"

At that point, Hannah squeaked and Isaac's face turned toward the sound and he realized we had an audience. I dropped to my knees so I matched his height, and took his face in my hands, bringing his face back to mine. "Yes," I whispered against his lips, before burying my face in his neck. "A thousand times, yes."

Hannah almost tackled us. She was crying and squealing, and doing that weird jumpy-hug thing she did, somehow managing to do it on her knees. We got pulled up to our feet and only after we were hugged by everyone, did we put the rings on with shaking hands.

Whether it was the squealing noise from Hannah, or the other excited voices and laughter, we soon had another visitor.

Brady.

I called him over, and crouched to my knees so I could give him a hug. He seemed to smile back at me, with happy eyes and his tongue lolling to the side, so I hugged him again.

Then Isaac's hand was on my shoulder, and he knelt beside me. He ran a gentle hand over Brady's forehead and gave his dog a hug.

Isaac sat back on his haunches, took my hand and sighed. "I owe everything to Brady," he said quietly.

I leaned over and kissed his cheek. "So do I."

The End

ABOUT THE AUTHOR

N.R. Walker is an Australian author, who loves her genre of gay romance. She loves writing and spends far too much time doing it, but wouldn't have it any other way.

She is many things: a mother, a wife, a sister, a writer. She has pretty, pretty boys who live in her head, who don't let her sleep at night unless she gives them life with words.

She likes it when they do dirty, dirty things... but likes it even more when they fall in love.

She used to think having people in her head talking to her was weird, until one day she happened across other writers who told her it was normal.

She's been writing ever since...

ALSO BY N.R. WALKER

Blind Faith

Through These Eyes (Blind Faith #2)

Blindside: Mark's Story (Blind Faith #3)

Ten in the Bin

Gay Sex Club Stories 1

Gay Sex Club Stories 2

Point of No Return – Turning Point #1

Breaking Point – Turning Point #2

Starting Point – Turning Point #3

Element of Retrofit – Thomas Elkin Series #1

Clarity of Lines – Thomas Elkin Series #2

Sense of Place – Thomas Elkin Series #3

Taxes and TARDIS

Three's Company

Red Dirt Heart

Red Dirt Heart 2

Red Dirt Heart 3

Red Dirt Heart 4

Red Dirt Christmas

Cronin's Key

Cronin's Key II

Cronin's Key III

Cronin's Key IV - Kennard's Story

Exchange of Hearts

The Spencer Cohen Series, Book One

The Spencer Cohen Series, Book Two

The Spencer Cohen Series, Book Three

The Spencer Cohen Series, Yanni's Story

Blood & Milk

The Weight Of It All

A Very Henry Christmas (The Weight of It All 1.5)

Perfect Catch

Switched

Imago

Imagines

Imagoes

Red Dirt Heart Imago

On Davis Row

Finders Keepers

Evolved

Galaxies and Oceans

Private Charter

Nova Praetorian

A Soldier's Wish

Upside Down

The Hate You Drink

Sir

Tallowwood

Reindeer Games

The Dichotomy of Angels

Throwing Hearts

Pieces of You - Missing Pieces #1

Pieces of Me - Missing Pieces #2

Pieces of Us - Missing Pieces #3

Lacuna

Tic-Tac-Mistletoe

Bossy

Code Red

Dearest Milton James

Titles in Audio:

Cronin's Key

Cronin's Key II

Cronin's Key III

Red Dirt Heart

Red Dirt Heart 2

Red Dirt Heart 3

Red Dirt Heart 4

The Weight Of It All

Switched

Point of No Return

Breaking Point

Starting Point

Pieces of Us

Tic-Tac-Mistletoe

Lacuna

Bossy

Code Red

Free Reads:

Sixty Five Hours

Learning to Feel

His Grandfather's Watch (And The Story of Billy and Hale)

The Twelfth of Never (Blind Faith 3.5)

Twelve Days of Christmas (Sixty Five Hours Christmas)

Best of Both Worlds

Translated Titles:

Italian

Fiducia Cieca (Blind Faith)

Attraverso Questi Occhi (Through These Eyes)

Preso alla Sprovvista (Blindside)

Il giorno del Mai (Blind Faith 3.5)

Cuore di Terra Rossa Serie (Red Dirt Heart Series)

Natale di terra rossa (Red dirt Christmas)

Intervento di Retrofit (Elements of Retrofit)

A Chiare Linee (Clarity of Lines)

Senso D'appartenenza (Sense of Place)

Spencer Cohen Serie (including Yanni's Story)

Punto di non Ritorno (Point of No Return)

Punto di Rottura (Breaking Point)

Punto di Partenza (Starting Point)

Imago (Imago)

Il desiderio di un soldato (A Soldier's Wish)

Scambiato (Switched)

Galassie e Oceani (Galaxies and Oceans)

French

Confiance Aveugle (Blind Faith)

A travers ces yeux: Confiance Aveugle 2 (Through These Eyes)

Aveugle: Confiance Aveugle 3 (Blindside)

À Jamais (Blind Faith 3.5)

Cronin's Key Series

Au Coeur de Sutton Station (Red Dirt Heart)

Partir ou rester (Red Dirt Heart 2)

Faire Face (Red Dirt Heart 3)

Trouver sa Place (Red Dirt Heart 4)

Le Poids de Sentiments (The Weight of It All)

Un Noël à la sauce Henry (A Very Henry Christmas)

Une vie à Refaire (Switched)

Evolution (Evolved)

Galaxies & Océans

German

Flammende Erde (Red Dirt Heart)

Lodernde Erde (Red Dirt Heart 2)

Sengende Erde (Red Dirt Heart 3)

Ungezähmte Erde (Red Dirt Heart 4)

Vier Pfoten und ein bisschen Zufall (Finders Keepers)

Ein Kleines bisschen Versuchung (The Weight of It All)

Ein Kleines Bisschen Fur Immer (A Very Henry Christmas)

Weil Leibe uns immer Bliebt (Switched)

Drei Herzen eine Leibe (Three's Company)

Über uns die Sterne, zwischen uns die Liebe (Galaxies and Oceans)

Unnahbares Herz (Blind Faith 1)

Sehendes Herz (Blind Faith 2)

Thai

Sixty Five Hours (Thai translation)

Finders Keepers (Thai translation)

Spanish

Sesenta y Cinco Horas (Sixty Five Hours)

Código Rojo (Code Red)

Chinese

Blind Faith